HARD
TO HANDLE

Also by Raven Scott

Hard as Ice

Hard and Fast

Published by Dafina Books

HARD
TO HANDLE

RAVEN
SCOTT

Dafina
BOOKS

Kensington Publishing Corp.
http://www.kensingtonbooks.com

DAFINA BOOKS are published by

Kensington Publishing Corp.
119 West 40th Street
New York, NY 10018

All Kensington titles, imprints and distributed lines are available at special quantity discounts for bulk purchases for sales promotions, premiums, fund-raising, and educational or institutional use. Special book excerpts or customized printings can also be created to fit specific needs. For details, write or phone the office of the Kensington Special Sales Manager. Kensington Publishing Corp., 119 West 40th Street, New York, NY 10018. Attn: Special Sales Department. Phone: 1-800-221-2647.

Dafina and the Dafina logo Reg. U.S. Pat. & TM Off.

ISBN-13: 978-1-61773-543-1
ISBN-10: 1-61773-543-4
First Kensington Mass Market Edition: September 2016

eISBN-13: 978-1-61773-544-8
eISBN-10: 1-61773-544-2
First Kensington Electronic Edition: September 2016

10 9 8 7 6 5 4 3 2 1

Printed in the United States of America

For my daughters, Sierra and Naima.
You are both such talented, funny and interesting people.
Thank you for making my life so rich,
and for always tolerating my crazy schedule.

ACKNOWLEDGMENTS

To my mom, sisters, and brothers; the last year of my life has been a crazy rollercoaster, and through it, you have all been amazingly supportive. Thank you for keeping me grounded and making me laugh even as I cried. To my friend, Fay; thank you for being such a good listener, and always sharing your positive insight. To my agent, Sha-Shana Crichton; thank you for your years of support and guidance. I couldn't have gotten this far without you. Lastly, to my editor, Mercedes Fernandez; it was great fun working on this exciting series with you. Thank you for your insight, ideas and passion for a great story

CHAPTER 1

"Come on, you can do better than that!" taunted the silky female voice, laced with a cultured British accent. "Looks like you've gotten soft lounging around on this side of the pond."

Samuel Mackenzie grit his teeth and hammered the punching bag with two quick left jabs and a hard right upper cut. His friend and employee Renee Thomas chuckled at his obvious annoyance.

"What are you doing here, Thomas?" Sam demanded in a deep, rich Scottish accent while his focus remained on his boxing workout. He wore long, loose workout shorts low on his lean hips, but his thickly muscled upper body was naked and slick with sweat.

"I work here," replied Renee as she walked across the expansive gym inside the Fortis headquarters near Alexandria, Virginia. At almost six-thirty on a Friday evening, the building had only a handful of employees still working. The gym was empty except for the two of them.

"Not right now you don't," he retorted, still pounding at the heavy-duty, leather-bound apparatus. "You were shot less than two weeks ago, little lass. You're not approved to be back for at least another week."

The tall, lean woman stopped next to him, with a teasing smile on her milk chocolate face, and not the least bit put off by his gruff reprimand.

"Yes, I know. But I'm not an invalid. It's just a flesh wound," she insisted. "I was just in today to help with some research in the U.K. Nothing the least bit strenuous. So don't worry, you still have a little more time to train before I knock you on your arse."

Sam snorted, and gave her a quick glance. Renee was five feet, eight inches tall, but at six feet, four inches and a solid two-hundred and forty pounds, he towered over her.

"Not in this lifetime, sweetheart," he said, working through another combination of boxing moves.

"Any problems in Toronto?" she asked, watching him with a mix of respect and amazement. For a big guy, Sam was surprisingly fast and almost graceful in his moves.

"Nope. Smooth as silk," he stated, throwing a powerful uppercut before finally stepping back and gripping the punching bag to still its swinging movement.

Sam owned and managed Fortis with his two best friends, Lucas Johnson and Evan DaCosta. It was a full solution security and asset protection firm of twenty-three specialized field agents, technicians, and operations analysts with elite government experience and training. He had been in Toronto for three weeks on his last assignment, implementing a cutting-edge, virtually impenetrable security solution for one of their current clients, Magnus Motorsports. He had flown back to Virginia that morning, heading straight to the Fortis compound to finish up some paperwork.

Renee handed him a clean towel from the stack on the supply cart nearby. Sam used it to wipe off the moisture dripping from his face and head, leaving his dark blond mop of damp hair in a tousled mess. He draped the towel across the back of his neck, soaking up even more sweat as he picked up his discarded T-shirt from a bench nearby.

"Lucas says you're off for the next two weeks?" she said as they walked toward the gym entrance doors that led outside near the parking lot of the building.

"Yeah," Sam confirmed, sounding less than thrilled about it. "My mum was supposed to come for a visit, but she had to cancel at the last minute."

"Wow! Stood up by your own mum. That definitely explains your relationship issues."

"I wasn't stood up. She closed a big deal with a new corporate client for the inn and spa she runs near Inverness, and they needed some immediate accommodations," he explained, tossing the used towel into a laundry basket nearby. "And I don't have any relationship issues."

"You mean, you don't have any relationships," Renee shot back, shaking her head. "Probably also due to your generally sour disposition."

Sam pulled on his cotton T-shirt, effectively

hiding a smirk. He and Renee had worked together for several years as security advisors within MI5, the U.K. security services, before he moved to the U.S. five years ago to join Fortis. They had stayed in touch since then, until Sam successfully recruited her that spring to join the team. It was good to have her around, even if she was one of the few people who could easily see beneath his bad-ass exterior and took every opportunity to tease him.

"So, what are you going to do with all that time off?" she asked.

"Not sure yet," he admitted, grabbing his car keys and cell phone from the counter along the wall. "There's some work needed on the house that I haven't had a chance to do for months now."

"Well, try not to do anything interesting. You might actually have fun," Renee shot back, rolling her eyes with exasperation.

"Not likely," declared Sam, grinning broadly with his bright blue eyes sparkling in amusement. "Are you leaving now? Do you need a lift home?"

"I just have a couple of things to finish off at my desk, but I'm fine to drive. It's only a twenty-minute drive to my place."

"You sure? I can wait for you and drop you off."

"I'm fine, Sam," she insisted. "Almost as good as new."

Sam looked at her hard, clearly skeptical that she was telling the whole truth.

"Okay, but send me a note when you get home," he insisted.

"Sure, old man," teased Renee. She punched him hard in the shoulder, but he didn't even flinch.

He watched her turn and walk across the gym toward the entrance to the Fortis offices; then he pushed through the heavy exterior door and stepped outside. It was a warm evening in late June, with a cool breeze that carried the smell of a brewing rain storm. Sam strode smoothly to his car in the small parking lot, unconsciously noting the other cars. One was unfamiliar and stood out as a luxury rental with darkly tinted windows. Seconds later, as he was about to pass it, the driver's door opened, causing the muscles in his stomach to tingle with caution. It was like a sixth sense telling him he wasn't going to like what came next.

Two shapely legs swung out from inside, smooth as melted caramel and wearing very sexy, very high, black stilettos. And Sam knew exactly who they belonged to, even before the rest of the woman emerged from the car interior. Draped in a body-hugging black dress and oversized dark sunglasses, her thick, shiny, chestnut-brown hair brushed over the top of her shoulders.

For a brief moment, Sam thought about ignoring her. He could just walk a few more steps to his car and drive away as though she didn't exist. It was what he had been trying hard to do since the last time he saw her four years ago, but it had never actually worked. So he strode right up to where she stood, stopping just out of arm's reach.

"What are you doing here?" he demanded bluntly.

Her full pouty lips parted, but no words came out. Sam could feel her nervousness and apprehension but refused to care.

"Well?" he growled, leaning forward.

She straightened her shoulders and lifted her chin.

"I need to hire a security consultant."

Whatever he had expected her to say, it wasn't that.

"Then you've made a wasted trip. Evan is out of town until Monday," he told her, then made a move to walk past her.

"I know. I want you," she added in a soft voice.

Sam stopped and clenched his fists tight until his keys were cutting into his flesh. "And why the hell is that?"

"My boss needs protection. He's in the middle of a big real estate bid, and he's been getting threats from one of our competitors."

"Your boss," Sam repeated, turning back to face her. "Who is he?"

"Terry Antonoli. He's a developer with a North American head office in New York and project bids in several cities in the Northeast."

"Does your father know you're here?" he asked.

"This has nothing to do with him," she replied, evasively.

He looked down into her face, still a good six inches from his, despite her heels. Though her dark brown eyes were covered by the shades, Sam knew exactly what they looked like—sparkling bright and rimmed with long, silky lashes.

"Tell your boss that we don't do babysitting," he finally stated with a dismissive sneer. "Call Evan on Monday and I'm sure he'll refer you to several good bodyguard services based in New York."

"Sam, wait. I need your help," she insisted as he turned his back to her and started walking away. "I think Terry is in real danger."

"Call Evan," he snapped without pausing or looking back.

Mikayla Stone-Clement was still standing beside her rental car as he drove out of the Fortis parking lot.

Sam was on autopilot for the drive to his house, which was just a few minutes south of the office, his thoughts fixed on this complication he would prefer to forget. His mind wandered between the memories from the past and her pretty pleas for help now. Both made his blood boil with anger.

He had met Mikayla over four years ago while on a mission in Maryland for her father, George Clement, and his newspaper and magazine empire, Clement Media. It had been a random encounter, and seemingly innocent at first. While completing an investigation into suspected corruption at one of the smaller Clement newspapers, Sam had found a very pretty and slightly injured woman falling in the alley outside the offices of the *Baltimore Journal*. She had introduced herself as Kaylee Stone, a staff writer who had sprained her ankle on uneven concrete while rushing to do an errand. Of course, Sam helped her with immediate medical care. Then one thing led to another, and he found himself at her place over the next few days as they got to know each other better.

By the time he discovered her real identity, an unforgivable line had been crossed. Not only was she his client's daughter, she was his friend, Evan DaCosta's, fiancée.

Mikayla Stone-Clement was the worst kind of trouble then and, judging by how damn hot she was looking tonight, she was even more trouble now.

Sam parked his car in front of his house and entered the cozy, secluded cottage situated on a large wooded lot along the banks of the Potomac River. Once inside, he headed straight into the bathroom for a long, hot shower. After towelling off, he walked naked back into his bedroom to get dressed in jeans and a gray shirt. It was only shortly after seven o'clock, and he felt a nervous energy to do something or go someplace where he was less likely to spend the next few hours thinking about a woman he could never have.

He picked up his cell phone, intending to call Lucas, but paused when the phone vibrated with a new email message. It was from Mikayla.

Please listen to this message left for Terry this afternoon. I hope you'll reconsider. I'm staying at the Hilton Crystal City hotel until tomorrow morning, room 815.

Her phone number was listed beside her name at the end of the note. Sam paused for several seconds before he clicked on the audio file she had attached.

"We've warned you to keep your foreign money out of our business interests. But you don't seem to be listening. So we'll just have to make it real clear for you. Pull out now or your bitch will pay the price. And she won't be so pretty when we're done with her."

Sam listened to the deep, distorted voice on the recording three times, trying to assess the validity and seriousness of the threat to the woman indicated. Who in Terry Antonoli's life was the intended target? His wife? Girlfriend? Mikayla?

Sam quickly called Renee.

"Are you checking up on me?" she asked as soon as she answered the call.

"I need your help," Sam stated bluntly. "Are you near your computer?"

"I can be in about ten minutes. Why?"

"I need you to pull up any information you can find about Terry Antonoli, real estate developer."

"Okay. What's going on?" Renee asked.

"I'm not sure yet, but we might have a new client."

"I thought you were on vacation?"

"Yeah, supposed to be. But looks like I might have to postpone it," Sam explained. "Send me whatever you find on the developer."

"You got it," Renee confirmed before she hung up.

Then Sam called Mikayla at the number she provided. After three rings, it went to voicemail. He didn't leave a message. Instead, he went into the walk-in closet of his bedroom and opened a concealed cabinet at the back of the space. From it, he took out a Beretta nine-millimeter pistol, checked the magazine, and then tucked it into the back of his pants. He called her number two more times as he strode out of the house and got into his car. She still did not answer, and the tingling in Sam's stomach was now an incessant cramp.

CHAPTER 2

"Terrance Antonoli is the youngest son of Salvador Antonoli, a very wealthy businessman in the construction and property development industry," Renee stated through the speaker phone in Sam's car about fifteen minutes later. "Salvador's originally from Greece, but married a French girl and has lived in Paris for the last thirty years."

Sam skillfully maneuvered his matte black Jaguar XKR-S across two lanes of the Jefferson Davis Highway to the off-ramp a few blocks from Mikayla's hotel.

"And the kid, Terrance? Anything noteworthy about him?" he asked Renee.

"Nothing to suggest he's into anything shady," Renee noted. "Twenty-nine years old, typical rich kid. Looks like a bit of a playboy. He went to Yale University in the United States, then went back to France to work for daddy's company. Married the daughter of a diplomat, then launched the U.S. branch of Antonoli Properties about eighteen months ago."

"So the threat could have been for his wife," Sam added. "Where is she?"

"Selina Antonoli lives in Paris. According to Instagram, looks like she's about six months pregnant with their second child."

"Okay. I'm pulling up to the Hilton now. Send me anything else you can find on this Terrance kid that could explain what kind of shit he's involved in."

"Sure thing, boss."

They hung up as Sam pulled in to the alley behind the airport hotel. It was narrow and empty except for two large garbage bins and a stack of wooden shipping crates. As he strolled around the side of the building, he tried Mikayla's cell phone number again, but there was still no answer. The tension in his spine grew stronger as he thought through various scenarios in his head. There were many reasons why Mikayla Stone-Clement would ignore his multiple phone calls in the last twenty-five minutes, and almost all of them were innocent. But Sam couldn't ignore the slim possibility that she may be the target of the threat made to Antonoli. Particularly if his wife was all the way in France.

Sam walked through the main floor of the hotel toward the bank of elevators, where he could see several people waiting with an assortment of luggage and bags. But his eyes quickly landed on a single man, standing off to the side and pacing back and forth with an intense energy. The man was big and bulky, with hunched shoulders and a barrel chest under a long, black leather jacket. One of the elevators arrived as Sam was halfway across the open space, and the group of people slowly filed in, including the thug. Even as he burst into a hard sprint, Sam knew there was no way he could get there in time. The heavy metal doors closed softly just seconds before he reached them.

Pressing the call buttons with rapid impatience, Sam scanned the floor indicators above the four elevators and weighed his options. The elevator he had missed stopped at the third floor. He considered how long it would take to run up eight flights of stairs to Mikayla's floor, but knew it would be too long. One of the other three elevators was descending from the twelfth floor and, with any luck, would arrive without any stops along the way. That would put Sam only about three and a half minutes behind the thug.

The elevator he had missed was on the move again. Sam watched as it passed the fifth and sixth floor, then held his breath after the seventh. It stopped on the eighth, just as the descending elevator dinged to announce its arrival on the ground. He stepped aside as several occupants filed out slowly, covering his edginess beneath a calm, polite veneer. Alone in the cabin, he selected the eighth floor and pressed hard on the button to close the doors, though he could hear calls to hold and wait for other passengers.

Very aware of the security camera mounted in the corner of the lift, Sam placed a firm grip around the butt of his gun, which was secured against his back and concealed under the loose cotton of his shirt. About twenty seconds later, he finally stepped onto the eighth floor. The hall was empty and quiet. The directional sign on the wall sent him to the right. He walked forward, listening intently for anything alarming or out of place. At the door marked 815, Sam carefully leaned forward until he could press his ear to the surface. There was only silence. Maybe his instincts were off and the man in the leather jacket was just another hotel guest, despite the unsavory look of him.

Sam was about to pull back and knock on the door when he heard movement on the other side of the thick metal slab. He had only seconds to prepare before it swung open with the same thug ready to step out of Mikayla's room and back into the hallway. The man paused for a couple of moments, clearly surprised to find Sam standing only inches from him and wearing a ferociously menacing expression. Sam used the opportunity to punch the stranger in the nose with a quick jab. The man's head snapped back, and his blood sprayed forward from the fracture of his bridge. Unsatisfied, Sam pulled back and shot the heel of his palm into the man's neck, crushing his windpipe.

The thug stumbled back into the room, clutching his face and making desperate gurgling sounds as he struggled to breathe. His face and hands were quickly stained red as he bumped into the wall behind him. Sam then slammed a hard right hook into his temple, and watched dispassionately as the dead weight of the large man slid to the floor, out cold. With a quick step back to scan the hallway,

Sam was relieved to see that it was still empty and otherwise silent. He entered the hotel room and shut the door behind him, then quickly removed the loaded handgun from the man's shoulder holster. Then Sam drew his own gun and cautiously crept forward to clear the rest of the room. The man on the floor was likely a lone assailant, but he knew better than to make any assumption.

The bathroom was directly across from the front door, with the small living room and dining space off to the side. The bathroom was still damp and steamy from a recent shower, but all three areas were empty. Sam continued forward, starting to feel hopeful that Mikayla was not in the room. Maybe she had showered, then gone out for dinner or on an errand, managing to escape whatever her attacker had intended. But the moment he looked into the bedroom, he knew that wasn't the case. He heard her rapid, shallow breathing from the opposite side of the room before he spotted the top of her head just above the edge of the mattress.

Sam lowered his weapon and rushed around the king-sized bed, trying hard to stay calm and prepared for anything, but failing miserably. He found her sitting on the floor with her knees folded and arms wrapped tightly around them. She had changed out of the black dress and into slim, stretchy yoga pants and an oversized tank top. Her feet were bare. There were no signs of blood or obvious injury.

"Mikayla!" he stated softly.

She jumped, clearly startled by his voice, then

looked up at him with rich brown eyes that were wide with fear and trepidation. Sam quickly looked back out toward the front door to confirm her attacker was still knocked out, resisting the urge to inflict more damage.

"Are you hurt?" he asked, stepping a little closer.

She shook her head to say no.

"Okay. Stay here and don't move," Sam instructed. "I'll be right back."

He waited for her slow nod of acknowledgment before he turned away, shoving his gun into the waist of his pants. Back at the front entrance, he stepped over the prone assailant to enter the large bathroom, and found two hotel robes hung on the back wall near the shower. Sam quickly pulled off the belts and stepped back outside to find Mikayla standing a few feet away just outside the bedroom.

"Is he dead?" she asked, her hands clasped tightly in front of her.

"No," Sam told her as he noted that the blood flow appeared to have stopped and the man's windpipe had opened up enough for shallow breathing. "He'll live, at least long enough to provide some information."

He quickly got to work restraining the attacker by flipping him on his stomach and hog-tying his wrists and ankles together with the belts. But he could feel Mikayla's anxiety and her eyes watching his every move until he was satisfied that the thug was completely immobilized.

"Why don't you have a seat and tell me exactly what happened," Sam suggested as he straightened up and walked over to the small bar area in the living room. She let out a deep sigh and took his suggestion, lowering herself gracefully into the small two-seater sofa. Sam took out a miniature bottle of brandy from the small fridge and poured the liquid into one of the glasses on the counter. Mikayla accepted it and took a small sip before she began speaking.

"I was in the shower for a while, and when I got out, I saw that you had called a few times," she explained in a quiet but calm voice. "I was going to call you back after I finished packing my suitcase. Then there was a knock at the door. I just assumed it was you. But, still, I asked who it was. He said it was a delivery."

Mikayla took another, bigger drink of brandy, then squeezed her eyes tight as the liquor burned its way down her throat.

"I should have known something was wrong, I wasn't expecting anything," she admitted. "But I opened the door, just a crack, and it was enough for him to shove his way inside."

She paused, as though not wanting to finish the story.

"What did he do, Mikayla?" Sam prompted in an even, dispassionate tone.

There was a pause for a few seconds, until she let out another deep sigh and closed her eyes as though trying to block out the memory.

"He shoved me up against the wall with both his hands around my neck. Then he squeezed so hard that I couldn't breathe. I think I blacked out a little, except I could still hear him laughing. When I opened my eyes again, I was lying across the bed, like he had thrown me there."

Sam shoved his hands into the front pockets of his jeans.

"Anything else? Did he say anything?"

Mikayla cleared her throat.

"He laughed again, then said: 'Tell Antonoli that the message wasn't a threat, it was a promise.'"

"Then what happened?" he prompted.

"That's it. He walked away and I rolled off the bed. Then I heard the scuffle at the door before you came into the bedroom."

"How's your throat? Did he hurt you?" Sam asked, resisting the urge to check for injuries himself, very aware that he had no right to console her now. Not after she had come to him for help and protection earlier that evening and he had so cruelly dismissed her concerns. Still, the urge to touch her was so strong, he had to physically hold himself back.

"No, not really," she replied, placing one of her palms over the long stretch of her delicate neck. "I might be a little bruised, but nothing serious."

"Okay. Why don't you finish packing?" he suggested. "I'll take care of him."

She looked up into his eyes with an alarmed glance.

"What are you going to do?"

"Get some information about who hired him for this job and anything else he knows. I can be very persuasive," he added at the skepticism written clearly on her face.

Mikayla finally nodded before draining the cup

of the remaining brandy and putting the empty glass on the coffee table in front of her. Sam watched as she walked back into the bedroom and slid the pocket door closed behind her. He planted his hands on his hips, reviewing everything he already knew about the rapidly evolving situation. Whoever was trying to squeeze Terrance Antonoli out of the very competitive real estate development market was obviously serious and quick to back their words with action. But tonight's attack only created more questions for Sam. Like why had the son of a successful European builder chosen to branch out in the U.S., and how had he managed to piss off a faction of organized crime so quickly? Because there was no doubt that the fellow he'd tied up, and who was finally showing signs of coming to, was working for an established syndicate.

Sam walked over and crouched down next to the assailant, whose breathing was almost back to normal.

"Seems like you've landed yourself into a spot of trouble, mate," he said in a deceptively calm voice. "Why don't you save us all a lot of bother and tell me what I need to know?"

The guy tried to speak, but it came out as a series of grunts.

"What was that?" Sam asked.

"I don't know nothing," the stranger finally choked out.

"Why don't you let me be the judge of that? Let's start with who sent you on this assignment."

"I don't know," the man replied.

Sam nodded, not at all surprised or put off by the response.

"All right, then let's start with something easier," he continued as he took out his cell phone and took a picture of the man's face, then sent it as an attachment in a quick email to Renee. "Like your name, for example. But keep in mind that, in about five minutes, I'll know everything there is to know about you, mate. So my question is just to establish a rapport, demonstrate how reasonable I can be if you make this exercise an easier one."

"Nick."

"Come on, you can do better than that. Nick what?"

Sam watched him struggle to swallow.

"Francesco. Nicolas Francesco."

"Good job, Nickie-boy. Now how did you end up in this hotel room with a very specific message to deliver?"

"I got a text message with instructions, that's it."

"Well, you must work for someone, Nickie. So why don't we start there?"

"I don't work for anybody, not official-like. I just take the occasional job, no questions asked."

"Okay, okay. So what about this text message you received? Do you still have the number?" Sam asked patiently.

"Yeah, in my cell phone."

"Good. You've done pretty good so far, mate. But I think you can do better," Sam continued as he quickly fished the phone out of Nick's jacket pocket.

"Who's your contact for these occasional jobs you do? Who sent the text message?"

"I don't know, I swear!" Nick insisted. "I got connected through a friend of a friend. I've never met anyone directly."

"And this friend of a friend?"

"His name is Lucky. That's all I know!"

"Okay, Nick. I believe you," Sam stated as he straightened up. "I'll be sure to tell the police how cooperative you were."

He walked back into the living area while dialing Renee on his cell phone.

"Did you get my email?" Sam asked as soon as the Fortis agent answered the call.

"Yeah, I'm searching the Virginia and FBI databases now," Renee replied.

"I'll make it easier for you. His name is Nicolas Francesco, and it sounds like he does only very low-level work."

"Okay. And how did he end up with a busted nose and a bloody face?" the younger agent asked, clearly anticipating a good story.

"That, my friend, is a great question. Let me conference in Lucas and I'll get you both up to speed."

Sam then spent the next five minutes providing a summary of the situation to Renee and one of his business partners, Lucas Johnson. Sam, Lucas, and Evan were equal partners in the firm, and worked together to discuss strategy for each mission. They also led the major engagements in the field, based on their elite skills. With his background as a CIA agent, Evan ran covert operations. Lucas was a cyber genius and led all major system security cases. Sam specialized in physical security and protective services, with skills honed as a British security agent with MI5.

"Sam, Terry Antonoli's assistant is listed as Kaylee Stone on the company website," Renee interjected. "But you called her Mikayla Stone-Clement. Are we talking about the same person?"

Sam clenched his jaw. It had been a long time since he'd heard the name Kaylee Stone.

"Yeah, one in the same," he finally confirmed, working to keep his tone even and without a trace of resentment. "Ms. Stone-Clement comes from a pretty wealthy and well-known Virginia family, and likes to use an alias when she doesn't want anyone to know who she really is."

"So, what now?" Lucas asked.

"Well, Mikayla came all the way to Alexandria to hire a bodyguard, so it seems to me that we have a new client," Sam suggested.

"Maybe, but it's pretty clear that Antonoli needs more than just a security detail," Lucas added. "Based on what happened tonight, he'll need threat assessment, maybe neutralization, depending on which parties are involved."

"I've confirmed Francesco's identity," said Renee. "You were right, Sam. He's not directly connected to a crime family. And he's from Baltimore."

"Interesting. They sent him forty-five miles to deliver a message," Sam mused.

"Maybe that's where the client is based," suggested Lucas.

"Maybe," echoed Sam.

"What about Mikayla? Where does she fit into all of this?" Lucas asked.

"I know only what she told me outside headquarters earlier this evening," Sam said. "But I'm moving her to a safe location for the night, so I'll see what else she knows about Antonoli's business dealings."

"Sam, the police will arrive in about five minutes to take Francesco into custody for trespassing and assault charges," Renee confirmed.

"What about Evan?" asked Lucas. "Should you advise him of the situation?"

"He's on the last three days of vacation with his girlfriend. We can wait until he's back on Monday to let him know his ex-fiancée is in the middle of our latest assignment," determined Sam.

CHAPTER 3

After closing the hotel bedroom door, Mikayla got down on her knees to fish out her small handgun from under the bed, where she had quickly hid it when Sam had called her name. She straightened up and stowed the weapon in the case at the bottom of her small suitcase, then finished packing her clothes, leaving out a light cardigan. It didn't take long, so she then spent the next ten minutes sitting on the bed, listening to the low tone of Sam's voice and thinking through what to do next.

As frightening as it had been, the attack tonight could not have come at a better time. Judging by the very cold reception from Sam earlier that afternoon, only hard evidence was going to sway him to help her and her boss, Terry. Sure, there was the risk that whoever had been sent to enforce the threats against Terry could be overzealous and really try to hurt her, but it was minimal. Whoever was responsible only wanted Terry out of the bidding process for government building projects, and could not afford unwanted police attention.

So, they would only see her as a means to achieve
their goals. And, hopefully, that was as far is it went,
with her gun and Sam Mackenzie as extra precaution. She and Terry had worked too hard on estab-
lishing Antonoli Properties in New York and New
Jersey to let thugs and criminals hold them back.

Mikayla checked her watch. It was almost eight
o'clock. Ninety minutes since she had approached
Sam outside the Fortis headquarters.

Asking for his help was the most difficult thing
about this whole situation, but there was no way
around it. She needed professional protection, and
there was no one else more capable than Samuel
Mackenzie. He might never forgive her for how
they had met, but he would still help her. His obvious disgust with her seemed just as strong four years
later, and she was counting on it. Sam was a very
smart man, but if he saw her only as a cheating,
opportunistic woman, he wouldn't look any deeper.
At least not at first.

Evan DaCosta, on the other hand, would know
something was fishy right away. He and Mikayla had
grown up together and had been good friends
long before they'd started dating. He would never
understand why she would give up her dream of
being a journalist to work as an administrator in
the building industry. And he would never support
her doing so while facing threats of physical danger.

Mikayla was deep in thought when there was a
knock on the bedroom pocket door. She stood up
and slid it open. Sam Mackenzie filled the open
space with his tall frame and broad shoulders.

They stared silently at each other for a few awkward moments until Mikayla glanced away.

"Are you all packed?" he asked.

"Yeah, except for a few toiletries in the bathroom," she replied.

"Okay. The police will be here in a minute to take your visitor into custody, and I'd like to move you to another location for the night."

"Does that mean you're taking the assignment?" Mikayla demanded, meeting his eyes again squarely.

"We'll see."

"No," she countered. "Either you agree to take Antonoli Properties on as a client or I'm staying right here until my flight tomorrow back to New York."

Sam's eyes narrowed a bit but the rest of his face remained impassive.

"We can discuss the details once we have you somewhere safe," he insisted.

"What else is there to discuss for you to make a decision? You heard the threat and saw what happened," Mikayla replied, pointing at the man still tied up at the front door.

"There's no need to be stubborn, darling."

"I'm not being stubborn, only practical," she shot back, annoyed by his patronizing tone. "I'm very grateful for your intervention. You're still a very gallant knight. But I need more than that. I've offered you the job, so either take it or leave so I can find someone else."

Sam slowly crossed his arms across his chest and planted his feet wide.

"All right, we'll take the assignment," he finally

agreed. "But you and your boss, Antonoli, will have to tell us everything there is to know about your business dealings."

"There is no we, Sam. I told you we're hiring you and you only. And it requires full confidentiality."

"It doesn't work that way, darling. I am Fortis. You hire me, you hire the whole company. That's the deal," Sam stated, spreading his legs wider as though to take an even firmer stance. "There is no confidentiality between me and my partners."

Mikayla did not miss the broader point he was making, and looked down at the space between them.

"I'm sorry, but that's the deal," she returned.

"Why?"

"You know why, Sam."

"Evan."

"He could never see me as a client. Our families are too close, and he would feel honor bound to tell my parents what's going on."

"From what I can see, Evan has moved on with his life, so maybe you're not giving him enough credit."

Mikayla smiled sadly at the attempted jab.

"It's not a risk I'm willing to take. My dad has been through enough in the last few years. I don't want him to worry needlessly about me."

"Looks like he should be worried," Sam added with another condescending twist of his lips. Mikayla refused to take the bait.

"So do we have an agreement or not?"

"I told you, if you hire me, you're hiring Fortis.

Besides, I've already given Lucas and one of our
analysts an update. Kinda hard to unring that bell,
lass."

She stepped closer to him and planted her hands
on her hips.

"You're a pretty capable man, I'm sure you'll
figure it out."

One of his eyebrows twitched.

"So, Mr. Mackenzie, do we have an agreement?
Or should I start searching for another security
consultant?" she insisted.

There were several moments of tense silence
during which neither of them blinked, until there
was a hard, loud knock at the front door.

"Get the rest of your things together," Sam finally
growled before turning to walk across the hotel
room.

Mikayla hid a smile as she followed a few steps
behind, pulling on the cardigan. She turned into
the bathroom just as Sam let the uniformed officer
inside. It took only a couple of minutes for her to
collect toiletries and supplies into a cosmetic bag.
When she stepped back out into the front hallway,
her attacker was being taken away in police custody.

"All set?" Sam asked. He had brought her luggage and purse out of the bedroom.

"Yes," she confirmed as she loaded the cosmetic
bag into the suitcase. "What about the police?
Don't I need to give a statement?"

"I've taken care of it," he stated simply, then ushered her out of the room with her luggage in tow.

"Where are we going?"

"Not far."

Mikayla stayed close to him as they went downstairs on a service elevator, through a long hallway, and outside to an alley at the back of the building. Sam opened the front passenger door of a slick, black sports car and helped her get seated. She heard the trunk open and shut before he folded his large frame into the driver's seat. The engine purred to life, and they were out on the street, moving swiftly through traffic at an aggressive speed. While Sam remained silent and focused on his driving, Mikayla tried not to think about how strange it felt to be next to him in the confined space.

They had known each other for such a brief period of time four years ago. Just a few days. Yet his presence created the same nervous anticipation in the base of her stomach, as though something exciting was about to happen. Only, this time, Mikayla knew from experience that excitement wasn't always a good thing, and she vowed not to let it beguile her into rash and regrettable behavior. She was trying to accomplish something with Antonoli Properties, and while Sam Mackenzie was necessary to do this, his presence could not be anything more than that.

The drive was only five minutes north to a small townhouse complex on the other side of the airport. Sam slowly drove the car down a narrow lane to the end of the street, then turned into the last driveway on the right. The door to a single-car garage slid up automatically, and he parked inside, closing the garage door behind them.

"Is this your place?" Mikayla asked as she stepped out of the car and looked around at the neat, organized space.

"No, it's a safe house," Sam said curtly. "Let's get inside. We have a lot to sort through."

Mikayla silently followed him into the two-floor house through an entrance near the kitchen. Sam switched on lights as they walked through to the living areas on the main floor. It was plain white, with unadorned walls and sparse furniture. Sam placed her suitcase near the staircase in the middle of the space, then started a thorough inspection of every external door and window, all of which were covered with utilitarian white blinds. She let out a deep breath, trying to ease some of the tension that had been building steadily since she'd stepped out of her rental car to speak to him just two hours earlier.

"Okay, Mikayla," Sam said as he walked back to her. "Start from the beginning and tell me everything you know about this real estate bid your boss is involved with and these threats."

Mikayla backed up to sit in the dark blue sofa against the wall. Then she took a deep breath and told the story of how she'd ended up in New York.

"I had met Terry about a year and a half ago at a charity auction for the Clement Foundation, the nonprofit organization for adult literacy that my mother runs," she explained, looking up into his eyes with a steady gaze. "He wanted to expand his family's real estate development business into the

U.S. and was here for a few weeks, meeting with business associates for potential investment opportunities. Last fall, he reached out to ask if I would be interested in a job. Antonoli Properties had just opened their North American office in New York and wanted to focus on city projects. Terry needed an executive assistant with a strong communications background who could help complete municipal government contract bids. I was ready for a new challenge so I accepted the job and have been working with him ever since.

"We now have three small projects under way in Brooklyn and Queens. Six weeks ago, one of our subcontractors told us about an open bid in Paterson, New Jersey, for a new government office building. We submitted a proposal last Monday, three weeks before the deadline. The contract will be awarded on August fourth."

Sam was now pacing slowly in front of her while he stroked the thick, silky blond beard near the line of his jaw.

"When did the trouble start?" he asked.

"Last Wednesday, a couple of days after the submission," explained Mikayla. "Someone showed up at our office claiming to be from the city of Paterson, asking very aggressive questions about building permits and insurance coverage. Terry and I were at one of the other building sites, but our receptionist was there, and said the gentleman suggested the review process for new vendors to work in Paterson was very extensive and could result in very crippling fines if there was any suggestion that we had misrepresented our credentials. Of course, I called the city development office right away, and they had no record of sending anyone to meet with us.

"On Monday morning, we found the glass in the front doors of our offices smashed and the computers and office equipment all destroyed. That's when I told Terry we needed to hire security. I arrived here two days ago."

"They knew you were in Virginia, alone, when they left that voicemail message," he stated solemnly.

"It appears so."

"Why you?"

"What?"

"The message was 'pull out now or your bitch will pay the price.' Why you and not his wife?" he asked in a deceptively soft voice.

Mikayla knew the answer, had been fully prepared to lay everything out from the beginning so that Sam would see her as she needed him to and be satisfied with only providing his protection services. But now the words were stuck in her throat and she just could not push them out. Not yet.

"I don't know," she lied, looking down briefly. "Terry travels a lot back and forth to France, so I've become the face of Antonoli Properties here. I'm sure I'm just the easiest target."

"You're also working for him under the name Kaylee Stone. Why?"

"Old habit, I guess? My dad is still very influential in many circles even if he doesn't run Clement Media anymore. I've never wanted anyone to think I was using the family connections to further my career. This way, I don't have to worry about it."

"That sounds like a pretty way of saying you prefer to lie about who you are, deceiving the people around you."

Mikayla let out a deep sigh as she stood up to stand in front of him. It was inevitable that they would get here eventually.

"Sam—"

"Does Antonoli know?"

"Yes," she insisted, sounding much more defensive than she wanted to. "I told you, I met him while I worked for my mother's charitable foundation. So he knows who I am. I mean, he calls me Kaylee, like everyone I've met since high school. But only my family still calls me Mikayla. And Evan's."

He looked down at her with a fierce stare, his jaw clenched hard. She could feel his dissatisfaction with her statement, and his silent need to challenge her words. The impending conversation was four years in the making.

"Sam—"

"What else do I need to know?" he demanded, cutting her off again.

"That's everything I can think of."

He nodded, seemingly calm on the outside, but his sky-blue eyes burned hot with intensity.

"Okay. This whole thing should be pretty easy to resolve once we find out what other companies bid on the same work." He looked at his watch. "We need to rearrange flights to New York for tomorrow morning, and I'll meet with Antonoli as soon as we arrive."

Kaylee nodded. "Thank you." Her voice was just

above a whisper. "I know I'm the last person you wanted to see again, so I really appreciate your help."

"It sounds like a pretty simple job, Mikayla, so hardly a big effort. And we both know that Evan would kick my arse if I didn't take the case."

She smiled sadly at the dry attempt at humor. Then she closed her eyes and said the words that needed to be spoken.

"I never meant to deceive you, Sam."

He stepped back, and Kaylee reached out and grabbed his wrist, trying to stop him from walking away. Sam froze, his whole body stiff and his eyes fixed over her shoulder.

"Let go of me."

"Please. Just let me explain."

"There is nothing more to explain!" he roared, low and deep, pulling his arm away so she was forced to release her grip. "Because of you, I did the most dishonorable thing a man could do, Kaylee. Evan is my business partner. My mate. One of two men that I respect the most. And I slept with his fiancée! There is no coming back from that. There is no explanation that makes that right! Not then and not now."

"But we didn't know. It wasn't intentional, Sam."

"You think that matters? That it changes anything?"

"Yes!" she yelled, stepping in front of him so he was forced to meet her eyes. "Yes, it matters. I'm the only one to blame. I was engaged to him and I let myself get . . . caught up with someone else. I didn't know who you were, but it was still my mistake. Not yours. Evan would have understood that."

"Don't you think I thought about that at the time, Kaylee? Do you think I've wanted to keep this secret? But do you know what's even worse than sleeping with Evan's fiancée just weeks before his wedding?" he demanded in a low growl as he took hold of her shoulders, pulling her so close their bodies were only a hairbreadth apart. "The fact I still wanted you. Even knowing who you were and what you had done, I still wanted you for myself. That, sweetheart, is unforgivable."

Kaylee didn't have time to react before Sam lowered his mouth onto hers in a deep, punishing kiss.

CHAPTER 4

After four years, Sam had Kaylee in his arms again, with his lips sweeping over her and his tongue delving into her warm, wet recess. He was vibrating from the sensation she created within him. Hot, sweet arousal and unrelenting need for the intoxicating flavor of forbidden fruit. She sighed and relaxed into the embrace, opening her mouth wider to him. God, he wanted her, just like before. Maybe even more.

His hunger for her was natural, right? Any man who tasted something insanely good only once, then was forbidden from accessing it again for years after, would crave that thing like a drug. He would dream about it, recall its color, scent, texture with absolute clarity until he was certain he had created it with his imagination. Then, if that thing was put in reach again, any man would have a greedy, uncontrollable urge to consume it. It was instinct, biology, and Sam Mackenzie was not immune to it.

Sam took her head in his hands to kiss her deeper, demanding access and controlling her response.

He sucked on her lips, nibbled roughly on their edges, and pulled at her tongue. Every caress sent fresh tendrils of arousal down his back until his legs tingled. Only Kaylee made him feel like this.

He pulled back to look down at her face, with her skin flush red-brown and her eyes closed. Her full lips were swollen and pouty, glistening from the wetness of his own. Then her lids slowly folded back until she looked back at him and his urgent need was clearly reflected in the brown depths of her eyes. His heart pounded harder.

With deliberate slowness, Sam reached down between them to hook his fingers into the edge of her yoga pants and tug them down her hips. Kaylee wiggled a little and helped push them lower until they pooled on the floor. Then she reached her arms up and placed them on the tops of his shoulders, steadying herself to step out of the pants. Their eyes were still locked. Sam reached around and gripped the curves of her ass in both hands squeezing their full firmness and pulling her up against his semi-hardness. Kaylee gasped, and ran her tongue along her top lip.

She was tempting him. Purposely trying to break his control. Sam clenched his teeth and rubbed his length against the base of her stomach, but resisted kissing her again. If this was going to happen, it would be on his terms, the way he wanted it.

Kaylee looked down at his lips and slid her hands farther up his neck and along his jawline. She brushed one of her thumbs across his lower lip, swiping just inside and stroking it back and forth. Sam's cock pulsed and hardened further against her body, and Kaylee sighed loudly. He stroked his tongue along her finger, sucking it into his mouth and biting on the pad. Hard. She gasped in surprise, and her eyes widened dramatically, but she didn't pull it back out. Sam bathed the spot with his tongue in tiny circles, and her breathing deepened. He watched her intently, soaking up every sign of her building arousal and almost forgetting that this was his show. Almost.

Sam pulled back his head and looked down between them. Her nipples were hard and peaked beneath her clothes. He quickly pulled off the light sweater so she was left in only the loose tank top and her underwear. Her body was almost as he remembered. Petite with lean lines and soft curves, though now a little fuller than before. Silky soft, russet-brown skin with a golden undertone. Feminine features that were still incredibly responsive to his touch. Sam just knew that she was now dewy and slick between her thighs. Just the thought brought him to full, impatient hardness.

God, he wanted to kiss her again. Her lips looked deliciously sweet. But he held back, trying to hold on to his control in the situation. Letting go of her ass, he quickly undid his belt, unsnapped the waist of his jeans, and lowered the zipper. As though clearly reading his mind, Kaylee trailed her fingers down his stomach and slid one of them right under the band of his underwear. She took hold of his cock in her small, soft hand, pushing down the cotton boxer briefs with the other. His thick length sprung free, stretching upward, and Sam could only watch breathlessly as she stroked over it with a tight hold. Jesus Christ, it felt insanely good. She added her other hand, using both to stroke him up and down with just the right speed and grip to drive him nuts.

Sam let out a low hiss as his balls tightened unbearably. Any moment now, she was going to make him come, way too fast. He could already feel it building hard, gripping his spine with its intensity. A few more strokes and he'd be a goner. He threw back his head to hold in a deep, carnal groan. But then she released her hold, and Sam wasn't sure if he was relieved or about to die from frustration. He took a deep breath and looked back down at her. The little minx was grinning, fully aware of the torture she was creating. It was such a pretty smile. And for the first time in a long time, Sam wanted to laugh out loud for no real reason at all.

"Kaylee," he whispered, despite his vow to keep this purely physical. But then she was lowering herself down onto her knees in front of him, and Sam forgot whatever he was going to say anyway. *No, no, no,* his brain screamed, but his cock was pleading, *yes, yes, yes,* much more loudly. Kaylee took hold of his length at the base and slowly sucked the thick tip into that beautiful mouth. He could not hold back a deep groan. She lowered over him until he hit the back of her throat, though she was still a couple of inches from the base. Then she pulled back all the way and did it again. And again. Sam was transfixed. It was the most purely perfect blowjob he'd ever witnessed. Then she sucked hard on his head, teasing the underside, and scraping lightly over the sensitive top with her teeth.

"Blimey!" Sam swore as sweat broke out on his forehead.

She was back to the long, sucking strokes, this time faster, purposeful. Sam couldn't take his eyes off her as he added this moment to the small repository of memories that he could draw on later. But the force of his impending orgasm was back, harder and more urgent than before. Way too soon to satisfy all his cravings. Sam reached down to cup the back of her head, and eased himself out of her mouth. He groaned from the loss of contact, but then watched unblinking as she stroked her hands over the long length, still slick and wet from her saliva.

Sam was convinced she was trying to break him.

"Stand up," he demanded, sounding rougher than he intended.

Kaylee closed her eyes, but allowed him to help her off the floor. He then led her up the stairs to the second floor. On the landing there were two equal-sized bedrooms with a full bathroom in the middle. Sam went into one of the rooms and opened the closet. There was a packed duffel bag on the floor with three or four days' worth of clothes, toiletries, and other emergency essentials. He opened a side pocket and took out an unopened box of condoms.

When he stood back up, Kaylee was standing beside the bed watching him. She suddenly looked so small and vulnerable in her oversized top and bare feet.

Sam paused, remembering the incident that had brought them together. It should have made him stop or at least slow things down dramatically. But it didn't. He was still rock hard, and there was a dark hunger driving him—a primal need to take her, on his terms. Possess her in the most carnal way, and her look of fragility in the sterile bedroom only fanned the flames.

Sam tore open the condom packet as he walked to her and effortlessly rolled the thin membrane on. She watched. He quickly unbuttoned his shirt and tossed it aside, pulled her into a tight embrace, and bent low to bite at her neck. Kaylee gasped, running her hand over his shoulder, gripping the thick bulge of his biceps. She moaned appreciatively. His cock pulsed against her abdomen.

"Sam," she whispered, but he didn't want her words.

He gripped her hips and turned her around. She cried out softly in surprise as he pushed forward until she bent at the waist with her arms braced on the bed. Her legs were closed and that round ass was perfectly displayed. Sam gripped both curves to lift her higher, aligned with his thrust. He knew he was being rough, callous, selfish, but he didn't stop. He just pulled aside her obviously expensive lace panties, gripped them like a handle, and stroked deep. She was so wet and tight.

Kaylee moaned deep. Or maybe it was Sam, he didn't care. He was too buried in her silken sheath to know the difference. Every inch of his body was alive with the sole focus of taking her hard and fast so that he couldn't tell where his flesh ended and hers began. It didn't last long.

Sam came in minutes with adolescent gracelessness. He roared with it, bucking his hips from the force of the shudders. It was both insanely good, and horribly unsettling. The intensity left him boneless in his wake. He wrapped his arms around Kaylee as they both fell onto the bed, then rolled them over so she wasn't crushed by his considerable weight. They lay there, breathing hard for several minutes.

The remorse came soon after. It tasted pretty bitter. He hadn't even taken off his pants.

Sam got up and went to the bathroom next door to discard the protection and clean up. He returned a couple of minutes later to sit on the bed beside her, his legs wide, hands clasped between them, head bowed.

"I'm sorry," he finally stated into the silence. "That was unacceptable and uncalled for."

Sam heard what sounded like a sniffle and his heart cracked. He looked over to see that she was lying on her back, arms straight by her side, staring widely up at the ceiling.

"Kaylee." A thin river of wetness trailed from the corner of her eye and into her tousled hair.

Uncertain of how to handle this, he lay down on his side, wrapped his arm across her waist and pulled her closer, draping one of his denim-clad legs across her naked ones until she was buried in the cocoon of his body. "I'm sorry," he repeated softly.

She let out a deep sigh with just a hint of sorrow.

"Did I hurt you?" he asked, hoping desperately that he hadn't.

"No. No," she assured him. "It was just—"

"I know. I had no right to take you like that," Sam acknowledged, swallowing around the awkward knot in his throat.

"No, it was fine," she told him, still looking up at nothing. "It was . . ."

"Rough," Sam muttered when she seemed to struggle with the right word.

"Yes. And I think I needed it like that." She let out a light, nervous laugh. "Sorry, I didn't mean to get so emotional. But it's been a long day, and I think that's exactly what I needed."

Sam let out a breath, caught off guard by her words. Kaylee never seemed to react to things the way he expected.

Finally, she turned her head and looked up at him, her eyes clear and honest.

"And I know that this doesn't change anything between us," she added softly.

He looked back at her for a few long moments. No, this didn't change anything. But it did give them a little more time to enjoy this unique physical connection, even though there was no possibility for more. He brushed his fingers across her cheek and traced the line at the edge of her face, along the jaw. She bit her lip, and Sam leaned down to taste their fullness.

They kissed slowly, tenderly, taking their time to explore a softer connection. They helped each other remove the rest of their clothes, then kissed some more exploring the swells and contours of each other's bodies. When she was flushed and slick, Sam lay her back down, slipped on a condom and slowly penetrated her heat. Their eyes locked, and they rocked gently, slowly increasing speed and urgency. Sam lifted her legs higher on his waist, deepening his thrust, and entwined her fingers with his above her head. They raced together in a rhythmic gait until Kaylee crested, gripping his length so tight in her sheath that he orgasmed moments later.

He held her close until her breath deepened and she was asleep. Then Sam carefully climbed out of the bed and took a shower. Back downstairs, wearing only a towel, he did a quick security check, then called Lucas on his cell phone. It was almost ten-thirty.

"What's the verdict?" his friend asked as soon as he picked up the phone.

"Sounds like your garden variety of coercion," Sam confirmed, then relayed a summary of what Kaylee had told him earlier in the evening. "I'll take her back to New York tomorrow and look into it. But with one complication. Looks like I'll be spending my vacation doing this pro bono."

Lucas laughed. "Really? And why is that?"

"Evan," he replied simply. "She's convinced that if he knew about the threats, he would feel obligated to tell her father. And since she doesn't know that Evan can keep a secret like a professional spy, I couldn't exactly convince her otherwise. She wouldn't leave the hotel with me until I agreed to her terms, so I told her what she wanted to hear."

"So, that's your plan? Work for free?" Lucas asked, clearly not supportive.

"Seems like the best solution. I only have to follow her direction and accept her terms if she's a client. And she's only a client if she's paying our fees. Otherwise, I'm doing her a favor during my time off," Sam reasoned.

"And when she finds out that you've lied to her?"

"Then she'll hardly be in the position to be vexed, now will she?"

"Geez, Mac, you really don't know anything about women, do you?"

"I know enough to be dangerous," Sam quipped, and listened to Lucas laugh. "I'll need Renee to stay on the case. Nothing physical right away, just eyes and ears for me when needed. Can we afford it?"

"Yeah, sure. I was going to keep her on desk duty for another couple of weeks. So now I can blame you for the lack of field work."

Sam shrugged. "She would have taken it out on me anyway."

"What about Evan?"

"I'll bring him up to speed next week, when I know more about the extent of this threat," Sam confirmed. "But with any luck, we'll have this thing sewn up tight in a few days."

"Do you need anything before you leave?"

"No. I have a bag at the safe house. Should be enough for three or four days. I'll buy whatever else I need."

"All right, keep me posted," Lucas requested.

They hung up, and Sam rummaged through the fridge and cupboards for water and snacks, then spent another thirty minutes securing a private plane for a morning flight.

CHAPTER 5

Kaylee remembered the day she'd met Samuel Mackenzie with absolute clarity, even four years later. It was the day that had changed her life in more ways than one.

At twenty-four years old, she had been living her dream, working as a staff reporter at the *Baltimore Journal.* The *Journal* was one of the smallest publications owned by Clement Media, and the perfect place to start her career in journalism with complete anonymity, writing as Kaylee Stone. Only the chief editor and the head of human resources knew who she really was, and both had strict instructions from George Clement not to provide any special treatment or let anyone else know that his daughter was working in the company.

The arrangement had worked fine for over a year. Kaylee had started in research, then earned her way up to writing about city politics. Her editor, Jason Holt, had seemed like a good guy, though a little lackadaisical in his job. She'd made good friends at the paper and among the city staff. She'd become close with one friend in particular, Rosalie Anderson. Rosalie worked in the mayor's office and often provided information that gave Kaylee the edge on breaking news.

It was a Tuesday in late April when Kaylee and Rosalie had met for coffee after a particularly heated city council meeting to review the budget.

"Are they really projecting a two-million-dollar overspend this year?" Kaylee asked.

"Honestly, I think that's conservative," Rosalie replied in a low voice, looking around to ensure they weren't overheard. "It's not all from this year. They saw the problem last fall after the budgets were already approved and decided to carry most of the spending over into this year so they'd have more time to balance the books."

"How can they do that?"

Rosalie leaned closer. "I only know that they delayed paying some invoices."

"Like renegotiating terms, or just making the payments?"

"I don't know exactly how."

"But for how many vendors? That's a lot of money," Kaylee added.

"That's the thing. Most of the overspend is for only two contracts," Rosalie explained.

"What? How is that possible?"

"It's not that unusual, really. Especially for infra-structure projects. The bids all look good on paper, then a year later, they are all delayed and way over budget."

Kaylee could only look at her friend with her mouth agape. "How is that possible? Isn't there any oversight or fines? Or someone responsible for making sure that doesn't happen?"

"You would think so."

Kaylee was ready to ask a load of other questions, but Rosalie looked around with obvious concern. "I have to go," she said, slipping on her purse and picking up her still full coffee mug. "Do me a favor? Keep this to yourself for now?"

"Rosalie, this is huge. You know I can't do that."

"Please? As a favor to me?"

"Okay," Kaylee conceded. "I won't do anything with it for now. Not until I can get more information from other sources."

"Thank you. I have to go or I'll be late for a meeting."

Kaylee watched Rosalie walk away with a feeling of excitement bubbling wildly in her stomach. Something definitely smelled wrong, and every instinct told her there was a big story at the heart of it. She just needed a little bit more information to corroborate the facts.

At the next meeting with her boss two days later, Kaylee mentioned the debate at city hall about a potential budget overspend, and that she wanted to pursue a story on what was behind it.

"How much overspend?" he asked, barely looking up from his computer.

"About two million dollars," she explained.

"For the whole fiscal year? That's nothing." Jason dismissed it with a wave of his hand. "It's probably just an accounting error. They'll sort it out at some point."

"I don't know," Kaylee persisted. "Councilman

Marchesi seemed pretty adamant that the mayor's office was mismanaging the budget and was demanding an answer."

"Everyone knows that Emeril Marchesi is planning to run against Mayor Lyle Gordon in next year's election. So, there's the real story, Kaylee," he explained in a patronizing glare. "This all sounds like political posturing more than anything else. You better get used to it, 'cause it's going to be a long and messy campaign."

Kaylee was well aware of Emeril Marchesi's political aspirations. And while she had the urge to provide more information about potential vendor favoritism for infrastructure projects, she also remembered her promise to Rosalie. Once she had more evidence from other sources, she would give Jason an update. Then of course he would support her story.

For three weeks, Kaylee tried to uncover any information to substantiate the rumor that two building companies were overcharging the city, but hit a wall at every turn. She talked to several people in the various municipal offices responsible for city building contracts. Kaylee also tracked down a copy of the budget update shared at the last city council meeting, but it had only very high-level line items, not enough information to support or disprove her theory. None of her usual contacts knew anything more specific, nor could they point her in the right direction. Finally, she tried the Department of Audits, hoping to uncover any known incidents of waste or fraud related to building contracts, but with no useful results.

The next morning was a Friday, and Jason called her into his office as soon as she arrived at work.

"What were you doing at city hall yesterday?" he demanded before she could sit down.

"What?" she stammered, caught off guard.

"I just got off the phone with Norma Sanders. As in the city of Baltimore comptroller, Norma Sanders. She wanted to know why one of my reporters was harassing her executive assistant yesterday—"

"I wasn't harassing anyone!"

"Harassing her executive assistant and making threats to uncover mismanagement in the contract bidding process."

"I never made any threats!" Kaylee insisted.

"I don't give a shit what you did, Stone. You were out of line! Now what the hell were you doing in the comptroller's offices?"

Kaylee bit her bottom lip.

"I was following a lead on a story," she replied, softly.

"On what exactly?" Jason snapped back.

"The forecasted budget overspend."

"What?"

She lifted her chin, straightened her shoulders and repeated her words.

"Are you kidding me?" he yelled, slapping the top of his desk with the palm of his hand. "I told you to leave it alone! There is no story there!"

"I know, but I have information from a very credible source—"

"Who?" demanded Jason, leaning forward aggressively.

Kaylee stepped back as tingles of dread began

creeping up her back. She had known there was a risk that her boss would be mad about pursuing the story, but this reaction was way beyond what she had expected.

"I can't say," she told him in a strong, steady voice. "But there is something going on there, Jason. I know it."

"You know nothing," he snapped. "And I don't need city officials calling my office, questioning the conduct of my reporters. So as of today, I'm reassigning you to Arts and Culture."

"You can't be serious!" Kaylee protested, unable to believe what was happening.

"Deadly serious," Jason replied as he sat down behind his desk and started sorting through the litter of documents on top. "You're just lucky the comptroller didn't call the chief with this or you would be out of a job. Now, get the hell out of my office."

Kaylee spent the rest of the day in a fog, thinking through the conversations she'd had the day before with city workers. Yes, she had spoken to Andrea Butler, the executive assistant to the comptroller, and asked some pointed questions about managing contractor invoicing and overspend. But there had been nothing threatening or aggressive in Kaylee's comments or tone. But obviously someone, the executive assistant, the comptroller, or someone else, wanted to ensure the questions stopped, by making a formal complaint to her boss.

By the end of the day, she was too angry to let it go. Rather than hang out with her girlfriends after work, she walked twenty minutes straight home to her Harbor East apartment, quickly packed an overnight bag, and drove an hour in her car to her parents' home in McLean, Virginia.

"Miss Mikayla!" exclaimed the family housekeeper, Ida Fuentes, with a big smile. "I didn't know you'd be home this weekend."

"Hi, Ida," Kaylee replied as they hugged. "It wasn't planned. I tried calling my mom, but I got her voicemail. Are my parents home yet?"

"Not yet, but I'm expecting them soon," Ida explained. "Your brother is home. He's watching television in the kitchen."

"Okay, thanks."

"Are you in town to see Mr. Evan? I didn't know he was back in the country," Ida continued as they walked through the large house.

"No, he's still in Europe for another couple of weeks I think," Kaylee told her. She and Evan had been engaged for over three years, with the wedding less than eight weeks away in early July.

"Well, I'm sure Mrs. DaCosta will be happy to see you anyway. There are still so many details to be finalized for the big day."

They entered the kitchen to find her brother, George "Junior" Stone-Clement, eating a sandwich and watching a reality television show. He barely looked up to say hello to his sister, or his mother, who also walked into the room from the entrance to the mudroom and garage on the other side.

"Yes, there is a lot to do," stated Elaine Stone-Clement, referring to the wedding plans. "And most of it still requires your decisions, Mikayla. The planner is starting to think I'm the one who's getting married."

"Hi, Mom," Kaylee said as she walked into her mom's arms for a long hug.

"Hey, baby. I just got your message when I pulled up to the house," Elaine explained. "It's so good to see you. Are you staying for the whole weekend?"

"No, just until tomorrow," replied Kaylee. She went to the fridge to get a glass of water, slapping her younger brother in the back of the head on the way. "Will Dad be home soon?"

"Probably not until later this evening. He has a dinner meeting with the board," her mom explained. "Now let me go get changed. We have a lot of decisions to make. Let's do it over dinner."

Kaylee smiled, though it felt very forced. The last thing she wanted to do was talk about frivolous, meaningless wedding details when her career was going backwards. But she did it anyway, for almost three hours, and it wasn't nearly as painful as she'd imagined. Her mom had a whole portfolio of options, pulled together from months of discussions and debate among Elaine, Kaylee, and her future mother-in-law, Cecile DaCosta, who had also been Elaine's best friend for years. All the options they had shortlisted were beautiful, elegant and timeless, making it easy for Kaylee to just pick one of everything with little debate. At least, that's what she told herself as she smiled back at the look of joy and pride on her mom's face when they were all done. But, deep in her stomach, Kaylee knew she needed to seriously figure out why she had little real interest in planning her nuptials to a man she loved.

"Mikayla! When did you get home?" George Clement asked as he walked into the living room at about ten-thirty that evening. He leaned down and kissed the cheeks of both his wife and his daughter.

"Hey, Dad," she replied with a broad smile.

George was a big man with a portly stature and a jovial disposition. He was a multimillionaire and CEO of one of the largest media conglomerates in the United States, which he had built from the ground up, yet he was always present for his family.

"George, you'll be very happy to know that we finally have the wedding plans finalized," Elaine stated a she walked over to the bar at the side of the room and poured a glass of aged scotch for her husband and glasses of cabernet sauvignon for the two women.

"Really?" he replied. "That's great! Now we can all get some sleep."

Elaine rolled her eyes at his sarcasm.

"I'm going to give Cecile a call with an update. At least she will appreciate our efforts, right, Mikayla?"

"Right, Mom," she agreed, but gave her dad a big wink on the sly as her mom walked out of the room with her usual long, confident stride.

"How's work going?" her dad asked as he sat down beside her on the deep soft brown leather sofa.

"I don't know, to be honest," she said with a deep sigh. Now that she had the opportunity to address the issue that had originally brought her back home, Kaylee was having second thoughts. She had always been so adamant that she would not use her family name to further her career, yet here she was, complaining to her daddy because she didn't like a decision made by her boss.

"What's wrong?"

She looked at the man she loved but also respected greatly.

"If I get your advice on something, will you promise not to do anything about it?"

"Okay. What is it?" he easily agreed while sipping at his drink.

Kaylee took a deep breath and told her dad a very brief summary of what had happened since the contentious city council meeting and her coffee chat with a friend in the mayor's office.

"Did I do the wrong thing, Dad? Should I have stopped pursuing the story when Jason told me to?" she asked when his expression remained completely unreadable.

"That depends on why you did it," he replied, watching her closely.

"Because! I think there is a real story here," she insisted passionately. "I know a couple of million dollars is not a big deal in the scope of the full city budget, but that's not the point! How are vendors allowed to overcharge the city that much without someone knowing about it? And if it's happening, why would anyone hide that from the rest of the city council?"

"Well, if that's what you think, then you did the right thing, sweetheart. The job of a journalist is to uncover the truth, and that's not always easy or convenient. But the key is to focus on the truth, not what you want to find," her dad stated with deep seriousness.

"So you're saying I might be wrong?" she asked, confused.

"It's not about being right or wrong. It's about pursuing the facts, wherever they lead," he patiently explained. "As long as that's your true intent, you'll always be doing the right thing as a journalist. And sometimes that comes with consequences."

Kaylee let his words soak in for a couple of minutes as she silently tried to figure out how they applied to her current situation.

"Looks like you have some decisions to make," her dad continued as he drained the last mouthful of rich, golden scotch from his glass. "In the meantime, tell me again about the conversations you had yesterday at city hall?"

"Why?" she asked with some concern. "I told you, Dad, I spoke to three people from a few departments of the city comptroller. But they were just basic questions about processes and regulations. I did ask a couple of people straight out if they knew about companies that over-billed. But that's it. I would never harass anyone or make threats. That's just a lie!"

"Sweetheart, I know that," George insisted, patiently tapping her knee. "I just wanted to understand what happened, that's all."

She let out a deep breath, suddenly very exhausted.

"Why don't you get some sleep?" he continued. "I know you're disappointed about moving from city politics to the society page, but it doesn't have to be a bad thing. It's also an opportunity to broaden your experience."

Kaylee nodded and tried to smile, but it looked more like a painful grimace.

"Thanks, Dad."

He leaned forward and kissed her forehead.

"Now, if you'll excuse me, I have a quick call to make before I'm off to bed also," George stated. "I'll see you in the morning."

While Kaylee finished her wine and made her way upstairs to her childhood bedroom for a dreamless sleep, she didn't realize that her father was calling Fortis to start an investigation into corruption at the *Baltimore Journal*.

CHAPTER 6

By Monday, Kaylee had a calmer attitude about the whole situation. Her dad's words had given her a new perspective. While she didn't regret pursuing the story on potential vendor abuse at city hall based on the information Rosalie had provided, three weeks was enough time to pursue that truth, and there was nothing to show for it. Following the facts had led to nothing, and now it was time to accept the consequences and move on. How bad could it be to write for the Arts and Culture pages? The Clement family was connected to many influential people in Virginia, D.C., and Maryland, so her new assignments might actually be fun.

She also spent time searching her feelings about Evan and their engagement. There was something missing from the equation, something that should be a critical part of a relationship for two people who were about to get married. Was it passion, intimacy, the need to feel completely connected to your partner both emotionally and physically?

None of those things had ever been huge in their relationship, but up until recently, Kaylee had considered that a positive thing. That was why they got along so well, and easily tolerated a long-distance relationship while Evan was working overseas. That was what allowed her to focus on her education and career, versus the many other women in her circle who could only think about china patterns and babies.

But more recently, as the date of the wedding inched closer, comfortable and easy started to feel like ambivalence and detachment. While Kaylee knew that she loved Evan, she could no longer confirm that she was *in love*, and she instinctively knew that Evan wasn't either.

Once she came to terms with that fact, there was only one answer. When Evan returned from Europe at the end of the week, Kaylee was going to end their engagement. Their parents would be upset and disappointed, but ultimately they would also see that it was the right decision.

Feeling lighter than she had in months, Kaylee went back to work with new determination. She spent the morning and the lunch hour doing research and reviewing previous articles written by other staff reporters. She had a meeting with Jason that afternoon when she was expected to pitch story ideas for her first few stories. The meeting went smoothly, though Jason seemed a little distracted and impatient. At first, she thought he might still be annoyed with her about the complaint from the comptroller's office, but he barely responded to her story suggestions, except to nod occasionally while repeatedly checking his phone. Kaylee left his office thirty minutes later feeling relieved that he was not about to penalize her with micromanagement or additional scrutiny.

The next couple of hours were uneventful. Kaylee worked quietly at her desk, taking notes and planning her schedule to attend various social and community events. She also sent a text message to Rosalie, suggesting they meet for coffee or lunch that week so they could catch up on things. It would be an opportunity for Kaylee to let her friend know that she was no longer assigned to city politics and therefore would not use the budget information shared weeks earlier.

At about quarter to four o'clock, she went to the bathroom, which was located on the opposite side of the floor beside one of the staircases. Though Kaylee was distracted while leaving the facilities, reading emails on her cell phone, she paused after pushing the exit door open a crack. Jason Holt's voice was low, but her name rang clear in the narrow pathway as he walked by.

"Stone has been shut down. I told you on Friday . . ."

Kaylee closed the door and paused there for several seconds, processing the words while her heartbeat started thudding hard in her chest. *Shut down?* What did that mean? She slowly pushed the bathroom door open, listening intently for Jason's voice or any sign of where he had gone. The hallway to the bathroom was empty and quiet. Kaylee looked at the exit to the staircase on her right, then crept over and pushed on the heavy door so it opened slowly just a little, then leaned in close to listen for any sound. He was in there, maybe one flight down and speaking in a nervous, urgent tone, but too quiet for her to hear all the words.

"I did what you asked. . . . When?" he demanded, clearly frustrated.

Seconds later, his footsteps echoed loudly, suggesting he was moving again. Kaylee quickly let go of the door and rushed back to her desk, trying her best to look normal. She looked around her work area, but no one else seemed to notice her flustered, agitated state. Only about sixty seconds passed before Jason emerged from the hallway, walking with determined steps toward his office, which was not far from her desk. He was no longer on the phone, but his eyes were fixed on its screen as he tapped actively at an application. Kaylee quickly looked at her computer, holding her breath as he passed by. She glanced over her shoulder when he disappeared into the office and out of view.

"Jason, do you have a second?" It was Albert Thompson, one of the staff photographers, walking up to the editor's door. "I need to show you those pictures. They're due in production within the next five minutes."

A moment later, Jason walked out and followed Albert across the room. Kaylee noticed right away that he did not have his cell phone. She looked around. Everyone else in the office seemed to be going on about their business. She stood up, taking her phone and a few sheets of paper with her, and walked to Jason's office. A quick glance over at

Albert's desk told her both men were sitting in front of his computer screen, intently focused on the images displayed. Kaylee took a deep breath and walked into the room, immediately spotting Jason's cell phone, face up on the desk. As she approached it, the device vibrated with a message notification and the screen lit up to display the message.

Kaylee paused to look back at the office entrance, listening to see if she could hear anyone nearby. Then she quickly opened the camera app on her phone and took a picture of Jason's cell phone screen, capturing the message details.

"What are you doing in here, Kaylee?" Jason demanded in a harsh voice.

Kaylee quickly turned around, placing the papers in her hand over his cell phone.

"I was just dropping off the first draft of the central library article," she improvised in a calm voice, quickly walking past him and out of his office.

"Kaylee!" She closed her eyes tight and took a deep breath before turning back around. "These pages are blank!"

He now stood behind his desk, accessing his cell phone with quick taps.

"Sorry! I must have grabbed the wrong ones," she explained with an embarrassed smile. "I'll bring them in a sec."

"Just email it," he replied with a dismissive wave of his hand, his eyes still glued to the small screen.

Kaylee nodded, then rushed away, barely breathing as she stopped at her desk just long enough to quickly pack up her laptop and power cord into her tote bag. Then she rushed to the elevators with her cell phone still clutched in her hands. She was about to press the call button when she caught a glimpse of Jason as he emerged from his office and looked around the floor. Afraid he was looking for her, and somehow knew what she had done, Kaylee almost ran to the staircase by the bathrooms and rushed down the eleven flights of stairs. It wasn't an easy escape while wearing a fitted white shirt and a black narrow knee-length skirt in black pumps with four-inch heels. By the time she pushed through the heavy doors on the ground floor and out to the alley at the side of the office building, she was sweating and her thighs felt weak and rubbery.

She paused for only a couple of seconds, trying to get her bearings and decide what to do next. Figuring that, if Jason was going to come after her, he would probably assume that she would go onto the main street at the front of the building, Kaylee decided to go through the back parking lot and find her way to another street. Then she could stop somewhere safe and decide what to do next. She was making her way through the alley in a slow, painful jog, looking back over her shoulder continuously, when her heel caught on the edge of uneven concrete and her ankle twisted painfully. Kaylee went flying forward, her cell phone tossed into the air as she instinctively reached out her hands to stop her fall. It all seemed to happen in slow motion, but she could not stop the momentum. Her shout of painful surprise echoed against the brick walls.

* * *

"I got you," Sam said as he wrapped his arm around the woman's waist from behind just before she would have hit the ground. He had easily fallen to his left knee, with his other leg bent at a right angle, and pulled her body so it landed against the firm brace of his right thigh.

"Arghhh!" she moaned in a softer tone, awkwardly reaching out for something to grab on to while looking around wildly. Her elbow knocked him hard in the nose before her right arm hooked around his neck in a choking grip.

Sam held her more securely for another few moments, allowing her to calm down before she could do any real damage to his body. Then he looked down at her face, partially covered by tousled black hair. Deep dark brown eyes stared back at him, open wide with apprehension and sparkling with flecks of gold. Her silky, russet-hued skin was dewy, and her cheeks were darkly flushed. Full, soft lips were parted slightly from her shallow, rapid breathing.

"I got you," he repeated softly, unable to think of anything else to say. The woman just stared at him for another few moments until a door closed somewhere nearby. She sat up quickly and tried to stand, but Sam immediately felt her freeze with a sharp gasp.

"Are you hurt?" he asked, using his arm and legs to ease them both upright. She barely reached his shoulder, even in stiletto heels.

She remained silent, but her slender frame rigid as a board. He looked down to see that she was on only one foot; the other was obviously swelling up.

"Your ankle?"

She nodded, clenching her jaw hard and obviously trying not to express her pain.

"Okay. I'm going to carry you to my car," he explained softly. "It's just a few feet away in the parking lot."

She nodded again, then held her breath and gripped her tote bag as he easily lifted her into his arms.

"My cell phone!" she gasped as they started through the alley, pointing behind them.

"I'll come back for it."

"No! Please. I need it," she insisted, gripping him tightly around his neck with both arms.

Sam retraced his steps and lowered her next to the phone so he could pick it up.

"Thank you," she whispered as he handed it over and lifted her into his arms again.

"I'm Sam, by the way," he said easily, barely noticing her weight. "Samuel Mackenzie."

Their eyes met again, and he could tell she was trying to assess if he was dangerous or not. Sam gave her a small smile, softening his usually stoic expression.

"Don't worry. I'm harmless," he continued, trying further to ease her obvious nervousness. "To a bonnie, injured lass, anyway."

Her brows quirked.

"Well, that's a relief," she replied, smiling wide and revealing glossy white teeth, the two front ones slightly longer than the others. "Kaylee."

"Nice to meet you, Kaylee." They reached his black SUV, which was parked against the wall next to the back entrance of the *Baltimore Journal.* "I'm going to sit you down in the passenger seat, okay? Then I'll have a look at your ankle."

Kaylee nodded and allowed him to put her down inside the car.

"Sam, is everything good?"

The question came as a young man with coppery-tanned skin and long, wavy dirty-blond hair walked over to the truck. He was dressed similar to Sam, in a dark fitted shirt and utility pants, and stopped next to the passenger door.

"Kaylee, this is my colleague, Raymond Blunt," Sam said as he gently lifted her left leg at the knee so he could inspect the ankle more closely by running his hands over the bone. "It's swollen, but not broken. Likely a slight sprain. I'll take you to the medical center. You'll want to wrap it up and keep it elevated with some ice."

"No, that's okay," she insisted, looking around. "It's starting to feel a little better, so I'll just take care of it at home. It will probably be fine in a few hours."

"Are you sure?" he asked. "It's no bother."

Kaylee looked between them, obviously embarrassed to be causing a fuss. "Yes, I'm fine. I've obviously interrupted your work—"

"Not at all," Raymond interrupted with an easy smile. "We were just finishing up here."

"See?" Sam said. "I'm completely at your disposal. And you can't drive in this condition anyway."

"I was going to take a cab," Kaylee explained, looking down. "I'm just a few blocks away so I usually walk to work."

"Then I have no choice," Sam declared as he gently lowered her leg so she could sit back in the grey leather seat. "I am honor bound to assist you home."

"There's no point in rejecting the offer, Kaylee," Raymond added when it was clear she was about to protest. "Sam here can be a little stubborn. And don't worry—you are completely safe in his hands. I can personally vouch for him."

"And who's going to vouch for your judgment, mate?" Sam shot back, sardonically.

"Dude, you're not helping," Raymond quipped, raising his hands dramatically

Sam snickered, but was pleased to notice that their banter seemed to amuse her. She looked much more relaxed, and less likely to hobble away in fear.

"Seriously, Kaylee. You could not be safer than with this guy, despite his scary demeanor," Raymond continued. "But here is my business card, in case you're still concerned. Just call me if he steps out of line, and I'll handle him."

That made her giggle as she took the black stationery and looked closely at both sides. It had his contact information, and a website for Fortis Consulting, the front company used by field agents while working a case. If she was inclined to look it up, the unsophisticated site described the firm as simply providing security solutions and protective services to small or medium-sized companies.

"Okay, enough smart remarks, Blunt," Sam said. "I'll take her home and connect with you later back at headquarters."

"Sure thing, boss. Nice to meet you, Kaylee. Take care of that ankle."

"Thanks, Raymond. Nice to meet you too," she replied politely.

The two men nodded to each other, and Sam got behind the wheel and started up the truck.

"Where to, ma'am?" he teased, with a quirk of his lips. Kaylee giggled again. It was a really nice sound and made him smile wider. She gave him an address in East Harbor, right next to the marina.

Sam wasn't familiar with all the Baltimore neighborhoods, but knew that one was pretty high end. He looked over at his passenger, thinking he would check her identity later, if Raymond didn't do it first.

"How are you feeling?" he asked after driving in silence for a few minutes.

"My ankle is sore, but I think my pride hurts the most," she told him, her face turned away as she looked out the window.

"You looked like you were in a rush when you left the building," he commented. "Do you work at the *Journal*?"

"Yeah, I'm a staff writer. I was just running late to do an errand. Nothing important."

They lapsed into silence again for the remainder of the drive. When he drove up to her building, Kaylee directed him to the underground visitors' parking. The security guard on duty checked his driver's license before opening the garage doors. Sam noted her prudent actions; by having him use the indoor parking versus something outside, she ensured his identity was documented before allowing him up to the apartment with her.

Pretty *and* sensible, he thought.

"This is a nice building," Sam said as they stepped out of the elevators on the fifth floor. He carried her bag and held her firmly around the waist while she held on to his shoulder to hobble forward without putting weight on the right foot.

"Thanks," she replied briefly.

At her apartment, the door had a keyless lock. Sam politely looked away as she entered the access code into the key pad. Inside, large creamy marble tiles in the entranceway led toward rich, darkly stained exotic wood floors throughout the space. As he helped her farther into the unit toward the main living area, Sam had the impression of simple furnishings with clean, modern lines and neutral, richly textured materials.

"Over on the couch would be fine," Kaylee said after they had passed the high-end kitchen and a powder room.

Sam slowly helped her lower onto the tailored sofa so her right leg was stretched out straight on upholstered light grey wool suiting fabric. He gathered a few of the pillows on top, tucking two under her calf and one behind her back against the sofa arm to ensure she could recline comfortably.

"How is that?" he asked, stepping back to check his work.

"This is perfect," she replied with a sigh. "I can't thank you enough for your help. I don't know what I would have done if you hadn't been there."

"You can thank me after I've finished the job," he

teased. Her eyes widened with confusion. "That ankle needs to be wrapped, and I want to make sure you can move around on your own."

"Honestly, I'll be fine," she insisted, sitting up straight. "See, I can already move it around a little. You've done more than enough already. I'll just call one of my friends for help if needed."

"Do you have a tensor bandage or first aid kit?" he asked, walking back toward the kitchen.

"There's a kit in the guest bathroom, near the front door," she told him.

"Okay. Any freezer bags?" Sam continued, looking around the neat, organized space. The only thing on the granite counter was a complicated-looking espresso machine and a paper towel holder.

"In the third drawer, next to the sink."

"Painkillers?"

She let out an audible sigh. His back was to her, and he grinned a little.

"The last cupboard, on your right."

Sam followed her directions, getting all the necessary supplies together. He could feel Kaylee's eyes on him, watching his actions the whole time. Fifteen minutes later, he was kneeling on the floor next to the sofa, inspecting his work. Her swollen ankle was wrapped with a roller bandage and had a cold compress pressed on it, and she had two aspirins and a glass of water within easy reach on the coffee table.

"Okay, now you can thank me," he declared.

Kaylee raised her eyebrows, assessing him with those rich brown, gold-flecked eyes.

"Okay. Thank you for your high-handed, stubborn assistance," she said with a sugary-sweet smile.

Sam chuckled easily.

"You're welcome, darling."

The endearment hung in the air, inappropriate for their brief acquaintance but accurately reflecting the easy connection. Kaylee looked down at her wrapped foot, but Sam's gaze remained fixed on her very pretty face. Something about this petite stranger pulled at him, stirring up an odd mix of affection, protection, and attraction. Now that she was patched up and comfortable, he should say his good-byes and leave, get back to work, close out the Clement Media investigation. But Sam found himself lingering, looking for another opportunity to tease her, put another smile on those very sweet lips.

Kaylee looked up at him again, and they glowed with awareness. Then she glanced down at his mouth.

Shit. He liked her. A lot. And the realization hit him hard and deep in the gut.

Sam's phone vibrated with a message, breaking the tense silence. Kaylee looked away again. He took it out of his pocket to read the note from Raymond.

Kaylee Stone, Staff Writer at BJ, works for Holt.

"I have to get back to the office," he said.

"Of course."

"Do you need anything else before I go?"

"No, I'll be fine."

Sam took a business card similar to Raymond's out of his pocket and put it on the coffee table next to the aspirin.

"Send me a message to let me know how you're doing. But don't hesitate to call me if you need to," he instructed as he stood up.

"You don't have to—"

"I know," he interrupted. "I want to."

Kaylee looked up at him with surprise, and he felt a tangible connection between them.

"Okay," she finally replied.

Sam smiled, transforming his usually stern expression into one that was boyishly charming. Kaylee grinned back before he walked silently out of her apartment.

CHAPTER 7

"Jason Holt isn't very good at corruption," Sam said.

It was close to six o'clock that evening as he and Raymond reconvened in a meeting room on the ground floor of the *Baltimore Journal* building. Their client, George Clement, was joining the meeting by video conference from his corporate head office in Washington, D.C. The grainy digital image clearly revealed the angry determination on his face.

"We have now confirmed three instances where Holt has accepted bribes, in cash, for influence at the *Journal*," concluded Sam. "The good news is that he appears to have acted alone, and we have not found any signs of wider-spread corruption."

"Sir, we've sent you a final report with all the details," Raymond added. "But as you suggested when you hired us on Friday evening, he has been compensated for directing newspaper coverage toward, or away from, certain stories. As far as we can tell, all three bribes appear unrelated and opportunistic. He was paid in cash, but there was plenty of evidence, between his messages on his personal cell phone, banking transactions, and purchase records."

"How much was he paid?" George Clement asked.

"We're not certain, but we estimate somewhere between twenty- and forty-thousand dollars in the first two cases," Sam explained. "We intercepted the cash for the third payment late this afternoon. It was fifty thousand."

"As you'll see in our report, the first two were with local businessmen who paid to have articles written for extra publicity," Raymond continued. "The last is not as clear."

"Mr. Clement, on Friday, you suggested the briber was somehow connected to city hall, maybe the comptroller's office?" Sam questioned.

"Yes, based on the information I was given," George confirmed.

"The challenge is that all the communication to Holt was done through an untraceable mobile phone," explained Sam. "We know he received a call from that unregistered number on Thursday afternoon, and he called back on Friday. There were several calls between them on Monday, with a final text message at four twenty-seven PM saying, 'The package is on its way.'"

George Clement sighed with obvious frustration.

"Sir, do you have any idea who at city hall may be involved?" asked Raymond.

"No," George stated. "I only know that Jason pulled a writer off a story after she questioned city employees. I just assumed someone there was involved."

"Maybe," Sam mused, stroking his short beard. "But it would have to be someone pretty high up and very ballsy. They would have done some pretty fast research to know that Holt could be bought."

"Or they had worked with him before," suggested Raymond.

Sam nodded at the possibility. "In either case, we'll start with what Holt knows."

"I've asked my chief editor at the *Journal*, Mark McMann, to handle the dismissal," George explained. "He's asked Jason to stay for a late meeting, and I'll ask Mark to question him about who paid the bribe."

"Okay. While this concludes our original mission for you, Mr. Clement, we would be happy to start a new assignment, pursuing the identity of who paid Holt. In which case, one of our agents can assist with his questioning."

"Thank you, Sam. You and your team have delivered the results I needed, as promised. And I appreciate the offer, but let's see what Mark discovers, then I'll decide what to do next. I have your number if I need it," George said before they ended the meeting.

Sam and Raymond began to pack up the various computers and devices for their makeshift control center.

"I have one of the analysts at headquarters running a security check on all the other employees at the paper," Raymond noted. "Should we hold on that until we get further instructions from Clement?"

"How long will it take to complete them?" asked Sam.

"A couple of days, at least."

Sam thought for a moment. "Let's limit it to just the writers and editors for now. It would be helpful to have them completed if he wants to look further into the situation."

On Tuesday, just before six o'clock in the evening, Sam was tapping lightly at Kaylee Stone's apartment door after being announced by the front doorman. She opened it wearing a black tank top and grey pants in a soft, jersey fabric. Her face was fresh and clean of makeup, and her hair was pulled back into a ponytail.

"What are you doing here?" she asked after waving him in and limping toward the kitchen.

"I told you earlier in my text message that I would check on you," Sam reminded her, shutting the door and following her slow path.

"I thought you meant with a phone call or something," she explained with a sigh.

Sam shrugged. "I was in the neighborhood." She raised her brows with obvious skepticism. He shrugged. "How did you make out through the day?"

"My boss wasn't in the office today, so I was able to work from home," Kaylee explained as she eased carefully into a dining room chair.

"Are you still in pain? Maybe we should take you to the medical center, or your family doctor," he suggested, bending down on his haunches to look at her still bandaged ankle, now visible below the hem of her pants. It looked much less swollen.

"It's tender but not too bad. I'm sure it will be fine in a couple of days," she told him.

Sam straightened his back to look up at her from his low position. She looked sweet and comfortable in her casual clothes, yet with a hint of sensuality simmering just beneath the surface, as though enticing him to uncover it. And there was no doubt he was enticed. Thoughts of her had continuously disrupted his attention and focus over the last fourteen hours.

What about Kaylee, exactly, had captured his attention? At twenty-nine years old, Sam met pretty women all the time. He had a great appreciation for the wide variety of feminine attributes that made them all uniquely attractive. He enjoyed their company when it was mutually convenient, but moved on once the connection ran its course. His relationships in their various forms had all been effortless and uncomplicated. Yet the incessant feeling in the pit of his stomach was telling him that Kaylee was anything but that.

Even now, as they looked at each other for longer than was polite or casual, Sam knew he was well off his game.

"So, how did you develop such a good bedside manner?" she asked with a teasing smile. "On-the-job training?"

Sam chuckled. "You could say that. People occasionally get injured in my line of work. Knowing what to do in a pinch comes in handy."

"That sounds intriguing. What exactly do you do?"

Sam slowly straightened up until he was standing. "Security consultant," he told her, walking toward the kitchen. "Can I get you anything? Something to drink?"

"Hmmm. Coffee would be great."

"I could murder a cup myself. Okay, let's see if I can figure out this machine," Sam added as he inspected the fancy and obviously expensive espresso machine. There were four glass mugs stored on top.

"It's easy, fully automatic," Kaylee explained. "The beans are already loaded, so you just need to press the green button."

He shot her a sheepish look, then followed her instructions.

"How do you take it?"

"Black," she answered. "But there's cream in the fridge and sugar in the cupboard."

Sam took out both for his brew, and walked back over to the dining table with both.

"Thank you."

They savored the rich flavor for a couple of sips.

"Security consultant. Is that like a bodyguard or something?"

He smiled. "Or something." Kaylee raised her brows at his evasiveness. "It's a little more complicated."

"Very intriguing," she said in a dramatic whisper, her eyes twinkling. "So, shouldn't you be guarding someone or something right now, instead of baby-sitting me? Not that I don't appreciate the attention. And the coffee."

"No need to be concerned. I'm between assignments right now," Sam told her with a charming grin. "You can appreciate the attention, guilt free."

Her lips split into a wide smile, and she burst

out laughing. It was a soft, rich, genuine sound, revealing the sweetest dimples in her cheeks. Sam could not hold back his own deep laughter.

"Are you always this charming?" she asked when they had both quieted down.

He shook his head, chuckling again. "No, not at all, actually."

"Really? Then you must be a natural. You're pretty good at it."

Sam rubbed at his stubble-covered jaw, hiding another grin. They shared another few moments of fleeting glances and knowing smiles.

"Any plans for the evening?" he finally asked while standing up and gathering their empty coffee mugs.

"I was going to go dancing, but I'm open to other suggestions," Kaylee quipped with an impish shrug.

"How about dinner? We could order something in."

"Okay, dinner it is," she agreed. "There's a pretty good Chinese restaurant nearby."

She placed the order, requesting her usual, and Sam nodded at each without any additional suggestions. He helped her get settled on the sofa, where they chatted about their backgrounds until the food arrived. Kaylee was great at asking questions, so it was mostly about Sam and his move from Britain to the United States two years ago. His condescending anecdotes about "Yanks" had her doubled over with laughter.

"Was it difficult, relocating to a new country?" she asked when they were both finished eating and sitting on the living room sofa.

He shrugged. "Not really. I traveled a lot in Europe and had worked here for a few months prior to that," Sam explained.

"Doing the same thing? Security work?"

"Law enforcement."

"You were a police officer? That doesn't surprise me," she acknowledged, looking him over with an assessing eye. "Do you miss home? Your family?"

"It's just my mum and dad. They're still in Scotland, outside the tiny village near Inverness where I grew up."

"A country boy?"

Sam nodded. "Dad still runs the farm, mostly growing vegetables and raising sheep. At one point, when I was about four, we had some cattle. I remember watching my father milk the cow every day and really wanting to try it. Then one morning, Dad was doing a fence repair or something, and I decided I could do the milking on my own." He smiled at the memory. "I got the bucket and stool he always used and set it up beside the nearest cow and I started tugging away, squeezing like how I had seen him do it. But nothing happened. I was only at it for a few minutes, until Dad came up behind me and he said: 'Little Mac, that's not a cow. And, son, that's not a teat.'"

Kaylee's eyes opened wide.

"Turns out I was giving the bull a good time," he finished, and she burst out laughing. "I swear that bull had his eyes on me for weeks after."

"He fell in love!" she gasped, pressing a hand to her chest while trying to catch her breath.

"Seems so," he admitted while chuckling.

"Do you still have magic fingers?"

Sam stretched out one of his large hands between them, turning it back and forth for examination.

"They're not as soft anymore, but I haven't had any complaints."

He held his breath as Kaylee brushed her fingers along his palm. The light touch sucked the breath out of his body.

"I guess some like things more rough," she teased softly. But the second the words came out, soaked in sexual innuendo, her eyes widened with awareness. She immediately sat back from him and tried to get up on her still sore ankle.

"Hey," Sam said, immediately reaching out to steady her with a light hold on her arm. But Kaylee shuffled away farther, moving until she was standing beside the sofa, holding on to the arm for balance.

"Sorry, I shouldn't have said that," she stammered, looking down at her feet. "I was just joking around. It was stupid."

"I know that, Kaylee," he replied, staying a couple of steps back from her with his hands in his pockets. "Don't worry about it."

She let out a deep breath, clearly still embarrassed.

"Thank you for dinner," she added, still not looking at him. "And everything else."

Sam nodded, sensing her withdrawal and feeling really disappointed.

"Would you like me to go?" he asked, preferring to speak directly.

Kaylee finally looked straight at him. Her rich brown eyes glittered brightly with mixed emotion.

But she didn't reply right away. Sam took a step closer, as though drawn by the intensity between them.

She let out a deep breath. "I think that's probably a good idea."

"Okay," Sam told her with a soft, patient smile. "I had fun."

He intended to walk past her in front of the sofa, toward the front door, but Kaylee looked up the moment their shoulders were adjacent. He was struck by the vulnerability and disappointment on her face and could not resist the urge to reach out.

"Kaylee," Sam whispered in a low voice, not sure what exactly to say. She leaned forward, closer, and he did the same until they were so close they were almost touching.

Sam paused, waiting for a sign that she wanted him to stay, and very aware that she had just told him the opposite. Her eyes flickered over the features of his face before dropping to his lips, but still he resisted the urge to kiss her. He raised his hand up, the same one she'd brushed so gently only moments ago, and stroked the back of his fingers along the line of her cheek. They both gasped at the spark that flared from the touch, and Sam slowly leaned close until his lips touched hers.

The first brushes were light, hesitant, and tentative, testing the waters, confirming the welcome. She felt soft and so sweet. Addictive.

She moaned, deep in her throat, and Sam was a goner.

CHAPTER 8

Kaylee was floating on a cloud of sensations. Every part of her body was alive and tingling with anticipation, craving something so different than she'd experienced before. Sam Mackenzie had shown up, out of nowhere, in the most chaotic moment of her life, to create even more havoc.

His lips gently stroked hers, so deliciously, like the first taste of a decadent dessert that was so irresistibly bad. Sinful. Kaylee leaned into the warmth radiating from his body, and opened her mouth to stroke her tongue over his lips.

He responded by cupping the back of her head gently and pulling her even closer. The kiss quickly became hot, deep, and wet.

"Are you okay?" Sam asked, pulling back an inch. "Do you want me to go?"

Kaylee tried to remember that this was an experiment, an effort to further understand her instant and insane attraction to this man. Just a sample of raw, unfettered passion. And Sam's hesitation was the opportunity to stop it, now, before it went too far.

Sighing deeply, she placed both hands on his chest in an effort to push back from the embrace and end the moment. *Oh my*. The thick, rigid muscle jumped under her palms. Kaylee swept widespread fingers over the impressive contours of his body as a fresh wave of heated arousal spread down her legs.

"Yes," she finally replied in a low, throaty voice. "Stay."

Sam buried his fingers deeper into her hair, tugging a little so she looked up at him. His blue eyes were dark and stormy, and his lips flared sensually. God, he was so gorgeously masculine. Like a modern-day Viking, she thought. Then they were kissing again, with tongues intimately entwined. Kaylee was now drowning in arousal, and the ability to think about the consequences slipped away.

"Let's get you off that ankle," he suggested, then effortlessly lifted her into his arms. In a blink, she was sitting upright again on the edge of the sofa, with Sam on his knees in front of her. He pulled her into his arms so she was pressed against his chest and cocooned within his thick arms.

"You smell great," he whispered, kissing and teasing her earlobe "What is it?"

"Chanel," Kaylee gasped.

"It's pure barry."

"What?" she said, confused but incredibly distracted by the path his hands were taking down her neck and along the line of her collarbone.

"It's fantastic," Sam explained with his accent even thicker.

He kissed her again, stroking deep into her mouth with his long, firm tongue. Then those big hands were gliding gently down her back, teasing her sides before slipping under the edge of her top. Kaylee gasped loudly as the touch of his fingers on her bare flesh made her eager with anticipation. She pulled back from their embrace to quickly pull the soft T-shirt over her head, tossing it aside. Sam leaned back to run his eyes over her bra-covered breasts, and Kaylee tried not to feel self-conscious about her average size. She held her breath as he slowly brushed his hands over the delicate lace and exposed curves.

"You're beautiful," he whispered.

She relaxed a bit and smiled teasingly. "You like?"

"Oh, I like very much," Sam replied in a serious tone, his eyes again locked with hers. "The whole package is pretty incredible."

Kaylee would have giggled, but they were kissing again. The temperature in the room quickly rose several degrees. Her bra soon followed the top, and then she spent several minutes slowly pulling off his shirt.

"Oh my," she gasped at the sight of his naked torso. He was all hard muscle with strong, broad shoulders, square chest muscles and a washboard abdomen. Kaylee stroked her hands over his fair, sun-kissed skin, savoring every defined contour. He watched her movements with heavy-hooded eyes and an intense gaze, then groaned when she brushed her knuckles over the button of his pants.

She slowly undid the fastening, and slid the zipper down. But Sam took both her hands before she could continue her exploration.

"I want to touch you," he growled. "Everywhere."

Sam used his hold to smoothly turn her body and help her recline until she was lying flat on her back along the length of the sofa. They both worked to remove her loose pants and underwear until Kaylee lay naked before him, arms folded loosely over her head. She should have felt awkward and exposed, but there was only anticipation and heavy, throbbing arousal.

From head to toe, Sam worked his way down the lines of her body, briefly stopping at every peak and valley to explore the texture and taste, and eliciting a variety of verbal responses. She was almost panting by the time he stroked over the balls of her feet and the sensitive insteps.

"Turn over," he instructed, then helped her roll onto her stomach. Kaylee closed her eyes and turned her head to the side, facing him. While he nibbled on the line of her cheekbones, his hands stroked soothingly up and down her back until he reached the deep curve of her spine and the swell of her behind.

"So sweet," he mumbled, running his lips along the top of her shoulder. He palmed the plump cheeks of her ass, massaging the flesh, then slid one of his hands along the underside and between her thighs.

"Yes!" Kaylee gasped, so ready for his touch that she could hardly breathe.

"Open for me," he urged.

She spread her legs until one was hanging off the edge of the couch. Then he caressed the seam of her mound, teasing the slick lips until he was within the delicate, inner petals and exploring her secrets. Kaylee groaned with delight, gripping the fabric of the cushion beneath her. Sam reached farther to brush over her clit, then circled it repeatedly with gentle pressure meant to drive her over the edge.

"God, yes . . ." she mumbled low and urgent.

"Like this?" he whispered, rubbing a little harder and faster.

"Ahhh-huh—" Kaylee moaned, no longer able to use real words.

"Hmmmm," Sam moaned as he used his other hand to slowly stroke a finger into her tight, wet sheath. "So sweet."

Kaylee couldn't do anything but bury her face into the couch in an effort to stifle the desperate groans of excitement. The magic he was weaving was so intense it was almost unbearable. Her need built and built to the height of arousal until she was almost gasping for air. Then she peaked with a sharp intensity and made the slow, shuddering descent back to reality.

Sam was chuckling. Once she was capable of moving, Kaylee turned her head and peeled her eyes open to look at him.

"Are you laughing at me?" she demanded, too lethargic to really get offended.

"I'm laughing with you," he explained with a big, boyish grin. "That was spectacular."

"Well, I have to agree with you, but you really shouldn't be so boastful."

"No, that was all you, sweetheart. I was just along for the ride and very glad to be invited."

Kaylee gave him a lazy smile and sighed deeply. He continued to stroke her back and the curve of her ass with long, relaxing brushes. She felt comfortable and so deliciously satisfied it was easy to forget that he was almost a stranger. Eventually, she turned onto her side and sat up. Sam immediately pulled her back into his arms for a deep, arousing kiss.

"Do you have any condoms?" he asked.

The question reminded her that there was so much more to be discovered with this man, and new warmth bloomed in the base of her stomach.

"In my bedroom," she told him.

"Should we relocate there?"

"Seems prudent." The next moment, he lifted her by the waist and over his shoulder like a sack of potatoes, with her bare ass in the air. "Hey!"

Sam wrapped his arm around her thighs to stop her struggling movements.

"Relax," he instructed with a rich chuckle. "We wouldn't want you to re-injure your ankle."

Kaylee sighed loudly and tried not to move around as the blood rushed to her head.

"You don't even know where you're going," she protested, though he was almost there anyway.

"I think I can figure it out."

A few seconds later, he lowered her across the width of her bed.

"In the side table?" he asked. She nodded, raising up on her elbows to look at him, still half naked and incredibly hot.

Sam opened the small drawer and paused, then pulled out a small, rubbery device and inspected it with obvious interest. He pressed the small button at the bottom and the toy vibrated with a low, quiet hum. He looked back at Kaylee with his eyebrow raised and a huge smile on his face. She shrugged back, ignoring the flush of embarrassment that spread across her face and down her chest. Her nipples hardened in response, recapturing his attention. He put the toy back and took out a small packet of protection instead, while his eyes remained fixed on her like a physical touch.

"I want you," he growled, quickly stripping off his pants and underwear. "I want to taste you, touch you everywhere all over again. I want to be inside you."

Kaylee was speechless as he stood in front of her and rolled on the condom. His eyes burned with intensity, and his naked six-foot-four body was pure, hard perfection. She swallowed, eyes wide, as he stepped between her legs and stroked his hand along the inside of her thighs. One hand gripped her hip and pulled her to the edge of the mattress while the thumb of the other hand brushed over the silken flesh of her pussy. She could only watch with intense fascination, her legs now anchored around his lean waist. Then he replaced his finger with the broad tip of his penis, stroking over her tight bud. Kaylee turned her head, back arched from the need that radiated through her body.

"Kaylee," he growled roughly. She looked back into his eyes as he slid slow and sure into her body. "Oh yeah—"

"Sam!" she gasped when he reached full depth, the angle hitting a spot she hadn't even known existed.

"Yeah," he repeated as he pumped deeply again and again until they were both damp with sweat. Kaylee could only pant from the intensity on his penetration. Then he was rubbing her clit in that gentle circular caress, and it was too much, too good. . . . His stroke was now longer, faster, driving them toward an incredible peak.

"Oh god! Oh god! Sam—!" she shouted minutes later when the orgasm vibrated throughout her entire body.

He froze for a brief moment, then fell forward, pulling her close so their torsos were completely fused. His body was shaking as he came, as he chanted her name with his lips next to her ear.

Kaylee was half asleep when she felt him leave the bed at some point, returning a short time later to settle them both under the sheets with her back spooned against his front. When she woke, dawn was breaking and Sam was gently stroking her breasts. His hot and very hard erection pressed against her behind.

"Morning," he whispered while snuggling into her neck and brushing his lips along her neck. "Did you sleep well?"

Kaylee smiled. She felt completely rested and very content.

"I did. What time is it?"

"Early," he replied. "You don't need to get up yet, but I have to get going."

She wiped her eyes and turned so she was on her back. Sam smiled down at her with his short, dark blond hair in tousled spikes and his blue eyes glittering. He was still on his side, and one of his hands now rested softly on her lower abdomen.

"Okay," she acknowledged, not sure what was supposed to happen next. "Help yourself to anything in the bathroom."

"Thanks. How's your ankle feeling?"

She tested it, rotating her right foot.

"Better. It hardly hurts."

"Good. Then we can go out for dinner. Tomorrow night?"

"Oh. All right."

"Send me a note later and let me know the best time," he instructed.

Then he kissed her, hard, his tongue sweeping deeply to entwine with hers. "Go back to bed."

Kaylee didn't think that was possible. But after listening to his movements for a few minutes, she nodded off for another couple of hours.

They exchanged a string of text messages over the next day and a half, deciding on the logistics of their next evening together. Every time Kaylee's phone vibrated with a new notice, her heartbeat increased and she smiled with anticipation. For a few dozen hours, she allowed herself to live in a small bubble, where she was just a young woman starting a new relationship with an insanely hot guy. No work drama, family obligations, other attachments, or looming inconveniences like ending an engagement and the cancellation of a lavish, high-society wedding that had taken months to plan. There would be plenty of time for all that once Evan returned from overseas on Friday.

Until then, Kaylee chose to be completely selfish for the first time in her life, and steal a few more hours with Sam. Because it would likely be over once she told him everything.

She worked from home again on Wednesday and Thursday. Her dad had called her on Monday night to let her know Jason Holt would leave the paper, effective immediately, and Mark McMann would manage the local news desks until a new editor was hired. Of course, Kaylee asked if Jason's leaving had anything to do with what she had told him on Friday, but George Clement was very good at executive explanations, only saying that the timing was a coincidence and the decision had been in the works long before then.

Kaylee was skeptical, but too relieved to press further. Mark was a good man to work for, and he might consider returning her to city politics. She decided to wait a couple of days for things to settle down again before she raised the subject.

Thursday evening, at twenty minutes after six o'clock, Sam knocked on her apartment door. She looked at herself in the bedroom mirror one last time, wearing a short navy-blue dress, tailored to fit her body perfectly, and tawny-brown leather pumps with five-inch heels. Her hair and makeup done flawlessly to look like it had required minimal effort. She took a deep breath and opened the door.

There he stood, legs wide and arms spread open with his hand braced high on each side of the door frame. His head was dropped forward as he looked down at the threshold for several long seconds. His white cotton dress shirt seemed strained over the bulk of his shoulders and arms. The welcoming smile on Kaylee's lips wobbled with uncertainty. There was an unmistakably chilly vibe radiating from his stance.

"Sam?" she questioned, taking a step back. He slowly lifted his head to look at her, and Kaylee felt slapped by the coldness in his eyes.

CHAPTER 9

On Thursday afternoon, three days after meeting Kaylee Stone in the alley beside the *Baltimore Journal*, Sam strolled through the office at Fortis headquarters with two other field agents. They were returning from a mission to retrieve sensitive digital photos stolen from the computer of a high-level White House official.

"How did it go?" Lucas Johnson asked as he approached them.

"It was a little messy, but the job is done," Sam explained as Lucas joined him and they walked toward Sam's office.

"Whose blood?"

Sam looked down at his dark grey cotton top, now ruined with dark red smears.

"The wanker wasn't very willing to cooperate, and was bonkers enough to take a swing at me," Sam explained simply. "It took a little convincing, but he'll live."

"Anything on your calendar for the rest of the afternoon?"

"Nope. Just going to shower and change. What's going on?"

"Ice is here, and I thought we could give him an update on things."

"I thought he wasn't coming in until tomorrow."

Lucas shrugged with his usual easygoing attitude. "The life of a spook is unpredictable, I guess. We're in my office."

Sam nodded, then went into his office with the private bathroom. When he joined his friends wearing a fresh white shirt and dark grey slacks, Lucas was leaning back in his chair with a big grin on his face while Evan DaCosta was standing with his arms across his chest, looking as serious as ever. Dressed in his tailored designer suit and handmade Italian leather shoes, Evan looked the part of a vice president at the family business, DaCosta Solutions, a huge defense contractor for the U.S. federal government. Only three civilians knew his real job as a field operative for the CIA, with a lethal effectiveness that earned him the name "Ice." Two of those people were there in the room, and the third was Evan's father, the CEO of DaCosta Solutions.

"I was just telling Ice that I've already started planning his bachelor party," Lucas said, obviously enjoying himself. "I'm thinking a weekend in Brazil."

"What happened to Greece?" Sam asked as he and Evan clasped hands and bumped shoulders.

Sam had met Lucas early in his security career as a security agent with the MI5, the British secret service. They had both worked with Interpol to shut down a criminal organization that was targeting financial markets in the United States and across Europe, and the two men had remained good friends for several years later. Two years ago, Lucas had made Sam an offer, to join a new firm of elite professionals that provided specialized asset protection and security solutions to private-sector clients, and introduced him to Evan. As a consultant for the U.S. Secret Service and several other top government agencies, Lucas had genius-level skills in cyber security and intrusion detection. Lucas and Sam would be managing partners, leading a team of military and police-trained agents and analysts, with Evan as a silent investor.

Now, two years later, the three men had a strong business relationship.

Lucas waved a dismissive hand. "It's still under consideration. But Ice has a huge family in Brazil so we can have an even bigger party there. Enjoy the local dishes." His pretty, golden-brown face held a big grin.

Sam raised a brow to the man next to him. Evan's smooth, reddish-brown face held the look of exasperation, but he just shook his head tolerantly. He and Sam were of similar size and stature, with Sam just an inch taller. Lucas was the smallest at around six feet, two inches tall and had a more slender frame that neither of his best friends let him forget about. But the computer geek was just as lethal.

"The wedding is still two months away," Evan told his best man, Lucas. "Plenty of time to work everything out."

"Not for the party I'm planning, my friend. But we can discuss it later. You said you spoke with George Clement?" Lucas asked with more seriousness.

Sam knew that the DaCosta and Clement families were close friends and neighbors, and that Evan was engaged to their daughter, Mikayla.

"Yeah, I called him earlier to ask about the situation at the *Baltimore Journal*.

"He told me this morning that he wasn't moving forward with any further investigation into the matter," Sam said, a little confused. "Holt claimed not to know who paid the bribe, so Clement considered the matter closed."

"I know. I saw the update when my flight landed," Evan said, uncrossing his arms to plant them on his hips. "That's why I called him. The man I know would never let a situation like this go unresolved."

"What did he say?" Lucas asked.

Evan looked at the two men with sharp intensity.

"That he was resigning as CEO of Clement Media, effective immediately. He'll only remain on the board of directors."

Lucas sat up.

"What's going on, Ice?"

"I don't know exactly. But I think we've stumbled into something bigger than a bribe in the media," he replied. "George just turned fifty, and he loves his work. Every instinct I have says he's being coerced."

"So, we'll be looking into who is applying pressure," Sam concluded.

"No." Evan sighed while the other man looked at him with obvious surprise. "He's made me promise not to have you guys work on it any further. The assignment is closed."

"Are you sure about this, Ice?" Lucas asked.

"No. I think we should complete an investigation, find out who's involved and neutralize the threat. But we won't because I promised," Evan replied with obvious internal conflict. "But I did convince him that we should continue to monitor the *Journal* and all the other Clement publications for any other corruption. So that's something."

Sam nodded. "We have a full security review under way from the *Journal*. Raymond should have the results today or tomorrow morning. We can implement a similar plan across the whole firm."

"Good," Evan replied with a sigh.

"You boys want to grab a meal when we're done here?" Lucas asked, always trying to lighten the mood.

"Thanks, but I have plans for the evening," Sam told them.

"Huh. You do clean up pretty good, Sammy. Who is she?" Lucas teased, but Sam ignored him. "What about you, Ice? You look like you could use a drink."

"Yeah, all right. Tomorrow, I have to tell Mikayla that I told George she shouldn't work at the *Journal* anymore, and it won't be pretty."

"Clement's daughter works at the paper?" Sam asked, surprised. That information had not been shared with him or Raymond, nor had they seen the name Mikayla Clement on the employee list.

"Yeah, for the last year or so."

"Doing what?" asked Lucas, clearly just as unaware.

"She's a writer, but no one knows it's her," Evan explained. "I didn't even know until a couple of months ago. Mikayla can be pretty stubborn when she wants something, and she's always wanted to make it as a journalist without her father's influence. So she writes under another name."

Sam tried to stay calm and objective, but his heart was now beating like a drum. Somewhere deep in his gut, his instincts were on high alert and telling him something god-awful. He cleared his throat and worked his jaw before asking the question.

"What name?"

"Kaylee Stone," Evan replied completely unaware of the bomb that he had just dropped. "It's a nickname she's had since high school, and her mom's maiden name."

Lucas and Evan were talking, but Sam couldn't hear their words. He couldn't move, couldn't think. His head was filling up with every intricate detail of the last three days—the moment he saw her rush out of the building and falling from a turn in her ankle; the look of fear in those big, sparkling eyes; that stunning smile and the sound of her laughter at his silly, sarcastic comments; the smell of her skin; the sweet, tight feel of inching deep . . .

"Sam?" He looked at Evan, then Lucas, both of whom were staring at him strangely. "You okay, man? You look paler than usual," Lucas teased with a chuckle.

"Yeah. Fine," he replied vaguely. But nothing was fine. The reality of Evan's words were the exact opposite of fine. It was the most impossible, inconceivable truth. Sam had slept with his client's daughter, who also just happened to be engaged to his business partner. The wedding invitation was sitting on his desk at home, and Sam could clearly recall the printed words, though he had paid little attention to them before:

Mr. George Clement and Mrs. Evelyn Stone-Clement
invite you to celebrate the union of
their daughter Mikayla to Evan DaCosta . . .

"I met her," Sam finally said.

"Who? Mikayla?" asked Lucas.

"Yeah," he confirmed in a cold voice. "Raymond and I did, on Monday, outside the *Baltimore Journal* building. She had hurt her ankle walking through the alley. She introduced herself as Kaylee so I had no clue who she really was."

"Is she okay?" Evan asked with obvious concern.

Sam nodded, forcing the words out of his mouth. "She's fine. It was just a light sprain. I gave her a ride home."

"I spoke to her on Tuesday, and she never mentioned it," mused Evan.

Sam closed his eyes, formulating the words that should be spoken next, to tell the rest of what had happened. But he couldn't do it. Not right then, in front of Lucas. This was something he would need to reveal to Evan in private, man to man; then he would face the inevitable fallout. However unintentional it was, Sam had committed the biggest betrayal imaginable, and there was no way they would all walk away unscathed.

"I have to head out," Sam finally said, ignoring the raised eyebrows as he strode out of the room.

He was on autopilot, quickly walking to his office to open his laptop. As fate would have it, there was now a new message in his email inbox with a file from Raymond. The result of their security audit. Sam didn't bother to open it. He grabbed his car keys and left the building. Anger, disgust, and shame were clogging his throat, slowly choking him until he couldn't breathe. How the fuck had he let this happen?

It was so obvious now. The expensive apartment. Her incredible sophistication and graceful demeanor, like that of a society princess in an entry-level job. Kaylee worked for Holt. She had to be the one who had told her father about an editor taking her off a story. That she suspected interference from city hall. It explained why Clement had hired them only to investigate Holt and kept the scope so tight. He was worried about getting Mikayla involved, particularly if no one else knew she was his daughter writing for the *Journal* under an alias.

Sam didn't remember the drive from Alexandria to Baltimore that night. He arrived at her building just after five o'clock, but sat in his car for over an hour reading the many stories on the Web written about the beautiful and generous Mikayla Stone-Clement.

Even as he found himself knocking at her door, Sam didn't know why he was there. What did he intend to accomplish by confronting Mikayla with the truth? Did he hope that it was all a big, crazy misunderstanding? That his Kaylee didn't already belong to someone else—a good man whom he considered a friend? That there was some explanation that would make the whole thing less horrific? When he looked up at her standing in front of him, wearing a sexy dark blue dress and looking even prettier than before, he felt such hot rage that he was afraid to move.

"Sam?" she asked, stepping back. "What's wrong?"

Then he knew for certain. It was all true. Sam strode past her, into the apartment, careful to ensure they did not touch. He heard the heavy door close, then the soft clicking of her heels behind him as she followed his path into the living room.

"Sam?" she repeated. There was now a hint of real concern in her voice.

"What are you playing at here, Mikayla?" he finally asked, his back still to her.

There was a long pause. He clenched his teeth hard at the sound of her low gasp of surprise.

"Wait—" She stopped and only silence followed. Sam dropped his head and planted his hands on his hips, waiting for the lies, denials, pleas. Nothing came. Finally, after a few long minutes, he turned to face her. Kaylee was turned away from him with her arms wrapped around her waist, staring off into space with wide, unblinking eyes.

"You know who I am," she stated rather than asked.

"Mikayla Stone-Clement. Daughter of George Clement, CEO of Clement Media," Sam spat. "Engaged to Evan DaCosta, vice president of European operations at DaCosta Solutions."

"How did you find out?"

"Does it matter? How long did you plan to hide your identity?"

"I'm sorry," she whispered. "I didn't mean for this to happen."

Sam swallowed the torrent of filthy words that were coating his tongue.

"You're sorry?" he finally muttered.

She looked at him, but he refused to acknowledge the sadness and remorse in her eyes.

"You're sorry!" he yelled so harshly that she flinched. But she continued to look at him squarely, almost defiantly.

"Yes, I am," she repeated, clearly trying to stay calm. "I didn't plan this. It just happened. We connected, and I—"

"We connected. So you thought nothing of lying about who you are and cheating on your fiancé?" snarled Sam.

She swallowed. "It wasn't nothing. Obviously, I shouldn't have let it happen."

Sam felt sick all over again. "You cold, selfish bitch."

She slapped him, hard. It took Sam a few seconds for it to register. This tiny five-foot, four-inch woman had just had the audacity to hit him when she was the lying cheat.

"You don't know me," she shot back. "I've known you for five minutes, so you have no right to judge me. Yes, I screwed up. I made a mistake! And I'm going to have to answer for that, but you have no right to call me names!"

"I have every right," Sam yelled back.

"Why? Because we slept together? Look at you.

I'm sure this is a regular Tuesday for you," spat Kaylee. "So don't accept my apology, I don't care. Just get the hell out of my apartment."

Sam was speechless, and the look of pure disgust was etched on his face.

"And what about Evan? You're just going to marry him? Then continue sleeping around behind his back?"

"Of course not!" Kaylee yelled back, then slapped her hand over her mouth and turned away. But not before her eyes shimmered with tears. "You have to go."

Sam knew she was right. There was no point to this confrontation, nothing left to air out.

"Why don't you wear your engagement ring?" he demanded, trying hard not to sound like an angry caveman.

"What difference does it make?" she asked in a defeated tone.

"Jesus, Kaylee. I deserve more than just a polite sorry! I want an explanation!"

"Why, Sam?" she sneered, walking away from him. "So you can continue to chastise me? I'm nothing to you. Just some random girl that you gallantly patched up. And I think you've been adequately repaid for your help."

"Is that what you think? That I go around sleeping with every woman I run into? Or is it easier for you to pretend what happened between us was nothing."

She sighed and dropped her head in her hands.

"Maybe that would make this easier. I don't know. But I know it's not true," she said softly, turning to look at him from a few feet away. "It was something, at least for me. It just makes this ten times harder."

Sam felt some of the anger drain out of him. She was right. They had both felt that rare, intimate connection both in and out of her bed. And that was what was eating at him, creating the bitter, stale taste of guilt in his mouth. She was scheduled to marry Evan DaCosta within a few weeks. He had accepted the fucking invitation! But Sam still wanted her. Even now, with the truth of her unforgivable betrayal between them, he wanted her. And it made him sick.

"Why don't you wear your ring?" he asked again.

Kaylee looked away, her lips quivering.

"I do, when I'm in McLean. But a three-karat yellow diamond attracts a little too much attention in the bullpen at the *Baltimore Journal*."

They both stood there silently for a few minutes.

"Are you going to marry him?" Sam finally asked, needing to know.

"I can't," she whispered. "For months now, I knew that something wasn't right. But I couldn't figure out what. I love Evan. In a lot of ways, he's my closest friend. We're good together. It should be the perfect relationship. But something didn't fit, and as the wedding grew closer, so did the possibility that I was making a big mistake. I just didn't know why until recently. Three days ago, to be exact. I was going to end our engagement this weekend."

Sam clenched his teeth at what her words suggested.

"You and Evan. You've—"

"Yes. Of course we've had sex," interrupted

Kaylee. "It was . . . fine. He's a great guy. But it wasn't like . . ."

She turned away and covered her face. He tightened his fist, wanting to believe everything she said. But only so he didn't have to believe she was a completely heartless tart. Not that it mattered. Whatever the truth was, whatever her explanations were, what he wanted just wasn't possible.

"We have to tell him," Sam finally said.

Kaylee looked up at him with complete confusion. "We? What are you talking about?"

That's when the rest of it fell into place.

"You don't know," he mumbled.

"Know what?" she demanded, walking toward him. "What are you talking about, Sam?"

"Evan never told you about Fortis?"

"Fortis? The company you work for?" she asked, now standing right in front of him. "You know Evan. How exactly?"

"I don't work for Fortis, I own it." He crossed his arms at his chest. "I own it, with Evan and Lucas Johnson."

He watched her eyes and mouth open with shock. Some sick part of him wanted her to hurt, to fully understand the damage she had done with her lies and treacherous behavior.

"He's a friend. An investor in my company, Kaylee. And I've now slept with his fiancée." She gasped. "So, now you can see exactly why this is my business."

"Oh my God, oh my God," she whispered, bending

at the waist as though hyperventilating. "I didn't know."

He turned away from her, hating the immediate and instinctive urge to comfort her.

"Give me one day," she finally whispered. He looked at her again. There were tears streaming down her face, but her voice was unwavering and her expression resolute. "I was going to end it tomorrow anyway. I'll tell him the truth. That I love him like my best friend, like a brother, and should never have accepted his proposal. That's really what I need to explain. You and I aren't the real reason, Sam. So let me end it tomorrow. And after that, you can tell him whatever you need to. In the end, I'm the one to blame, and he'll understand that."

Sam felt something crack painfully behind his ribs.

"Please. Give me one day," she pleaded again.

When the words choked his throat, he could only nod.

Kaylee let out a deep breath of relief.

"Thank you," she told him with her lips trembling and fresh tears swelling forward. "Good-bye, Sam."

CHAPTER 10

Sam looked over at Kaylee from the corner of his eye. It was Saturday, the morning after she had walked back into his life, and they were sitting apart in a spacious private jet during the flight from Dulles airport to LaGuardia in New York. The plane was slowly making its descent for landing. Sam anticipated they would be on the ground by 8:30 AM.

Kaylee was reclined far back in her chair with her body and face turned toward the window and away from him. He knew she wasn't sleeping, but she was doing a pretty good job of pretending to be. It had been that way since they had boarded the plane over an hour ago, and Sam was pretty grateful for it. They had barely spoken at all since he had woken her up that morning, naked in the bed they had shared.

Sam turned back to the information he'd researched during the quick flight. It was a few dozen articles and social media postings on the activities of Mikayla Stone-Clement over the last few years.

Most of it, Sam already knew. When George Clement retired from his role as CEO at Clement Media, Kaylee Stone had quit her staff writer job in Baltimore, and Mikayla had resurfaced in the Virginia and D.C. social circles a few weeks later. There was gossip about her sudden breakup with the very eligible Evan DaCosta, with speculation about his womanizing ways, or her sexuality. She spent the next three years working for her mother's charitable organization, with lots of media coverage from as far away as Martha's Vineyard for their various successful fundraising campaigns. Then, last summer, she relocated to Manhattan, but was no longer in the social scene. The rest seemed to match her story.

Sam scrolled through dozens of her pictures from parties, dinners, and events with society's business and political elite. She always looked perfect—elegant, stylish but conservatively understated. Poised and polite but never quite approachable. And she only ever seemed to wear shades of black and grey, or the occasional dark blue, as though forever in mourning. She was never laughing, nor was there ever a hint of those dimples. When she smiled, it didn't seem to reach her eyes.

One of the more recent images captured Sam's attention. Taken at a Clement Literacy Foundation dinner last July, it was of Kaylee and her mother, but with a mature man between them showing some familiarity with both women. It wasn't her father or Evan. The caption didn't provide his name, nor did the original Web page for the article. They all smiled politely for the camera, but something in the man's expression made him uneasy.

Sam then switched to searches on Terrance Antonoli, but there was little valuable information about the property developer on the Web. He read through it all until they landed.

"I've let Terry know we'll meet him at his apartment at around nine o'clock," Kaylee said as they waited for their luggage in the baggage claim area. Sam nodded.

A driver met them at the exit, and they were on their way into Lower Manhattan a short time later. Sam called Renee during the drive.

"Did you get my email from last night?" he asked when she answered.

"Bleeding hell, old man. You really need to learn how to take a proper vacation," she replied, and Sam smirked.

"Stop taking the piss. I'm working on it," he conceded.

"Not hard enough. I'm looking into all calls connected to Francesco's phone, and I'll let you know if anything of interest comes up," Renee said. "I'll start working on any information about city projects in Paterson, New Jersey. We might find the information we need in public domain. But I'll bring in Raymond if we need to access more secure networks to find out who the competition is for the proposal Antonoli submitted."

"Thanks, but don't spend too much time on it over the weekend. We'll regroup on Monday."

"Okay, boss."

"Thanks, Thomas," he added.

"Who was that?" Kaylee asked, still looking out the rear passenger window. "Someone from Fortis?"

"It's none of your concern," Sam said dispassionately, aware that they needed some clear boundaries.

"It is if you were discussing my assignment. We specifically agreed that it would be confidential."

"I remember your conditions very clearly, Kaylee. But I'm not just your hired hand. I still have a business to run and other clients to support," he said, barely looking up from his phone screen. Kaylee didn't reply.

Their car arrived at their destination a few minutes later, in the Battery Park neighborhood of Lower Manhattan, and they stopped in front of a new, tall building. The driver helped her out of the car, then delivered their bags to the curb.

"Welcome back, Ms. Stone," said the older, portly doorman as he exited the building to greet them. His jet-black hair, full beard, and swarthy complexion suggested Middle Eastern descent.

"Hi, Ali. Nice to see you again," Kaylee replied with a genuine smile.

"Do you need any help with your bags?" the man asked politely.

"We're good, thanks," Sam said, draping the strap of his duffel bag over his shoulder and grabbing the handle of Kaylee's rolling suitcase.

The doorman nodded and opened the door for them to enter. Inside, the lobby was spacious and modern with lots of honed marble, chrome, and glass. They rode the elevator to the penthouse on the twenty-fourth floor.

"Does Antonoli know about the attack last night?" Sam asked as they walked to the apartment door.

"Yes, I called him while you were talking to the police at the hotel."

She pulled out a pass card and swiped it at the door to unlock it. They walked into the apartment to find a slender man sitting on the center of a large white sectional. He was watching three televisions mounted in a horizontal line on the wall, but immediately stood up and strode toward them with a bouncing gait.

Terrance Antonoli looked every inch the indulgent playboy. His dark brown hair was expensively styled, his creamy olive-tinged skin was darkly tanned, and bronze and designer logos adorned every piece of his clothing. His face split with a wide smile, revealing large, unnaturally white teeth.

"Kaylee, darling. It's good to have you back home safely," he said in a lyrical French accent. Then he pulled her into a close embrace, so tight her back was arched.

Sam cleared his throat, his eyes narrowed. A small white terrier came charging across the room and jumped up and down in front of Kaylee. She stepped back from Antonoli to sweep the ball of fur up into her arms and cradle it like a child.

"Hi there, Niko! I missed you too," she teased, scratching his belly to the dog's obvious delight.

Sam set their bags aside and walked further into the room.

"Ahhh, you must be Samuel Mackenzie," Terrance said with his hand extended. "Kaylee has told me about you. Thank you so much for your support in this unfortunate matter."

They shook hands while Sam could feel the heat of Kaylee's gaze.

"Kaylee and her family are well connected to my firm, so her safety and security are of the utmost importance," Sam explained, choosing his words carefully. "She's given me some information about this threat, but I have some additional questions for you, Mr. Antonoli."

"Please, call me Terry," replied the younger man. "I'll tell you everything I know, but Kaylee is better positioned to fill in any gaps, I think. Come. I was about to eat breakfast, and I asked our house-keeper, Silvia, to prepare extra in case you were both hungry."

Terry walked away toward the hidden area on the right side of the apartment. Sam looked over at Kaylee, who still had the dog in her arms. She looked back defiantly, then followed Terry. Finally, Sam did the same, finding them in the large white kitchen with a variety of pastries and fruits laid out on one of the Carrera marble counters.

"Would you like some coffee, Mr. Mackenzie?" asked Terry. There was a large French press on the round table off to the left, in front of wall-high windows and doors to a rooftop terrace.

"Sam's fine. And coffee would be lovely."

Kaylee was now sitting at the table with a flaky croissant and an assortment of fruit on her plate. Terry handed her a cup of coffee, black. Then poured two more, placing one across from Kaylee, and sitting down in the chair next to hers with his own brew. Niko sat down next to her feet.

Awareness tingled down Sam's spine. He looked back at Kaylee, holding her gaze steadily, trying to read the truth in her eyes. She looked back, unblinking, but her eyes were cloudy.

"Have a seat, Sam," Terry requested, gesturing to the chair across from Kaylee. "Ask the questions you need to."

She looked away to stare out the terrace door. Sam sat down and added sugar and cream to his coffee from the containers in the center of the table.

"Your family has a very successful business in France and other parts of Europe," Sam began after taking a sip of his drink. "Why expand to the United States?"

Terry nodded as though he'd anticipated the question.

"My reasons are both business and personal," he replied. "On the business side, much of Europe is still recovering from the recent recession and financial crisis. So the profitability of our business interests has diminished considerably in recent years. Diversification into new markets is necessary for us to remain competitive, if not essential. On the personal side, I have three older brothers. It is not easy for me to carve out my own path while under their shadows. So, I'm seeking to do so boldly in another country."

"You intend to move to the U.S.?"

"Perhaps, at some point, if our business here continues to grow," Terry explained.

"And your wife, Selina? Is she supportive of this objective?" Sam continued, flicking a glance at Kaylee. She bit into a strawberry and slowly chewed it.

"Ahh, my wife," sighed Terry, flashing a blinding smile. "Selina understands the possibilities of this venture and is, of course, very supportive. She is not opposed to perhaps living in America and raising our family here"

"That's right. She's pregnant. Congratulations."

"Thank you. We are expecting our baby daughter later this summer," Terry added, still smiling affably.

Kaylee popped a grape into her mouth.

"My understanding is that Antonoli Properties specializes in developing commercial properties, like shopping malls and retail plazas. And you recently built some vacation resorts in the Caribbean and Europe," Sam continued. "Yet, here, you've chosen to start with developing civic properties through government contracts. Why is that?"

Terry glanced at Kaylee, then took a drink from his cup.

"It is purely a financial decision, made with the guidance of my American investors," Terry explained, spreading his arms wide to suggest it as a simple answer. "The commercial development business is very competitive, requires a heavy cash outlay up front, and is high risk unless you have a certain percentage of committed tenants. That is very difficult to accomplish these days, particularly for a new developer. By starting with small, municipal construction projects, we have a guaranteed buyer and a contractual commitment from the start. These facts are very compelling, so I had to be agile in my approach and try a new path, as is necessary for any new venture."

Sam looked relaxed, but watched the Frenchman closely. Everything he had said so far made good sense, but Sam knew he was hiding something, if not outright lying.

"Well, judging by the trouble you've encountered recently, and the danger Kaylee is now in, it would seem municipal construction is just as competitive as commercial development," Sam noted. "Why didn't you withdraw your bid after the first threat?"

"Sam, Terry is a businessman," Kaylee interrupted. "He can't simply cancel projects every time one of his competitors gets their feathers ruffled."

"Sure he can, if someone might get hurt," Sam replied easily, with his impassive gaze still fixed on Terry. "He's not exactly hurting for profits."

"That's unfair," gasped Kaylee, pushing back her chair.

"Sit, darling. Sit," Terry insisted, waving his hand in her general direction. "I had two options for responding to these threats, Sam. Either retreat from the bid or hire professional protection to ensure that my staff and I remain safe. I chose the latter."

"And now that Kaylee has been physically attacked while traveling alone?"

"She assures me that you are the very best there is in physical security and protection. So it seems I made the right decision and we have little to fear going forward."

Sam wanted to punch the little wanker in the nose, but of course he didn't.

"Any other questions, Sam?" Kaylee asked, shooting daggers at him with her eyes.

"Aye, just one. Why do you think they've gone after Kaylee in order to coerce you? You have other employees, several of which are also women of a similar age. Why her?"

"I would think that was obvious," Terry replied, flashing his big, phony teeth again while reaching out to take hold of Kaylee's hand. "They must be aware of my affection for her."

"Your affection," Sam repeated, looking back and forth between them.

"Affection, fondness, attachment," Terry added, gesturing with a wave of his hand after each label. "These are all words meant to explain our rather delicate and discreet relationship of an intimate nature."

CHAPTER 11

However Kaylee had imagined the meeting between Terry and Sam would play out, it could not have been worse.

There was a long, tense silence after Terry's statement, and no one seemed to move. Always sensitive to energy, Niko leapt up onto all four paws and barked. Kaylee cleared her throat and reached down to ruffle the downy soft fur around his neck. Terry sipped his lukewarm coffee, and Sam remained still as though carved in stone.

Kaylee felt bad for Terry. While he'd done a great job through the questioning, he was completely out of his depths with a man like Sam. And he had no clue just how big a minefield he was now in the middle of. How could he? Kaylee had never anticipated that she and Sam would end up in bed together right out of the gate.

"Anything else, Sam?" she finally asked, putting an end to the unproductive stalemate.

Sam pierced her with his chilly blue eyes. "Naw, Kaylee. I think I've gotten what I need, for now."

She didn't look away, refusing to cower away from his glare. As a twenty-nine-year-old single professional, she could do whatever she wanted, with whomever she desired. His opinion about it didn't matter, only that he provided protection against the threats to her and Terry.

"So what now?" Terry asked.

"That depends on what exactly I'm being hired to do here," Sam replied with what Kaylee knew was false politeness.

"I thought that was clear," Kaylee interjected. "We need security protection for the next thirteen days, until the official vendor selection for the Paterson City project."

"Is that all?" he asked.

Terry looked at Kaylee, but she tried not to notice.

"What else is there? We've already explained that we're not prepared to withdraw our bid. And if we win, there's nothing anyone can do about it."

Sam looked between them, as though seeing far more than she'd like him to.

"Unless we uncover who is making these threats and take them down," he finally stated simply.

"I've already tried that," Kaylee told him with a sigh. "But in Paterson, all city proposal submissions are confidential during the bid process, except to a very small selection committee that includes the deputy mayor and other officials. So our only option is to install the right security."

"My family has come across these types of unsavory tactics on occasion, Sam," Terry added with a dismissive tone. "They will bully only those that seem weak, then scurry away at the first sign of strength. If they are watching us, and see your new security detail, I'm certain they will do just that."

"You're certain," Sam repeated, with obvious condescension.

Kaylee sat forward to put an end to the direction things were headed. "We've explained what we've hired you to do here, Sam. So let's move on to exactly how we make that happen quickly. Do we understand each other?"

"Yes, ma'am," he replied smoothly. "We understand each other completely."

"Good," she replied, lifting her chin defiantly. "Now, what do you need to get started?"

"First, I will need to secure all required premises. We'll start with this apartment, the Antonoli offices, and your house, Kaylee."

"I live here," she clarified. Sam's nose flared, but he didn't otherwise react.

"I will need a few hours to inspect the spaces, plan and install the required security and surveillance equipment," he continued. "Since the threat is specifically against you, Kaylee, I will provide your personal protection at all times outside of this apartment and the office."

"What about Terry?" she asked.

"We could have a security detail for him, but I don't think that's necessary. They need Terry healthy and capable of officially withdrawing from the city bidding process. Threatening someone he cares for is usually an effective way to ensure cooperation. Hurting or killing the head of Antonoli won't necessarily guarantee that will happen, so it wouldn't serve their purpose. And assaulting a powerful executive attracts way more attention and scrutiny than a lowly assistant. As long as you're Kaylee Stone, you're expendable."

Kaylee swallowed, taken aback by how succinctly Sam had summed up everything she already knew and was counting on.

"Well, that sounds like a good plan," Terry chimed in, standing up at the table. "And to make your job even more straightforward, I will be flying back to Paris tomorrow morning for several weeks for a family obligation and business meetings. Kaylee can effectively manage everything here while I am away."

"I'll show you around the apartment," Kaylee told Sam once they were all on their feet. "Then you can get started on your security plan."

"Sam," Terry said with his hand outstretched again. "It was a pleasure to meet you, and I'm sure my Kaylee will be in good hands while I'm away."

They shook hands, but Kaylee was certain that Terry winced at the force of Sam's grip.

"Now, if you both excuse me, I need to get ready for an appointment," the Frenchman explained with a bow of his head. Then he walked out of the kitchen, toward the bedrooms.

Kaylee let out a deep breath, relieved the meeting was finally over.

"You're bloody shitting me," Sam growled with his hands planted on his hips. "You and that smarmy git?"

"Terry is a great guy," she replied honestly, having

no clue exactly what he had just said but certain it was an insult.

"Christ, Kaylee! What are you playing at? He's married and his wife's pregnant, for bloody sakes!"

Kaylee flung up her hands to stop his tirade.

"I'm not doing this with you, Sam. Despite what happened last night, my relationships are not your concern. I don't appreciate your scrutiny of my life, and I certainly don't need your consent," Kaylee told him with icy firmness.

He stood there for several long seconds staring down at her, but she refused to back down or cower in shame.

"Now, are we doing this tour of the apartment or not?" she finally asked, folding her arms across her chest with a bit of attitude.

Sam smiled down at her, and it wasn't friendly.

"Lead the way, princess."

The penthouse was about twenty-one hundred square feet on one floor. Walking from the kitchen and small breakfast table, Kaylee showed him features of the great room. There was a powder room and a den-slash-library off to the right. To their left, she pointed out the doors to Terry's bedroom and office; then they walked into her bedroom and private bath. It was spacious, feminine, and comfortably furnished with a queen-sized bed, end tables, and a small antique dresser. The walk-in closet was lined with custom cabinetry and additional drawers. In the white bathroom, there were double sinks, a big, deep freestanding tub, a frameless shower, and a private water closet for the toilet.

"You don't share his bedroom?" Sam said as he

looked around, checking all the spaces and windows like he'd done everywhere else.

"I like my space," she replied simply.

"Any other areas I should see?" Sam asked as they walked back into the hallway.

"The laundry room, storage closet, and then the terrace."

"After you," he replied with a polite gesture of his hand.

His tone was so sickeningly polite. Kaylee rolled her eyes and marched forward, stopping at each space until they were outside of a large rooftop patio area. It ran the width of the apartment and had glass-panel railings around the perimeter. Sam walked to the edge and looked around in all directions, including up at the face of the building.

"Nice view," he finally commented, looking out at the clear view of the Hudson River, with the New Jersey shoreline across it and the Statue of Liberty to the right.

"Yeah, it is."

They stood there for a few minutes; enjoying the breezy air and June sunshine.

"What are you doing here, Kaylee?" he finally asked softly.

"Sam—"

"Just tell me," he demanded. "Why leave your family, your career, everything, to work as an assistant to this arrogant wanker? To allow yourself to be a pawn in dirty business practices? Is he coercing you in some way?"

"What? Of course not!" she replied, looking away. "It's complicated."

"Are you in love with him?"

"How can you ask me that, Sam?" she snapped back.

"It's the only thing that makes sense," he growled. "Why else would a woman like you live like this? It's not for his money or connections, is it?"

"Look, I don't expect you to understand this, but Terry and I have an arrangement that works for me," Kaylee explained honestly. "Like my job. I want it to be successful, even if there are some risks. He gives me lots of authority and I find it challenging and rewarding."

"Well, you're definitely the beauty and the brains of this operation," he quipped sardonically.

Kaylee looked over at him, remembering what a great sense of humor he had. She chuckled, and he flashed a brief grin, transforming into a stunningly handsome charmer right before her eyes. Her stomach tingled predictably in response.

"If we're going to work together over the next week or so, there needs to be an understanding between us, Sam," she finally said.

"Yeah, I know."

She took a deep breath.

"So, let's start over from here," Kaylee suggested as they both looked out over the river and the Manhattan cityscape. "You do what you do best, and I do my job. And we'll be civil to each other for the duration. Deal?"

She stuck out her hand, expectantly. Sam took a few seconds to search her face before he finally accepted her offer.

"I have to speak with Terry before he leaves. Do

you need me for anything else?" she asked, pleased with where they'd ended up.

"We should go over your schedule for the next two days and establish a routine for communication, but I'm good for now," Sam told her.

"And we need to find somewhere for you to sleep," she mused. "You can sleep in Terry's room while he's gone."

"That's not necessary. I can sleep anywhere. It's a well-known strength of mine."

Kaylee grinned, unknowingly flashing her dimples. "Or I can sleep there and you take my room? Or the den? We rarely use it, and I'm pretty sure it has a pullout sofa."

"Sure, the den works fine."

"Okay, well, just come find me when you need something."

He nodded and Kaylee left him out on the deck. She found Terry in his bathroom, dabbing a gel-pomade into his hair with absolute precision.

"Geez, Kaylee, you didn't really prepare me for that one, did you?" he protested as she walked in and hopped up on the counter to edge next to him.

"I don't think anyone can be adequately prepared for Sam in advance," she mused, using her finger to comb through his hair and properly shape the sophisticated spikes. "Thank you again. I know that was awkward."

"That's an understatement, my dear. When I told him so delicately that we were lovers, I was certain he was going to smash my nose in," Terry added, still looking at himself in the mirror. "I'm quite fond of this nose. I'm told it's very aristocratic and true to my Greek blood."

"It's a fantastic nose, Terry."

"You are mocking me, Kaylee, and it's very rude." She laughed.

"Where are you headed?"

"I do have a meeting that my father arranged with one of our business associates in the city. Then I must go shopping and pick out something special for Selina. Any suggestions?"

"She's Parisian, living in the center of designer fashion, fragrance, and culture, so it's hardly worthwhile to get something like that. You have to buy something quintessentially American," she insisted.

"Like a box of sugary donuts?" he joked.

"Twinkies, actually."

"What?"

"Just walk into any convenience store and the clerk will point them out. Insanely sweet and good."

"Again with the mockery," he sighed and walked out of the bathroom.

Kaylee smiled and jumped off the counter to follow him into the bedroom. It was as masculine as hers was feminine, with a giant king-sized bed, charcoal-gray fabrics, and dark wood furniture.

"Just go into Tribeca and find a trendy boutique with unique pieces or locally designed fashion. She'll love whatever you pick."

Terry pulled on a navy cashmere wool blazer over a white oxford shirt with stylishly narrow khakis on the bottom.

"All right, I'm off," he declared a short while later.

The two close friends looked at each other intently. "Are you sure about this, Kaylee?"

"Yes! Everything's fine! Go shopping for your very beautiful, very pregnant wife."

"No, I don't mean now. I mean this whole crazy situation we're in," he clarified seriously. "It's not too late to end it, you know. We've accomplished quite a bit in a very short period of time. We don't need the New Jersey contract."

"We've already gone over this, Terry. We've come too far to bow to pressure now. In another week or so, it will all be over, one way or another. Trust me."

"I just hope I don't live to regret your persuasive ability to talk me into things. Even if they are proving very profitable," he sighed.

"Just keep your eyes on the prize, my friend," Kaylee teased, tapping one of his cheeks affectionately.

"*Au revoir,*" he called as he walked out of the room.

Kaylee followed more slowly, then walked into her room. Her suitcase was now by the bed, and she could only assume Sam had put it there. She spent the next few minutes unpacking, dividing the clothes between the laundry and dry-cleaning bins, then putting away her toiletries, but her thoughts were elsewhere. They were on Samuel Mackenzie and the unplanned impact he was having on her psyche and her plans. The whole thing required his security services with a certain level of detachment. Professional but disapproving of her apparent lifestyle so that he would not look too far beneath the surface. Once a cheater, always a cheater, right?

Only, now, having spent the night with him, Kaylee didn't know if it helped or hindered her scheme. And she didn't know if it made it easier or more difficult to deceive him.

Kaylee spent another hour or so working in her room, then took a shower and got dressed for the afternoon in well-worn jeans and a black long-sleeved T-shirt with a light, pretty scarf draped around her neck. She slid her feet into comfortable but fashionable sandals; then she went to find Sam. The den had been transformed into a working space, with his laptop and other small equipment set up on the console table by the window. He also now wore a gun holster over his shoulders, with a weapon secured in it.

"Are you ready for an update?" he asked, looking over at her.

"Yes, and I have one as well," Kaylee explained.

"Okay, you go first. I can work around your schedule."

"Niko needs a walk in a few minutes. Then I have a hair and nail appointment in about forty-five minutes, at two o'clock." Sam raised his eyebrows. "What? It's a recurring appointment, every two weeks, otherwise it would be impossible to fit it into my schedule with my regular stylist. And it's too late to cancel."

"Fine, what else?"

"That's it really for today. Except Niko needs a walk around dinner and before bedtime," she added. "Then tomorrow, I'll go for a run in the morning. Most mornings, actually."

"You run?" he asked.

"Yes. But I'm not sure how that will work for security. Maybe I should just go on the treadmill for now."

"I'll run with you," Sam said. "Mornings?"

"Yes. That would be great."

"Now, let's get Niko out and work out the logistics for your hair appointment." He shrugged on a loose jacket to cover his weapon, then gestured for Kaylee to lead the way.

"It won't take long. There's a nice path around the building and a small park in the back," she explained. "And I usually just walk to the appointment. It's about twelve blocks, so fifteen minutes, tops."

Niko was a smart dog, well trained for their routine and already waiting for Kaylee. She hooked the leash to his collar, then they headed out for the walk. Along the way, Kaylee said hello to a few neighbors, then led Sam through the main floor and out one of the back doors.

"There's an indoor pool," he commented, noting the large facility surrounded by glass.

"Yeah, but I've never used it," Kaylee admitted as they followed Niko on his familiar route through a small city park. There were lots of people out walking, with and without dogs.

"Why not? You don't swim?"

"I do, but I just haven't had time."

"You've got to stop and smell the roses, sweetheart."

Kaylee snorted. "Somehow, I don't see you stopping to smell anything."

He shrugged. "I might surprise you. But I'm partial to orchids. My mum tried to grow them for a time. Brilliant scent."

She giggled.

Niko noticed a squirrel up ahead on one of the paths that cut through the dense trees and pulled hard on the leash to run after it. Kaylee found herself jogging forward to keep up with him.

"Let me take him," Sam offered, taking hold of the leash and holding the terrier back and in control with a firm grip.

"Thanks."

They walked a little farther in comfortable silence. Kaylee was looking off to the right, appreciating the beautiful weather and the rustling of the fragrant breeze through the trees, and she didn't notice Sam had stopped a couple of feet back so Niko could do his business. She followed the path around a sharp turn.

"Kaylee, wait!"

Startled, she turned toward Sam's voice just as a firm arm gripped her around her waist, dragging her inside the dense bushes.

CHAPTER 12

Sam had stopped for only a minute, catering to the dog while Kaylee strolled forward on her own. But he'd had eyes on her the whole time, alert in judging the distance between them and calculating how quickly he could secure her if needed. What he hadn't noticed was the fork in the path they were on, with one arm continuing straight forward, and the other turning sharply right, but well hidden from where Sam and Niko where standing. It took two seconds for Kaylee to disappear out of his line of sight behind a tall crop of trees and thick bushes, and only a second longer for Sam to run after her, shouting for her to wait for him, dragging poor Niko along.

When he turned at the trees, Kaylee was gone. Sam turned around, trying not to panic, then stopped and listened. He heard branches snapping and muffled voices coming from inside the dense bushes along the right side of the path. Niko barked in the same direction, and Sam tore into the shrubbery, barreling down anything in his way. More grunts, and a male voice swore. Sam ran faster, dodging low-hanging branches and hurdling over tree stumps.

"Let go!" he heard, finally seeing some color and movement ahead. Certain it was Kaylee, Sam wrapped the dog leash securely around the wrist of his left hand, then drew his Beretta with the right and released the safety as he quickly crept forward, pistol pointed downward as a precaution. Niko bounced around beside him anxiously. A couple more yards and Sam swept aside rough bushes to quietly enter the clearance, and stumbled onto the last thing he expected. Kaylee was on the ground, straddling some guy around his stomach and punching him in the face with her fist while he was trying to dislodge her.

Sam stepped back, completely surprised.

"Kaylee! What the hell are you doing?" he demanded, looking around to secure the area while concealing his weapon again.

"He tried to assault me!" she yelled, pausing in her attack.

The man on the ground took the opportunity to wildly swing at her, catching her across the face and successfully knocking her off his body. Sam ran forward to protect her, reaching them just seconds after the thug kicked Kaylee in her side, scrambled to his feet, and took off into the bushes. Sam's heart was thudding in his chest as he dropped to his knees beside her, and everything in his field of vision was suddenly red with rage.

"I'm fine," she immediately insisted, sitting up. There was blood dripping from a cut on her lip.

"Stay right here, and don't move an inch," he commanded, tossing down Niko's leash and jumping to his feet.

In his desperate rush to get away, Kaylee's attacker had left a clear path of waving tree limbs and bouncing leaves. He wasn't fast, and he was very loud, hitting everything in his path. Sam had eyes on him within a couple of moments, then took him down from behind minutes later. As they both hit the ground hard, Sam immediately placed a knee hard in the base of his spine. Grabbing both of the thug's arms, he pulled them back tight to disarm the assailant, then took out a handy zip tie from one of his jacket pockets and secured the guy's wrists together.

Sam then flipped the perp over and stepped over his body with satisfaction. Kaylee had managed to do some real damage. His nose was bleeding steadily and one of his eyes was already turning blue. Judging by how he'd curled into the fetal position, she may have also applied a good shot to his bollocks. Sam shook his head and started laughing. Once again, Kaylee had managed to completely surprise him.

Fifteen minutes later, they were all in the main area of the park and Sam was handing off the perp to the NYPD. Kaylee was sitting on a bench with Niko at her feet, touching at her swollen lip. It was no longer bleeding. Sam watched her for a few minutes, trying to piece together the various things that just didn't add up. Finally, he walked forward and sat down beside her.

"Let me take a look," he commanded. She co-operated, turning in her seat to face him.

It was a small, straight cut and looked pretty clean.

"I think you'll live."

"Good to know," she quipped.

"What about your side? Does it hurt?" he asked, remembering the kick she had received.

"No, it's fine. I might have a little bruising later, but nothing serious."

They sat in silence for a few minutes watching other people go about their leisurely activities.

"You can't leave my sight like that ever again, Kaylee," Sam finally said, now that he was calm enough to have the conversation. "Not for a second."

"I know. I didn't mean to. It all happened so fast."

"It always does. So you need to always be in my line of sight outside of any secure areas. That's non-negotiable."

"I get it. I know. It won't happen again," she vowed. "Do you think it was random?"

Sam looked around, noting everyone's movement and demeanor, constantly assessing the threat level around him.

"Looks that way. The cops have had a couple of complaints about similar sexual assault attempts in a few of the parks. They're checking if this guy matches any descriptions from other reported incidences."

"But you're not sure," she concluded.

"We'll see. But I don't like coincidences."

"Yeah, me neither."

"Do you still want to go to that hair appointment?"

She brushed a hand through her hair with a sigh.

"Do I look like I've just been assaulted in the bushes?"

Sam smiled and gently brushed a thumb across the tender spot on her lip.

"Only in a good way."

She gasped and slapped him. "That's terrible!"

"What? Too soon?" She gave him a disgusted look, but he could tell she wanted to smile. That seemed to be the goal of all his comments these days. "I'd feel more badly about it if that poor fellow's nose hadn't been busted, and his balls shoved up near his spleen."

Kaylee did laugh then.

"Hair appointment?" he repeated. "If we flag a cab, you might only be a couple of minutes late. Surely that's acceptable."

"All right, let's do it," she finally agreed and they both stood up. "What about Niko?"

"I'll hold on to him. He can keep me company."

They walked toward her building, where there were usually taxis waiting outside.

"We never did discuss your security plans," she reminded him. "What do you have in mind?"

"I've ordered a few enhancements for the apartment, as a start. They should be delivered by tomorrow."

"How's that possible? Tomorrow is Sunday,"

Sam shrugged. It was very convenient to have a business partner who also owned a defense contracting firm. Even the most cutting-edge equipment was an email away.

"I also have the floor plan for the Antonoli office, and I've drawn up a few options. But I can't finalize them until I can inspect the current equipment."

"You've been busy," she commented.

They had reached the main street near her apartment, and easily flagged an available taxi.

"I can take you to the office tomorrow if that would help," she offered once they were seated and on their way. Niko was standing in her lap, looking out the window.

"That could work, but let's play it by ear."

"Okay, that all sounds like a good start."

Sam nodded. "You know, eventually you'll have to tell me exactly what's going on here, Kaylee. Or I'll figure it out myself."

"What are you talking about? I've told you everything."

"Yet I still managed to be caught unaware." He narrowed his eyes. "For instance, you neglected to mention that you're a ninja."

Kaylee burst out laughing, but Sam was only half teasing.

"How else do you explain your ability to overpower an assailant that's at least half a foot taller than you and fifty to sixty pounds heavier? Particularly since his hobby is planning assaults on unsuspecting women. Which he's likely rethinking at this point, I might add."

She grinned up at him, her twin dimples making a rare appearance and her brown eyes sparkling with golden specks.

"You're ridiculous. I've taken a few self-defense classes, that's all. And I was pissed off."

Now Sam laughed deep and hard. She joined in, and they were both still chuckling when the cab reached the front of the salon. He paid the tab and took a hold of Niko.

"I assume you're keeping a record of your out-of-pocket expenses," she noted when they were outside.

"Don't worry, I'll just add it to your tab," Sam assured her.

"See that you do."

Sam and Niko spent the next hour and a half sitting in a very posh salon and spa watching her get spruced up. He didn't have the heart to tell her she looked just as pretty after as she had before, and that it hardly seemed worth whatever extravagant costs they charged. She had wanted to walk back to her apartment, but he insisted they take another taxi. As much as he teased her about the attack, he preferred that she get home quickly so she could rest.

The trip back was uneventful, and the apartment was empty when they arrived.

"What time is Terry expected back?" he asked, starting his perimeter security check. Even at their height, you couldn't be too careful. There was always the possibility of someone accessing the apartment from one of the adjoining suites.

"I'm not sure. He didn't say," she said, walking into the great room and turning on one of the three large televisions.

Sam completed his check, then returned to the front hall. "I'll be in the den then if you need me."

"Okay. I'll see what Silvia left for us in the freezer. Or we could order something."

"Whatever you decide is fine," Sam assured her before walking away.

In his temporary office, he logged in to his laptop and opened one of the Fortis secure portals. In there, he retrieved a folder labeled ANTONOLI and pulled up the contents. Pictures and documents tiled across the computer screen, creating a virtual picture of the mission so far. Sam stood back and looked hard at the information collected over less than twenty-four hours.

After four years with no contact, Kaylee had flown to Virginia, alone, wanting to hire Sam, and only him, for a security job. She was now working in New York for a development company, using her favorite alias. She was also having an affair with her boss that was not a well-kept secret. A competitor in the city contracting business wanted them to withdraw from a bid and was using strong-arm intimidation tactics. He'd sent a goon from Baltimore to attack her in her hotel room and pass on a message to her boss to pull out. Her attacker, a hired "freelancer," didn't appear to be a direct alliance or affiliated with a known organized crime family, or other organization. Those were the facts. The significance of the park incident was still undetermined, so Sam left it off the map for now.

Except for Kaylee's reaction to the assault that afternoon. Strong, capable, and unintimidated. Trained to defend herself.

Sam stroked his low beard. What was the statistical likelihood of a wealthy and privileged socialite who had never been victimized choosing to take self-defense classes long enough to be effective, then becoming the specific target in a coercion racket?

He really didn't like coincidences. Something wasn't adding up, and Sam was absolutely certain Kaylee was at the center of it. Either she was being manipulated or she was manipulating Sam. He just needed to figure out which.

His cell phone vibrated with a message. It was from Renee.

No luck accessing Paterson bid through public domain files. Will get Raymond on it on Monday. Hope you're enjoying your vaca.

Sam went back to examining the files and thinking. Kaylee was right about how difficult it would be to get the names of their competitors. It was one of the main reasons she and Terry cited for why they didn't want him to focus on identifying and neutralizing the threat. Was that all there was? After further review and consideration, he mapped out two immediate objectives, besides keeping Kaylee safe. One, get the name of the other competitors using Raymond's gifted digital skills. Two, try to discover why Kaylee had proactively developed solid self-defense skills.

CHAPTER 13

Terry returned in time to eat dinner with Kaylee on Saturday evening. They had beef stew, and Sam opted to eat his in the den. She watched television, and Terry packed for his trip to Paris. Then they went to bed, sleeping in his room. By the time Kaylee woke up at eight o'clock on Sunday morning, he'd already left for the airport. She returned to her room and quickly dressed for a run in knee-length leggings and a tank top over a sports bra. Her weather app said it was currently sixty-eight degrees with a warm day ahead.

Sam was already in the kitchen, drinking a cup of coffee, when she walked in to get some water. He was dressed in loose shorts, a technical T-shirt, and running shoes.

"You're all set," she said, a little surprised.

"I'm an earlier riser. Been up since five-thirty," he explained with a shrug.

"Really? I hope the sofa bed was comfortable enough," Kaylee stated, grabbing a bottle of water out of the fridge.

"It was fine, no complaints. I've been known to sleep standing up."

They looked at each other for a few seconds.

"Did you see Terry before he left?" she finally asked.

"I did. Don't worry—he still has all his giant teeth."

Kaylee almost sprayed water across the room.

"That's not very nice," she reproached, turning away.

"No, it wasn't," Sam acknowledged, cool as a cucumber. "Neither is taking off while your girl-friend is in certain danger."

Kaylee sighed, trying not to take the bait.

"That's why you're here, Sam. Right?"

"Am I a surrogate for all his duties, or just your safety and security?" he asked softly. "My skill set is pretty vast."

Kaylee just looked back at him, her lips tight with disapproval. Finally, he sighed, clearly disappointed that she wouldn't participate in the banter.

"I'm ready whenever you are," he finally stated, putting the empty coffee cup in the sink. "How long do you want to go?"

"I'm not sure. It's my first run in about a week so maybe just three or four miles? See how I feel?"

"How are you feeling after yesterday?" he continued, walking up to her. "Any soreness? Bruising?"

He was about to touch her side, but Kaylee stepped back out of his reach. Things tended to go sideways whenever they touched each other.

"I think it's okay. I'll probably take a long soak in the tub this morning when we get back."

"Good plan."

Kaylee pulled on her shoes by the front door just as the white terrier came bounding toward her.

"Let's give Niko a quick walk, then we'll head out."

Fifteen minutes later, they were outside the front entrance of her apartment, and Niko was back upstairs resting on his dog bed.

"Do you have a favorite route?" Sam asked as he looked around and double-checked his gear. No one would suspect that his nifty little cross-body knapsack had a gun, knife and a few other security essentials. He checked his watch, and looked around again, ever vigilant.

"Not really," she admitted. "I usually just start on the street and head over to the promenade at Battery Park."

"Right then, you can lead the way. But you need to stay by my side at all times, within reaching distance. I will stay on pace with you. Any instructions I give need to be followed exactly. If anything looks dodgy, we turn back."

"Yes, sir," Kaylee replied, hiding a smile. She noticed that when he got a little worked up, his accent deepened and he used words like "dodgy."

"Let's get off then," he urged.

Kaylee relaxed her shoulders and started running, choosing a pace that felt comfortable and sustainable. She focused on her feet, strides, arm swings, and deep breathing. It was a strong pace, and Sam didn't seem to have any trouble keeping up with her. He stayed on her right side, always right by her elbow and close enough to touch without crowding. About twenty minutes in, her breathing was louder, and her posture and alignment required more focus. But Sam didn't seem at all affected. Kaylee could hear the regular bounce of his goody bag against his back, but nothing else. Not his breathing or even feet striking the pavement. *How can such a big guy be so stealthy?* she wondered.

"How are you doing?" he asked at the thirty-minute mark, with no hint of being winded.

"Good," she gasped, taking a quick look over at him. Was he even sweating?

"We just hit three miles. One more?"

"Yeah, okay."

About ten minutes later, he signaled with a touch on her arm. They slowed to a walk, and Kaylee took in big gulps of air to bring her heart rate down. She used the edge of her top to wipe down her face. Within a few minutes, everything was feeling much better.

"Whew! That was pretty good, right?" she asked him, feeling a little giddy from the high.

"It was very good, I'm impressed." Kaylee laughed "How long have you been at it?" he asked.

"A few years now, off and on," she replied, breathing deep and loving the feel of it. "I had a friend in Baltimore who invited me to join her running club, and I couldn't believe how out of shape I was. Then the more I did it, the more addictive it became. I even started training for the Baltimore marathon."

"You didn't do it?" he asked as they headed back toward the apartment.

"No, I moved back to McLean, and I didn't have the time anymore," she admitted, trying to keep her tone light. "But I started up again last year when I started working for Terry. I ran the NYC marathon last year."

"Really? That's bloody impressive," Sam stated, sounding genuine.

"Yeah, well, it was my first and my last," Kaylee told him. "It was pure torture! Why would anyone put themselves through that on a regular basis? I almost threw away my running shows the next day."

Sam laughed. "So no more marathons?"

"Maybe a 10K. Or a half marathon. But that's it." He continued chuckling, his focus still very much on examining their surroundings. They walked the rest of the way in easy silence.

"So, what do you think? Can we do this every morning?" she asked when they were home.

"Probably, with a few concessions," he told her. "We'll need to change the time slightly each day and take different routes."

"That's fine."

"And I need to confirm your transport to and from the office. Then, we can decide on a running schedule."

"Yes, sir."

He scowled, but there was a hint of a smile. "Cheeky lass. Now, head off for your soak in the tub. I want to have a look at you after. At your side, I mean," he quickly added.

Kaylee looked down.

"Then we can head to your office whenever you're ready," Sam finished.

She nodded, cleared her throat, and walked away.

Twenty minutes later, Kaylee was reclined in her large bathtub filled with scented bubbles and Epsom salt. Pop tunes from the collection on her cell phone were playing through the built-in speaker system. She tried relaxing but couldn't. Things were not going according to plan, and she had to find a solution, fast.

On the surface, Kaylee should be happy with the progress. The Paterson bid had caught the attention of the right people. They'd applied some of the pressure tactics she'd anticipated. Engaging Sam had always been a strong possibility, and Kaylee had been fairly certain he would take the job on her terms. But he was supposed to believe that she was a lying, cheating slut. Someone who would have an open affair with her married boss. Someone thoughtless and selfish, undeserving of anything more than the basic security required by the job. That was the only way this would work.

Sam wasn't supposed to care about her motives. He shouldn't be making her laugh with his sarcasm and charm. And he definitely should not still want her. But he did, and now Kaylee had to rethink everything.

Maybe Terry was right. Maybe this whole thing had gone far enough. She certainly had enough information on Ross Construction to shut them down and write a great article on city corruption in New Jersey. They were the only other company to bid on the latest project, and it was very obvious they were the ones making the threats. But exposing Ross wasn't enough. It was just a small player. Operations like that one would continue to come and go, and if she made her play now, she would never get another chance to go after the really big fish.

No, she needed to see this through. It was the only way to see that the people responsible for destroying her family got what they deserved. But Sam Mackenzie's role needed to be re-examined.

What if she just told him the truth? Would he help her, or just shut it down? Was it worth the risk?

Her phone rang, interrupting her thoughts. She reached over to the stool where it was lying and answered the call on speaker phone.

"Hello."

"Hey, sis," replied her younger brother, George Jr.

"Hey, Junior, what's up?"

"You around this week?" he asked.

"Yeah, why?" Kaylee confirmed. "Will you be in town?"

Junior was a lawyer for a firm in D.C., but he occasionally had client work in New York.

"Yeah, for a few days. We're negotiating with a firm there. I'm flying in on Wednesday morning."

"That's great!" Hanging out with Junior was always a fun diversion. "Did you want to meet for dinner Wednesday?"

"Sure, that should be good. But I'll confirm in a couple of days."

"Okay. How's Dad doing?"

"He's good. The same," Junior replied. "I stopped by yesterday, but only for a few minutes. Mom's still in Martha's Vineyard."

"I know. I spoke to her last week. He's getting worse, Junior," she said softly.

"Yeah. He was drinking at ten o'clock in the morning. And it wasn't his first. We were supposed to go to the driving range at the club, but he didn't even remember confirming the plans."

Kaylee closed her eyes and tried to hold back the tears.

"Mom says he doesn't even go to any of their events anymore. He just sits in the house and broods," she added.

"Not since you moved to New York," her brother added.

"That's not fair."

"No, but it's true, Mikayla. Even Mom says so."

"I'm almost thirty years old, okay? I can't live with my parents my whole life, doing what they want me to do. It's not healthy or normal."

"I know," he mumbled. "Look, I'm sorry. I didn't mean to sound like I'm criticizing. It's just frustrating, that's all."

"It's okay. Don't worry about it," conceded Kaylee, trying to swallow the lump in her throat. "Anyway, let me know if you want to meet up on Wednesday. We'll get caught up."

"Sure, talk to you later."

"Bye."

They hung up, and Kaylee gave into the frustration, anger, and sadness. She sobbed quietly as tears poured down her face. None of this was fair for anyone in her family, but most of all for her dad. Four years ago, the happy, successful, and productive man she'd known her whole life had started to slowly fade away, and now the only thing left was an empty shell. He was controlling and bitter, and he drank too much, driving everyone away.

Only Kaylee knew exactly why, and only she could fix it.

Eventually, she got out of the tub and got dressed in slim jeans and a flowy black top, trying hard to put on a neutral face that hid the myriad of weighty issues swirling in her mind. She and Sam took a taxi to and from Antonoli Properties in Midtown, stopping to eat a quick lunch next door. They walked around the building so Sam could build his security plan; then Kaylee worked in her office for a bit while Sam did the same inspection inside the company offices. If he noticed her melancholy mood, he didn't let on.

They ate dinner at the apartment, reheating lasagna Silvia had made, then spent the evening doing their own thing. Kaylee was grateful for the space. She tried to watch television, but found her mind drifting off. Every once in a while, her eyes would fill up, and she would absently brush the moisture away.

"Kaylee, what's wrong?"

She jumped, startled to find Sam bent down in front of her.

"What?" she asked, blinking and trying not to sniffle. "Nothing—"

He cocked a brow at the obvious lie.

"It's nothing," she insisted, shifting to sit up straighter on the sofa. "Just silly girl stuff."

Sam looked at her steadily, clearly not put off.

"Did you need something?" Kaylee finally asked

to distract him. She picked up the remote control and started to flip through the channels.

"I still haven't looked at your side," he stated.

"Don't worry about it. I'm fine." She tried to dismiss him by focusing her attention on the television.

He didn't budge, and his expression suggested he wasn't going to. "Humor me, then you can go back to your girly weeping about nothing in peace."

Kaylee finally sighed and put down the remote. She leaned to the right and lifted the left side of her blouse to reveal the side of her stomach. There was a dark blue circle just below her ribs, but it looked worse than it really was. Just tender to the touch, but easy to ignore.

"Bloody hell, Kaylee! Why didn't you tell me?" Sam cursed in surprise.

"It's nothing, Sam," she insisted, trying to cover it back up. "Just a little bruise. I hardly feel it."

"Stay still!"

He held the fabric up and ran his fingers gently over the injury. Kaylee tried not to wince, but couldn't help it.

Sam swore again and stood up. "Stay right there and don't move."

He returned a few minutes later with a bag of ice wrapped with a dish towel. Kaylee gasped in protest as he briskly tugged her shirt off over her head, tossed it aside, and applied the compress to her side. She slapped away his hand and took hold of the ice.

"That wasn't necessary," snapped Kaylee, shooting him daggers and very aware that she was now sitting in front of him in her bra.

"It's very necessary. We should have done this yesterday," he snapped back. "Why would you hide it from me?"

"I wasn't hiding it," she insisted, looking away. They stayed like that for a long time, both stubbornly holding their ground.

"Let me see it, again," Sam finally urged, sounding a little less annoyed with her.

Kaylee pulled away the compress, and he leaned in close for another inspection, gently pressing the broader area. After the burning cold ice, his hands felt warm and soothing.

"Okay, that's enough for now," he proclaimed with his palm still placed softly over the bruised skin. "We'll ice it again before you go to bed. And you should sleep on a few pillows so it stays elevated. You were kicked near the stomach. There's always the risk of internal injuries when you're hit like that."

"Sorry," Kaylee finally conceded, looking down. "You're right. I should have shown you right away."

"Why didn't you?"

She opened her mouth, but didn't have an answer. Not one that would make any sense on its own, that wouldn't just create more questions.

"Look at me," he insisted, lifting her chin with one of his hands. She complied, meeting his intense gaze, hoping he couldn't read everything in her eyes, including her desires. His brows were curled, jaw clenched tight, and his eyes were a stormy blue. So purely masculine. Her mouth went dry, and her breath became labored. Kaylee swallowed hard and licked her lips. He looked down at

her mouth, brushing over it with his thumb. She
had no ability to stop herself from swiping his flesh
with her tongue. One of them groaned, and then
they were kissing, open mouthed and wet. She
shoved her fingers into his hair, stroked them over
his scalp, controlling the pressure and movements
she needed.

Sam picked her up by the hips, and then he was
sitting up on the couch with her straddling his
thighs. Their lips separated only as long as needed.
His hands raked over her back, down to squeeze
her ass, pulling her even closer against his body.
She clutched at his shoulders, invading his mouth
with her tongue in deep strokes. Sam bit at her lips,
then licked them soothingly. He deftly unhooked
her bra and dragged it off her arms, careful not to
agitate her bruise.

Kaylee broke their kiss to arch her spine and
leaned back with her eyes closed. Her need for his
touch had drained her of all hesitation and inhibi-
tions. When his hands finally cupped her breasts,
she cried out softly with pleasure. He stroked over
the sensitive flesh with the palms of his hands,
scraping their tips with his skin. She shivered, biting
her lips so as not to cry out. He circled the nipples,
tugging and squeezing gently until Kaylee was
almost panting from the sensations. Every stroke of
his finger sent tingles of desire down to her core.

Then his fingers stopped and his hands fell to her
hips. Kaylee moaned with frustration and opened
her eyes to find Sam looking at her. While his eyes
burned hot and his lips curled with arousal, there
was something else there that she couldn't quickly

identify. Or maybe she didn't want to. . . . She bit her bottom lip seductively, gripped his T-shirt, and started to pull it up. Sam grabbed her wrist to stop her efforts. They sat there for several heartbeats, eyes locked, both trying to read something from the silence.

"I can't do this," he finally stated in an angry tone.

Kaylee froze, and her heart stopped. She opened her mouth to say something, but her brain shut down. They still looked at each other.

"I won't play backup to another man, Kaylee," he said sharply. "Never again."

She was shaking her head as tears collected in her eyes, blurring his image. The look on his face and the loss of his touch hurt so much, leaving her breathless. *No, there is no one else*, she wanted to explain. But, of course, she couldn't. Instead, Kaylee finally looked down, climbed off his lap, and walked away with as much dignity as she could manage.

CHAPTER 14

"Ross Construction," Renee said. "They're the only other company to submit a proposal for the new government building in Paterson."

It was Monday afternoon, and Sam was sitting at a small desk near the front door of Antonoli Properties. That location allowed him to have eyes on Kaylee, and all access points to the offices. But it did not provide any privacy, so Sam had to take extra precautions. Wearing a headset, he was able to have a confidential meeting with Renee through his laptop on the digital platform with video image and document sharing.

"What do we know about them so far?" he asked, looking at the digital copy of the proposal in question.

"There's not much to know. They've been in business for three years, popping up out of the blue. They have two other Paterson city government projects on the go, all new building construction or renovations," she explained.

"Who owns it?"

"No one. They use the name Ross, but the owner is listed as PTL Inc. I looked them up too, and they don't exist."

Sam was quiet while he looked through some of the documents that Renee shared online.

"So they're a front for another company," he said, stating the obvious.

"The other interesting thing is that for all but the first project they worked on in Paterson, they were the only bidder for the work. And for the first project, their proposal was about twenty-five percent cheaper than the others submitted," she added. "So, it looks like they undercut everyone to win, then built a monopoly with the city, and Bob's your uncle."

"They would still need people working in the municipal offices to make this work."

"My thoughts exactly," Renee agreed. "I've started a security review on city employees and officials that are connected with vendors and subcontractors, from the mayor down. If we assume it's through bribes and greasing, there will be a money trail somewhere."

"Unless they're cooperating because of threats or other coercion. Sometimes, that's more compelling than money," Sam added. "But let's see what you come up with in the next few days."

"Will do."

Sam stroked his jawline, thinking. This whole job was starting to stink of something fishy.

"What about the perp from Friday? Francesco? Did you find anything useful in his phone records?"

"Nothing. He's a dud," she confirmed. "His friend

Lucky, aka Frank Pacini, is a little more interesting. He's a known associate for one arm of the Augello crime family, but hasn't done nothing noteworthy. A handful of arrests for petty crimes, one conviction. Based on what Francesco told you, I think he's more of a broker, finding local thugs to do work for cash, or that sort of thing."

"Anything that connects Lucky to Ross Construction or Paterson?" Sam asked.

"Nothing that I've found so far."

He checked his watch. It was just after four o'clock. Kaylee had a five o'clock meeting uptown, so they'd have to leave the office soon.

"Okay, thanks for the update, Thomas," he told Renee. "Let me know if you have anything at all on the city employees."

They ended the digital link, and Sam closed the collaboration portal. He looked up to check the room, and found the office quiet and secure, with the small number of employees busy with their various tasks. There were only two, in addition to Kaylee. Annie Chow was the receptionist. She was a middle-aged Chinese woman with flawless golden-hued ivory skin, a soft voice, and amazing efficiency from what Sam could see after one day. She sat behind a large desk in front of the entrance to the Antonoli office, with the company logo mounted high on the wall behind her. Sam's makeshift security desk was across from hers on the parallel wall, so he was able to watch her multitask expertly.

Paul Dixon was the second employee. He was a young recent graduate from a local community college with a diploma in urban planning and design.

Born and raised in Brooklyn, his pale complexion contrasted with his dark brown hair, secured in a man bun, and full beard. He worked at a desk in the center of the floor, next to the printer and small kitchen, and seemed diligent and hardworking.

Kaylee sat in one of two offices along the back of the space. She had spent most of the day in there on phone calls or working on her computer, only leaving to get water from the fridge or go to the bathroom behind Paul's desk. She ate lunch at her desk, a salad that Annie picked up from the deli next door.

Sam looked at his watch again, then back at his computer screen, opening another folder on his desktop. It contained one document and a sub-folder. The document had been created on Sunday evening and summarized the results of a search through all government crime databases, from local police to the FBI, with Mikayla Stone-Clement as the subject. There were only two items on the report, both speeding tickets from between three and six years ago. That was it. No record of her as a victim of an assault, or of threats or any kind of reported harassment. Once Sam reviewed those results, he started a second search.

Lucas Johnson was a genius at cybersecurity and digital applications. His latest creation was an advanced search portal with the ability to access every public and private domain that used standard, off-the-shelf network firewall software. That meant his system could access ninety-five percent of the Internet, then pull the results into a searchable database. Last night, Sam had created a database query with Kaylee as the target, using her real name and pseudonym, from junior high to the present. The search was now complete, and the results were available in a sub-folder on his laptop.

It was now four-fifteen. Sam had ten minutes to do a security check of the premises before he and Kaylee left for the day. A review of the search results would have to wait until that evening. Sam closed his laptop and collected his things into a soft leather messenger bag, then made his way through the office, out the back door, then around to the front again. Everything seemed normal, with no signs of a threat.

The only security protection currently in place in the building was a basic alarm system connected to the front door, the rear exit, and the ground-floor windows. Sam had ordered the video surveillance and motion detection equipment required to re-motely monitor activity inside and outside the building. The supplies would be delivered Tuesday morning, and Sam planned to have them installed by the afternoon. He had set up a similar solution at Kaylee's apartment on Sunday afternoon with all video feeds saved to a cloud-based portal accessible from Sam's laptop and cell phone.

Back inside, Sam waited by the front door as Kaylee left her office and walked toward him. She wore slim-fitting grey pants, a red blouse, and black shoes with very high heels. A large tote bag hung off her shoulders. She smiled and said good-bye to Paul and Annie. Her eyes met his fleetingly before she walked past him and out the front door. Sam clenched his jaw and followed silently.

Despite his annoyance, it was better this way. Whatever was going on with Antonoli Properties, Kaylee was trouble. She had the unique ability to mess with his head and destroy his willpower even while she lied to his face. Last night was proof of that. Sam might have to see her every day, watch her every move, but he needed to stay detached from her in every other way. This new coldness between them was the best way to solve this mission and to preserve his sanity and integrity.

"I had a car delivered earlier this afternoon," he told her as they walked down the front stairs to the street. "We'll drive to your meetings and appointments going forward."

There was a black 7 Series BMW parked at the curb, with dark tinted windows and large sport tires. Sam opened the passenger door so Kaylee could enter, then sat in the driver's seat and put his bag in the back seat. He started the engine, checked a few of the custom security features, then pulled out onto the street for the drive to the Upper East Side of Manhattan. Kaylee was meeting with a new vendor of commercial building supplies for the two New York projects Antonoli had under way.

They were silent to and from the meeting. Back at the apartment, Kaylee immediately went to her bedroom while Sam did his perimeter check. In the den, he logged on to his computer and quickly reviewed the day's worth of security footage for the apartment. All was clear. He took off his jacket and shoulder holster, securing his Beretta near the pullout sofa, where it was well concealed but quickly accessible. Then he changed out of his shirt and slacks and into athletic shorts and a T-shirt. Finally, he sat down and opened the folder with the report on Kaylee's past.

As expected with such wide parameters, there were pages of information on her. Sam was interested in only one thing. In the search field, he created a Boolean string for any reference to an injury, assault, or grievance. Anything to explain why she felt the need for self-defense classes and practiced to the extent that she could take down a serial attacker so effectively.

Several references were filtering in. Sam took a deep breath and read through them. Then he did another search string, and another, spending over an hour reading the results. There was nothing that came close to being important.

Sam sat back, frustrated with the lack of progress on his two main objectives. First, the only competitor for the building contract, Ross Construction, was a ghost organization. It was a front, and the people responsible for threatening Kaylee were not easily connected to that operation or the evidence so far. So Sam was no closer to protecting her by eliminating the threat.

Secondly, he was not closer to understanding anything about Kaylee and her role in this whole thing. There were too many odd facts that on their own seemed normal, but when put together just didn't make sense. And like Sam's dad always said, if it didn't make sense, it probably wasn't true.

He sat there, brooding for another few minutes. Then, on impulse, he did a search for Antonoli in her information. Numerous references came up.

He scrolled through them, starting with the most recent, and successfully resisted the urge to read the content. The last thing he needed was to learn more details about their current relationship. At the bottom of the list, he found two hits from about eighteen months ago, connected to a Clement Literacy Foundation event. One was an invite list, the other a photo of Antonoli and Kaylee from a media article. The last link was from seven years ago. It was an email distribution list for a high school reunion.

Sam leaned forward. Strathford College, a very exclusive private school, had sent an invitation to the entire graduating class for their five-year reunion. There were about sixty email addresses on the list in alphabetical order. Kaylee was under M, and near the bottom there was a T. Antonoli. Sam quickly opened the Internet browser and did a search on Strathford College. It was an exclusive private school in Arlington, Virginia, that offered boarding facilities and catered to international students. A few more Web searches and it was confirmed. Kaylee and Terry Antonoli had gone to high school together, graduating the same year.

He stood up and paced the small room. Kaylee had told him that she had met Antonoli at a Clement Foundation event. It wasn't a lie, but like everything else she had told Sam so far, it wasn't the complete truth. Why would Kaylee conceal how she really knew Antonoli? If they weren't friends, in a class of only sixty people, they had at least known each other. The man was married and sleeping with his employee; how could knowing him from high school make the situation any more ugly?

Sam felt a heavy black weight at the pit of his stomach. These lies and half-truths confirmed that Kaylee was manipulating him. Professionally, it was annoying and impeded his ability to provide the level of security required to ensure her safety. But he had no doubt that he would figure out the truth eventually. That's what he and the Fortis team did best. It just might take a little longer and require more resources than he'd anticipated.

But the feeling in his stomach was not professional. It was personal, and it was fueled by dark, rapidly growing anger.

Four years ago, Mikayla Stone-Clement had come close to destroying him. As Kaylee, she had sparked an excitement and attraction that he hadn't ever felt before. In those short couple of days, Sam had fallen for her, and he'd thought about the possibility of what they could share emotionally and intimately. For years after their time together, Sam would remember her in his dreams. Or he would be out somewhere and smell her perfume. He would kiss a woman for the first time, hoping to experience that electricity, but it never happened. Then, eventually, Sam was glad it didn't reoccur. That kind of desire for one woman was too dangerous, especially if she could never truly be his.

That desire had turned him into a man with no integrity. The stark truth was that he had unintentionally betrayed a friend, then knowingly kept it secret. And, every day since, Sam had regretted how he handled the situation, despised acting against his nature to hide the truth. Because, deep down, he knew that he had done it for Kaylee. But he was done being a fool for her, and he would not be manipulated again.

At eight-thirty, Sam went into the kitchen to get something to eat. Kaylee was not in any of the living areas. Roast beef and roasted potatoes were in a container on the counter, and a mixed green salad was in the fridge. Kaylee had explained yesterday afternoon that Silvia worked during the week, taking care of Niko, the shopping, and the housekeeping. She made dinner if needed and stocked the freezer with meals for the weekend. Sam put together a plate and ate at the table. He was walking back to his room when he noticed the large sticky note on a console table near the front entrance. It had his name on the top and provided written outline of Kaylee's schedule for the next two days, starting with a walk for Niko before bedtime. There was no mention of a morning run.

Sam clenched his jaw and folded up the note. He found a similar message on Tuesday night.

By Wednesday, the silence between them started to feel normal, and less awkward. If anything changed in her calendar, she would send him a text message with the details. The space was now wired with the new video surveillance and security equipment. He was able to watch the feed on his phone, and receive alerts of any unauthorized entry into the office. That day, they arrived at the office by eight-thirty. Then, later, Sam drove Kaylee to Brooklyn, where she spent most of the afternoon at a site visit for one of her projects.

They returned to Antonoli shortly after four

o'clock, and Kaylee went back to work at her
computer. Ten minutes later, Sam's phone vibrated
with a new message.

> I'm going out to dinner with my brother at
> six o'clock. He'll meet us here. Restaurant TBD.

Sam already knew the specifics on George Stone-
Clement, Jr., including recent pictures and current
activities. On paper, Junior seemed to be a typical
twenty-seven-year-old man from an affluent background. But by six-thirty, Junior had yet to arrive.
Annie and Paul had left about an hour ago. Kaylee
finally walked out of her office, obviously ready to
leave for the day. She wore a black dress that
hugged her body and ended just below the knees.
Her heels were black and white and impossibly
high, but she walked in them perfectly, her hips
swaying gently with each step.

He grit his teeth, and looked down.

"We'll meet him outside," Kaylee said as she
walked toward the front entrance. They were the
first words she had spoken to him that day.

Sam nodded. She stood beside him while he set
the security alarm; then he opened the main door,
holding it wide as she walked through.

"There he is," she said.

In the few seconds it took to activate the digital
lock outside, Sam saw Kaylee wave one of her hands
in the air and turned his head to look out at the
street. There was a young guy waiting on the opposite side of the street for the traffic to slow down so

he could cross. From a distance, his appearance matched the pictures of Kaylee's brother. Sam and Kaylee started down the front stairs of the brownstone when Sam's cell phone vibrated and chirped loudly with a very distinctive alarm. He didn't need to take the device out of his pocket to read the warning. It was a sophisticated and very sensitive radio-frequency sensor indicating that a bomb detonator had been triggered within a one hundred feet radius of their position.

With little time to react, Sam grabbed Kaylee around the waist and pulled her tight against his body so she was completely covered by his size, then twisted them both to face the building and leapt forward. They slammed down hard on the top landing just as the black BMW blew up, spraying burning metal and debris everywhere.

CHAPTER 15

Kaylee didn't understand what was going on. Suddenly, she was flying through the air, crashing to the ground, face down with a heavy weight squeezing the breath out of her body. An enormous boom reverberated around her, shaking the surface beneath her face like an earthquake. The chaotic sounds of shattering glass and ringing car alarms swiftly followed. But they were muffled, and her ears were ringing.

When she finally opened her eyes, it was to squint through the cloud of dust and ash that was blowing around her. It was so thick that Kaylee coughed uncontrollably the moment she tried to breathe deep.

"Kaylee?" The crushing weight eased up, and Sam's face was suddenly in her line of sight. Their eyes met, and his were an intense blue, his face creased with concern.

"Stay down," he demanded, still covering her body like a shield.

She nodded, coughing some more. Then she

remembered the sight of Junior about to walk across the street toward her.

"Junior," she gasped, trying to push up onto her knees. Her hands stung as they scraped over tiny shards of glass. "Where's my brother?"

But Sam still held her down.

"Where's my brother!" Kaylee yelled, now struggling to get up and look around. Fear and desperation were starting to overwhelm her. It felt like forever before she felt Sam grip her shoulder to help her up. It was only a couple of minutes.

When they stood up, Kaylee turned around to see exactly what had happened. It took a while for her to comprehend the scene in front of her. Not five feet away, the black carcass of a large sedan was engulfed in flames. Cars on the street were stopped in both directions with their drivers and passengers looking around. Several of them were on phone calls or taking pictures and videos. Pedestrians and shopkeepers were rushing around, trying to assess damage and injuries. Several people were lying on the street, either too stunned to get up or too injured to move. *Where is Junior?*

Sam was trying to move her. He had an arm around her waist and was pulling her back from the scene.

"Let me go!" she snapped. "I have to find my brother!"

"I need to get you off the street, Kaylee," he said sharply, forcibly moving her. "Get inside the building. I'll find your brother."

She looked up at him, eyes wide and glistening.

"I promise," Sam added. "I will find him. But I need to get you inside."

Suddenly the reality of the situation hit her. She fell back a step, looking around wildly. It had been a car bomb. Someone had just blown up the car Sam had rented two days ago.

"Let's go," he urged, standing behind her protectively while unlocking the office doors. There was a gun in his right hand. The narrow sidelights on either side of the entrance were shattered, with chunks of decorative glass littered everywhere.

"Stay right here, okay?" he continued when she was over the threshold. "The security surveillance will let me know if anyone tries to enter. Do you understand, Kaylee? Do not leave the office."

"They tried to kill me," she whispered, looking into his eyes.

"No. This wasn't a miss. They just got more coercive."

From the now empty gap next to the doorway, she watched Sam fly down the front stairs and onto the street, pistol held in both hands but pointed down. He walked around the burning car as though examining it, then took out his cell phone and took pictures. Then he ran to the other side of the street, stopping briefly to talk to anyone he passed along the way. There was an older woman lying down on the sidewalk in front of a flower shop with blood covering her shoulder. Sam crouched down beside her for a few seconds. Then Kaylee watched as he took off his jacket, folded it up, and gently tucked it under her head like a pillow. He spoke to her again, then was up and running.

Where is Junior?

Kaylee looked back and forth along the street from the narrow opening, trying to catch a glimpse of her brother's blue suit. Her eyes returned to Sam, who was now going door to door, looking inside each of the retail spaces. Finally, he came out of the deli with his arm wrapped around Junior. Kaylee gripped the window frame, weak with relief. But, from a distance, she could see that Junior was limping and had a cut on his forehead with a small amount of blood dripping down the side of his face.

The sound of sirens was now audible and getting increasingly louder. Within a few more minutes, the street was blocked off by several police cars. Three ambulances were on site attending to those injured, including Junior. It was so hard for Kaylee not to run out and hug her brother, but she stayed exactly where Sam had left her until he returned. And she was very aware that she had created this chaos, and that she was directly responsible for all the injuries and damage.

Once the area was secured by the NYPD, Sam ran back to join her in the Antonoli offices.

"How's Junior? Is he okay?" she immediately demanded, rubbing her hands together.

"He's okay," he told her with an assuring hand on her shoulder. "There's a superficial cut on his forehead, and he scraped his knee when he hit the ground. The paramedics are working on him now. He's going to be fine."

Kaylee swallowed, breathing deep and trying hard not to start crying uncontrollably.

"Can I see him?"

"Soon. He knows you're here, and you're okay. But I need to get you back to the apartment as soon as possible," Sam explained in a low, soothing tone. "I'll have a car here in a few minutes, then I'll take you both home."

"Will we be safe there? They must know where I live," Kaylee asked as panic started to rise up again.

"As safe as anywhere else at this point. But I'll be reviewing all options," he told her.

"Okay. Okay," she repeated, trusting him completely.

"Christ, Kaylee! Your hands," he cursed, grabbing both of her hands and turning the palms up.

They were scraped, torn, and crusted with dried blood. She suddenly became aware of how they throbbed.

"Come over here and sit down," Sam urged, leading her over to the receptionist desk and pulling out Annie's chair so she could sit in it. "I'll have a car here in just a few minutes. But let me get someone to have a look at those cuts."

"This is all my fault," she stated softly. "I did this."

"Kaylee, these fucking arses are dangerous cowards. You can't feel responsible for their actions."

"No, listen to me," she insisted, looking up at him with pleading eyes. "I have to tell you something."

Sam paused, as though reading the seriousness in her eyes.

"Let's get you cleaned up and back to the apartment. Then we'll talk."

She sucked in a shaky breath and nodded.

He quickly brought in a paramedic to clean and

bandage her hand, creating a mitten made from sterile gauze. It was almost seven o'clock when a dark SUV arrived, parked discreetly just outside the crime scene. Sam directed Junior into the back seat, then finally walked Kaylee out of the Antonoli offices toward the vehicle.

"Jesus, Mikayla!" her brother swore when she entered the vehicle and sat beside him on the back seat. They immediately hugged each other tight.

"Are you okay?" she whispered near his ear.

"Yeah, I think so. The explosion knocked me off my feet for a second. But it could have been worse, right?"

She didn't want to think about it.

"Who is that guy?" Junior asked when they finally pulled apart. He gestured with his head to Sam, who was now sitting in the front passenger seat and looking bigger than ever. The SUV took off, quickly heading toward Lower Manhattan.

"He just said you were safe and with him," her brother continued.

Kaylee sighed. "He's a friend and he's been helping out for the last few days," she replied evasively. "It's a long story."

"Is he a detective or something?"

"No."

"Well, he definitely acted like one, the way he directed everyone and got the street blocked off."

Kaylee just looked away. Now that she was away from the scene and sitting safely beside Junior, the adrenaline rush was slowly ebbing away. She felt physically exhausted and emotionally raw. Junior must have seen it reflected on her face. He wrapped his arms around her shoulders, pulling her up against him. Kaylee cried silently for the rest of the ride.

Moving from the car and up to the apartment felt like a military operation. Sam and the stranger who drove the car covered her from both sides, and they had Junior walking in front. Once inside the apartment, the stranger took a position by the door and Sam immediately got on his phone.

"Do you need anything?" Kaylee asked Junior as they walked slowly together into the great room. He brushed the cut over his eyebrow, held together with a butterfly closure, and winced in obvious pain.

"I wouldn't mind some pain reliever, if you have any," he admitted.

"Sure. Go sit down. I'll bring you some."

Kaylee brought him back some acetaminophen and a bottle of water. She sat beside him while he swallowed the pills. They were still for a while until, eventually, Junior turned on the televisions. One of the screens showed the evening news, with live coverage of the aftermath. The caption on the screen read: *Car explodes in Midtown. Police suspect foul play—investigation under way.*

Another forty-five minutes or so went by. Kaylee was aware of Sam talking on the phone and work-ing on his laptop, which was now set up on the kitchen counter. At some point, he handed her a bottle of water, which she gratefully gulped down. She and Junior were still watching the ongoing news coverage when there was a knock at the door. Kaylee looked up, and her heart immediately started thudding in her chest. The stranger who had driven them home immediately opened the door to three people standing in the hallway, only one of whom she recognized.

"Evan," she whispered, standing up. Junior stood also.

Evan DaCosta strode swiftly into the room while his other companions filed in behind him. Instead of his usual expensive suit, he wore black utility pants and a fitted top that stretched snugly across his wide chest. His handsome face showed fierce determination. Kaylee covered her mouth to hide its trembling. Despite everything that had happened, and what was yet to come, it was so good to see him.

"What have you gotten yourself into?" he demanded as he approached them in the great room. The gruffness of his voice was softened by the concern in his eyes.

Kaylee only shrugged before he pulled her into his arms, forcing her up on to her tippy toes.

"What are you doing here?" she whispered into his ear.

"If you're in trouble, where else would I be?" he replied before they separated.

"Evan, it's good to see you," Junior said as the two men shook hands and slapped shoulders.

Evan then stepped back, and Kaylee looked around at the four men and one woman who now surrounded her and her brother like warriors ready for battle. Sam seemed to understand her confusion, and he stepped forward to stand next to Evan.

"Kaylee, I've brought in the Fortis team to help with your security going forward."

"You should have told me," she protested.

"There wasn't exactly time for debate. And I think you'll agree that the situation has escalated beyond that of what you hired me for."

She clenched her jaw hard, forced to accept that he was right. One of the other men looked vaguely familiar, and he walked up to her. "Hi, Mikayla. I'm Raymond Blunt. We met briefly a few years ago."

Kaylee smiled a little. "Hi, Raymond. I remember. And thank you for coming here so quickly," she replied politely.

"And since these Neanderthals have no manners, I'll introduce myself," said the tall, attractive woman next to Raymond. "I'm Renee Thomas, Fortis agent. And that's David Ferguson, by the door. He's from DaCosta, and based in New York."

Kaylee and Junior nodded to each of them.

"Now that we have all the niceties out of the way, let's get set up and see what we're dealing with," Evan concluded.

She looked at Sam, but he had turned to talk with Renee and Raymond, pointing in the direction of the open dining area. That was when Kaylee noticed the four large metal boxes behind them, just in front of the apartment door.

"What's going on?" she asked Evan as people started moving in all directions, clearly executing a plan she had no knowledge of.

"We're going to set up some equipment to help us find these bastards and take them down," he replied.

"Wait a minute. Take down who? Why?" Junior asked with obvious confusion. "What's going on here?"

Sam joined them. "I think we should all put our cards on the table," he said bluntly. "We don't have time for any more bullshit. The risks are too high."

"What?" Junior questioned. "Kayla, what are they talking about?"

Kaylee looked at the three men in her life and wondered if it was fate that they were all together, now. Or karma. Either way, it was time for the truth. She took a deep breath.

"Sam's right. I need to tell you guys something." She looked Sam squarely in the eyes. "This is all happening because of me."

Junior was a smart man with the mind of a lawyer. He looked between his sister and the man he knew as owner of a major defense contractor for the federal government.

"The explosion," Junior finally said. "You guys know something about it."

"That's what I'm trying to tell you. I'm the one responsible."

"Mikayla, this is not your fault—" Evan tried to tell her, but she cut him off, raising her hands in frustration.

"Listen to me!" she finally yelled. "It is my fault. I did this."

Sam was the only one who considered that her words were literal. He stepped closer and leaned in.

"What exactly are you trying to say, Kaylee?" he demanded in a voice that sent chills down her spine.

"I'm saying that I set this whole thing up. These people came after me because I wanted them to."

CHAPTER 16

"I think you better start from the beginning, Mikayla," Evan suggested. "And don't leave anything out."

Kaylee swallowed, and dropped down on the couch, feeling overwhelmed by a mix of conflicting emotions. She was scared and regretful about what had happened that evening, but also certain that it had been necessary. Junior sat beside her and took her hand, silently offering his unconditional support.

"It started in Baltimore, when I was writing for the *Journal*," she began. "I was assigned to municipal politics and wanted to do a story on budget overspend. I had a lead from a friend that there were a couple of vendors that were always exceeding the costs they had originally quoted the city. So, I started looking in to how that was possible, maybe to expose flaws in the process or general mismanagement.

"I didn't find anything. No one in the mayor's office seemed to know or care about it, but my editor found out what I was doing and reassigned me to another page."

"Jason Holt," Sam said, his eyes squinting as he made the connection.

"Yeah. He was pissed because I had gone behind his back to follow my lead. Then someone from the city complained that I was harassing them. Which I wasn't, of course."

"Wasn't Holt the guy George hired you guys to investigate a few years ago?" Evan asked Sam.

"Yeah, it was our first case for Clement Media, and it was a pretty easy one. Holt had been taking bribes in exchange for press coverage," confirmed Sam.

"Wait," Kaylee interrupted, looking up at Sam with obvious surprise. "You were involved in that?"

Sam only nodded, avoiding her eyes. She didn't need him to spell out that it was the reason he had been at the *Baltimore Journal* that fateful afternoon over four years ago.

"I was pretty upset about being reassigned and accused of harassment, and wanted some advice from my dad," she continued. "He told me not to worry about it, that writing for another column was not a big deal. So I went back to work and tried to put it behind me. But then I heard Jason telling someone on the phone that he had 'shut me down' and that he had done what had been asked."

"Was he talking to the person from the city that had complained to him?" Junior asked.

"Maybe, but it was the way the conversation happened. Jason was talking in the staircase, and seemed really agitated," Kaylee explained. "It just looked really suspicious to me. So I tried to look at his phone, hoping to see who he had talked to."

Sam and Evan looked at each other.

"What did you find?" Sam finally asked.

"I didn't have time to go through the phone calls, and I didn't want to touch it in case it was locked or something and Jason would know I was snooping. But he did receive a text message, so I took a picture of the message with my phone. It said, 'The package is on its way.' Then I got scared about the whole thing and rushed out of the office."

"That was the day you tripped in the alley," Sam concluded.

Kaylee nodded, avoiding his eyes.

"My dad told me later that evening that Jason had been fired. Then, a couple of days later, Dad announced his retirement as CEO. I left the paper and started working with my mom."

"So, how did we get from then to now, Mikayla? What does Holt have to do with any of this?" asked Sam, folding his arms across his chest.

"A couple of years later, I was cleaning up my computer and found the picture I had taken of Jason's phone. I had looked at it a bunch of times before, but what I hadn't noticed was that his phone hadn't been locked after all, and his email inbox had been captured in the background. The text message had come in while the email application was open. The list of emails was blurry, but I could see the sender names. One was from Nate Battleford."

"Battleford? Doesn't he work for Groveland

Development?" Junior asked. "They do a lot of major infrastructure projects for Maryland and D.C."

"Yes, exactly. And they also do building projects for the city of Baltimore. At least they used to."

"I know the owner, Anthony Fleming, and I've met Nate Battleford. But what's the significance, Mikayla?" Evan asked. "What does this have to do with what's going on now?"

"It's about the government contracts," she explained. "My friend who told me about the budget overspend said the contracts were for building projects. At the time, I was more focused on city officials and the audit process. I wasn't thinking about the building companies. Until I saw Jason's emails. Why would the head of a building company be emailing my editor just days after I was at city hall trying to understand how city contractors billed the city? The same day that he tells someone that he shut me down?"

"You think Nate Battleford was the one who bribed Holt," Evan concluded.

"I know he did," she confirmed.

"It's likely," Sam added. "We weren't able to determine who it was at the time, so Battleford is as good a suspect as anyone. But that's hardly surprising or unusual. Corruption in government contracting is pretty common practice in big cities."

"Believe me, I know that, Sam," she replied with a trace of bitterness. "I know it's tolerated and ignored as long as everyone benefits. But, at the time, I was thinking it would still make a good story."

"I don't understand," Junior said. "What story? You aren't a journalist anymore."

"I know, but I wanted to be," she explained to her brother. "I was working for Mom, and liked doing charitable work. But I missed writing, and I wanted to go back to it. So, at the time, when I found this connection between Groveland Development and Jason, it felt like an inside scoop had fallen in my lap. I decided to reach out to Jason and see if he'd be willing to tell me what he knew, as an anonymous source."

"What did Holt tell you?" Sam asked.

"Nothing. Jason's dead. His car blew up about two months after he was fired from the *Journal*."

There was silence as the group looked around at each other.

"I assume that didn't stop you from digging into it more," Sam said sarcastically.

"I didn't know what to do. Two years ago, Groveland was all over the news. They were working on several high-profile projects in D.C., and Anthony Fleming was well known within our family social circles," Kaylee explained with a sigh. "So I asked my dad about Groveland, and he freaked out."

Evan straightened up. "What do you mean, freaked out?"

"He told me I didn't know what I was talking about and I should never bring it up again. When I said I had evidence that Anthony had had one of his men bribe Jason, he started yelling, forbidding me to look into it further," she explained, trying not to remember the anger and fear in her father's eyes. "He was drinking at the time, so I thought he wasn't really thinking straight. But after that, he started keeping tabs on me, constantly grilling me about what I was doing and where I was going. And his drinking got worse and worse. It took me a little bit of time, but I finally understood."

"Fleming had forced your dad to retire from Clement Media," Evan filled in.

"Jesus!" swore Junior.

Sam sighed, and the two friends exchanged a look.

"You knew?" Kaylee accused Evan with surprise and disappointment.

"No," he denied. "But I knew your dad was hiding something at the time. He didn't want Fortis to continue the investigation into who had bribed Holt. That wasn't like him at all, and when I tried to discuss it, he made me promise not to look into it further."

She sighed and looked at her brother. He was looking at the ground and he was angry.

"Why didn't you tell me all this, Kayla?" he finally demanded, standing to face her. "The whole time that we've watched Dad decline into a drunken mess, you knew the reason and you said nothing. Mom and I have struggled to deal with it, to figure out what was going on, why he turned his back on us and turned into someone none of us could stand to be around. And you knew the reason."

"Junior, I tried," she insisted.

"You didn't try!" he yelled back, leaning into Kaylee aggressively. "You didn't tell me or Mom. You just packed up and left. You moved to New York to work for your boyfriend and didn't look back."

"Junior," Evan interrupted, grabbing the younger man by the arm and pulling him back.

"He got so much worse after you left, Mikayla. And you didn't give a shit!" Junior finished.

"You know that's not true," Kaylee yelled back.

"Okay, let's calm down," Sam added, stepping between the siblings. "This isn't getting us anywhere."

Junior pulled his arm out of Evan's grip and walked a few steps away, clearly trying to control his anger.

"So, then what, Mikayla?" Evan encouraged her. "You think Fleming forced your dad to retire. What happened next?"

"It was more than his retirement, Evan. I think they threatened his family in order to keep him quiet," she said. "It's the only thing that explains his behavior, especially once I told him I have evidence on Anthony Fleming. And it's been eating him up."

"Then why did you leave, Mikayla?" Junior demanded, stepping to her again. "How could that possibly have helped the situation?"

"I had to, Junior," she snapped back. "Don't you get it? Nobody cares about how Groveland makes their money, or that politicians and city officials line their pockets with every contract they award. That people, good people like Dad, are forced to aid their corruption. It's just business as usual, nobody gets hurt."

She took a deep breath, trying to stay calm and factual.

"There's no story unless the public cares, and no one will care unless they see tangible damage."

Sam had been watching and listening to Kaylee's story with mounting frustration. Deep down, he had known the truth almost from the beginning, but hadn't wanted to acknowledge it. It was too crazy. But all the pieces finally fit together.

"Jesus Christ, Kaylee," Sam exclaimed, raking a hand through his hair. "You were the bait. Are you frigging mad, lass?"

"What does that mean?" Junior demanded, obviously too angry to see what was soon to be obvious.

Sam looked at her, teeth clenched against the urge to tell the rest of the story himself.

"I spent months looking into Groveland and how they did business, how they'd managed to become a monopoly for building projects in Baltimore," she explained, avoiding Sam's eyes. "It was so simple. They would undercut anyone who dared to bid against them, and then, after they won the bid, they just overcharged. Materials were more expensive, the project took longer. It had been going on for years.

"And it wasn't only in Baltimore. They were doing the same thing in several other cities across the Northeast under a bunch of different front companies," she explained. "If anyone complained or investigated, they were shut up pretty quickly. If the city started any sort of official audit or investigation, Anthony Fleming would just dissolve that company and reopen business under another name."

"You have proof of this," Evan asked.

"A year ago, I had plenty of proof that Groveland had monopolies in several cities operating under different names," Kaylee confirmed. "But that wasn't enough. Not to shut down Groveland and protect my family. I needed more than just aggressive business practices."

"You needed proof of criminal coercions," Sam said.

"Yes," she agreed. "And since Jason was dead and my dad wasn't well, I needed more evidence."

Junior finally stopped pacing and looked at his sister with something other than anger.

"That's why you started working for Terry?" he asked.

"Eventually. But only after I tried to find someone who was willing to come forward with real information. I couldn't use our family contacts without risk of exposure," she explained. "Then I ran into Terry at one of the foundation events, and it seemed like the perfect opportunity. If I was working in the building industry, I could witness their illegal tactics firsthand."

"You could be the witness," Evan finally deduced.

Sam shoved his hands in his pockets to keep from grabbing Kaylee by the shoulders to shake some sense into her. When she had claimed that the events earlier were because of her, Kaylee had meant it literally.

"Holy shit, Mikayla," Junior mumbled. "Does Terry know this? That you're using his company to investigate Anthony Fleming?"

"Terry knows some of it, but not all. And it's not his company, it's mine," she said. "I used my trust fund for the start-up and bought the right to use the Antonoli name in North America. But I couldn't present myself as the owner of a new building company; it would draw too much attention, even if I used the name Kaylee Stone. I couldn't risk that someone would realize I was the daughter of George Clement."

"But no one would pay attention to an executive assistant," Sam finished.

"Unless they needed leverage," Kaylee whispered.

"I can't believe this," whispered Junior. "This is what you set out to do? To make yourself a victim for men who use threats and force to get what they want? This is crazy, Mikayla!"

"Don't you see, Junior? It was the only way. Our family has been completely destroyed! Dad is slowly killing himself because of what these people have done. They need to be stopped, and I had the means to do it."

"Mikayla, your brother is right. This is insane," Evan added.

"Have you seen my dad lately, Evan?" she demanded. "When was the last time? Last year? You wouldn't even recognize him now. He drinks all the time, and it's killing him. So what was I supposed to do? Plan social events, golf tournaments? Go to dinners with these people and politely take their dirty money as donations? I couldn't do it."

There was heavy silence after that. The passion and determination of her statements echoed around them. Finally, Sam went up to Kaylee and touched her shoulder.

"What do you have on Fleming?" he asked.

Her shoulders relaxed a little, and she seemed grateful to move on.

"His people just blew up a car in Midtown so I'd say I finally have enough to stop him."

"No, you don't, Mikayla," Junior countered.

"Fleming is two hundred miles away, so you can't connect him to this. Don't you understand that? People like him are pretty much untouchable—that's why they do it. So, as far as I can see, you put us, and a lot of other people, in danger for no reason."

"Jesus, Junior, weren't you listening? I started Antonoli Properties specifically to compete against Fleming and force him to come out in the open. I've traced at least seven of his phony companies. I knew how he operated, so I outplayed him. He bid low in Paterson, and I just bid lower. Then the threats started. So there is no doubt who's responsible."

"Ross Construction is a front for Groveland," Sam said, and Kaylee looked at him with surprise.

"How did you know about Ross?" she asked.

"My team is pretty good at finding information, Kaylee. It wasn't difficult," he replied.

"They're obviously a shell company, but Renee's still trying to find out who really owns Ross," Evan reminded them. "What makes you think it's Fleming?"

"I'll show you," she said, before walking away.

Kaylee went quickly to the office between her room and Terry's. It was neat and looked unused, except for the storage space under the desk. She opened it up and took out a thick folder, which she carried back to the living room. Sam, Evan, and Junior watched silently as she laid out several documents on the coffee table.

"This is the statement of work from a project Groveland did with the city of Baltimore five years ago," she explained, tapping the first document. "Look at the last page, with the invoicing information. It's operating under Groveland Development, but the registered owner is PTL Inc."

"That's the same company that Ross has listed on their bid in Paterson," Sam remembered. "But that company doesn't exist."

"Not anymore," Kaylee agreed. "Somewhere between three to five years ago, Anthony changed the registered name of his company from PTL Inc. to Groveland Inc."

She pointed to two other city contracts dated more recently, and the new name was listed under each for invoicing.

"But he kept operating the shell companies under the original name," Evan concluded.

Evan looked down at the documents, rubbing a finger over his lips in thought.

"This definitely suggests that Fleming owns Ross. But it doesn't prove that he's responsible for the threats against you and Antonoli, instead of someone lower in the company."

"Maybe not, but it's enough to create a scandal." Kaylee insisted. "If I publish a story on Groveland winning state projects while it maintains shell companies that threaten its competitors, the business and political fallout would destroy him."

"No," Sam stated bluntly. "It's too risky, and you're not putting yourself in the line of fire anymore."

"It's not your call, Sam," she insisted, turning to face him with squared shoulders.

"I'm making it my call," Sam snapped back. "You're not putting this story out there. You're not in this alone anymore, Kaylee. You hired me to protect you, and that's what I'm going to do, whether you like it or not. And we'll take down Fleming in the process."

CHAPTER 17

At first, Kaylee looked as though she was going to argue with him. But then she glanced over at her brother and Sam was relieved to see her shoulders sag a little. She turned and walked a few steps away from the three men, remaining quiet and in thought for a few minutes. Sam looked over at Evan, who was frowning as he looked between Kaylee and his partner.

"Okay, you're right," Kaylee finally agreed, turning back to face them. "How do we get him?"

"We're not doing anything more tonight other than surveillance and reconnaissance," Sam said. "Once we know more about the car bomb, who planted it, and when, we can create a plan of action."

Kaylee nodded, looking tired and deflated.

"It's almost nine-thirty and I'm sure everyone's hungry," Evan said. "We'll order some food, get everyone settled in, then regroup in the morning."

"I have to get going," Junior said, brushing at his head wound again.

"Why don't you stay for something to eat?" Kaylee suggested.

"No, that's okay. I'll pick something up near my hotel," he told her, then turned to Evan. "I still don't understand how DaCosta fits into all this, Evan. But thanks for coming here to help Mikayla."

"I'm no longer the head of DaCosta Solutions," Evan explained. "Now I own Fortis with Sam and another partner. And this is what we do. We provide security solutions and asset protection for our clients."

Junior looked around at the operation that was being set up at Kaylee's apartment and then back at Evan. "Looks like I need to get caught up on a few more things."

Evan smiled and slapped him on the shoulder. "How long are you in the city?"

"I planned to stay for the weekend, but now I don't know," admitted Junior, looking very confused and a little disoriented.

"I'll walk you to the door," Kaylee offered, and the siblings walked away.

"So, what do you think?" Evan asked when they were out of earshot.

Sam stroked his chin, still coming to grips with everything Kaylee had told him and all that she had been through over the last few years.

"It was a crazy and reckless plan, but I can see why she did it," he replied.

"I've always admired her strong will and determination. But this is a whole other level of balls," Evan added.

"We need to solve this thing right away, before

someone realizes who Kaylee really is," Sam added. "They weren't trying to kill her today, just send a really strong message to Antonoli. But we both know that they are completely capable of murder."

"I know. And, if Mikayla is right, they've already killed one witness: Holt," concluded Evan.

"I'll order some food. Why don't you start updating the others, then we'll do a status review to see what else we know?" Sam suggested, taking out his phone to find a local restaurant that delivered.

"Wait, Sam," Evan inserted. "Is everything okay between you and Mikayla?"

"What do you mean?" Sam asked impassively.

"I don't know. There just seems to be a bit of tension between you. Beyond the obvious situation. And why do you call her Kaylee?"

Sam shrugged, feeling like a fraud.

"I just got used to it, I guess. That's how she introduced herself when we met four years ago, and the name she used when I took this assignment."

"Oh yeah, I forgot about that," Evan mused. "Anyway, thank you for taking this one while I was out of town. Particularly since you're supposed to be on vacation."

"Don't worry about it. I didn't have anything planned. But just so you know, she still thinks that I'm working for her. So maybe don't mention that this is all off the books."

"Yeah, Lucas mentioned that too. And now we know why she didn't want me to know what was going on."

Kaylee approached at that point, looking too exhausted to stand. "I'm going to get cleaned up."

"Okay. I'll let you know when the food arrives," Sam replied. Their eyes met for a few seconds.

Finally, she nodded with a ghost of a smile and went toward her room.

Sam ordered pizza, which the team devoured while it was still hot. Kaylee joined them about an hour later, wearing yoga pants and a cotton T-shirt, and looking a little less weary.

"Renee and I have reviewed all the surveillance footage from today, both from the apartment and the office," Raymond said as they all stood around the table in the kitchen. "No sign of any threats or unusual activity."

"Good. There was nothing after the explosion to suggest there was anything else in play," Sam told them. "So let's attack the problem in the morning."

"I booked rooms for the team at the Ritz-Carlton," Evan noted. "Or did you need anyone to stay here for extra support?"

"No, I'm good. We're wired up pretty tight here. I'll know the second something breathes too close," Sam confirmed. "You guys get some sleep."

The Fortis team left the apartment at around eleven o'clock that night. Renee, Raymond, and David Ferguson, the DaCosta consultant, said polite good-byes. Then Sam watched Evan and Kaylee hug, noting the obvious caring and friendship that they had for each other. But that was all it was, since Evan was crazy in love with his girlfriend, Nia. Yet that knowledge didn't stop Sam from clenching his jaw with unjustified annoyance.

Then he and Kaylee were alone in the apartment.

She was still in the kitchen, cleaning up the pizza boxes and empty cans of soda.

"Why don't I take care of all that?" he offered, piling up the dirty plates and used napkins. "You should get some rest."

"Is that it then? You have nothing else to say?" she asked, still cleaning up.

Sam put everything down on the counter and turned to face her. He really did not want to have this conversation right now. Too much had happened in a short period of time for him to focus on anything more than the mission. His personal feelings for Kaylee needed more time. Right now, all he felt was a slow, burning anger and stomach-turning fear for the risk she was in. And he didn't want to discuss any of that with her.

"I think you've said plenty this evening, Kaylee. Or are there more lies you need to confess?"

"No," she said softly, casually tossing things into the garbage can. "But I would like the chance to explain."

"I think you gave a pretty good explanation earlier," he replied, leaning against the counter with his arms and ankles crossed. "Despite what you think, I'm not an idiot. I knew you were lying to me from the beginning."

"I know you're not. I also knew you would know I wasn't being completely honest with you, but that would be true to form, wouldn't it?" she explained. "You would expect me to be deceitful and immoral. So why bother to question my situation? My motives."

"You forgot manipulative," he snarled, and she

flinched. "Is that why you slept with me? Then led me to believe that you slept with another man the very next night right under my nose? True to form?"

She sighed and looked away.

"Damn, you're cold."

"I'm sorry, Sam," she finally whispered, still avoiding his eyes. "I was desperate, and I did what I thought had to be done. So yes, I lied about Terry and I. But being with you at the safe house had nothing to do with this. I didn't plan it. How could I?"

Sam looked at her profile, trying to make sense of his tangled thoughts and emotions. He didn't know what to believe, and he didn't trust himself to objectively assess the facts. Kaylee had this unnatural ability to break down his barriers and stir uncontrollable desires. After four years, being around her still made him feel alive and charged, but also raw and unrestrained. It was too much too soon, just like before. And it was not a good sign for how it would all end.

"Antonoli. He's not your lover," he found himself stating.

She finally looked back at him.

"No. We've been friends for years, and he just wanted to help me out. And he really does love his wife."

He nodded, feeling marginally better, then annoyed that it mattered so much.

"Sam," she whispered with a soft, pleading look in her eyes.

He stepped back, using his anger and willpower to resist the allure of where this could go.

"Go to bed, Kaylee. We have a lot to figure out tomorrow."

Then Sam took his laptop and went to the den. He paused inside the room, immediately regretting the impulsive brush-off. Now he was the one being dishonest. It was a lie to let her think he didn't desire her when he did. That it wouldn't be so easy and so good to take her in his arms, be with her again. But walking away was the right thing to do.

And there was Evan. Sam needed to tell him what had happened four years ago. It was time, and it was necessary for their friendship and partnership. And for his integrity.

Now that he'd seen her and Evan together, as friends after their engagement, Sam felt less concerned about how the truth would impact Kaylee. Considering what she had dealt with virtually alone to go after some very bad people, Sam had no doubt about her ability to deal with Evan's reaction. So it was time and it needed to happen soon.

Purposefully putting Kaylee and his desires out of his mind, Sam reviewed the digital feed of the apartment surveillance, secured his gun near his pillow, and went to sleep on the small pull-out couch.

Thursday morning, the Fortis team met again in the dining room over breakfast. They had several high-powered computers set up on the long table to create a base of operation for the rest of the mission. Sam would continue to lead the operation and was ready to set their immediate objectives and assign tasks.

"The first thing we need to do is to have Antonoli

Properties withdraw their bid for the Paterson contract. That will take the heat off Kaylee and allow us to go on the offense and catch them unaware," he began. "Kaylee, can we talk to Antonoli this morning and make that happen?"

"There's no need. I have signing authority," she explained, readily. "But I'll give him an update."

"Then let's clarify our primary objective. Kaylee, would you agree that the target is whoever was or still is exerting influence over your father? Then we have to confirm who that is and why," he said, and she nodded with agreement. "We need to go back to our original assignment for Clement Media four years ago. Raymond, you should access the original security review from the *Baltimore Journal*, and the annual audits we do now, and review all of the data and information Kaylee has uncovered since."

"You're still doing work for my father?" Kaylee asked.

"Yes, since he retired. After Holt, he wanted Fortis to look for any signs of corruption on a regular basis," Evan explained.

"Evan, can you work with Kaylee to pull together a comprehensive review of all the known facts and the evidence associated with Holt?" Sam instructed. "For example, we know he was bribed over whatever Kaylee was investigating, based on the conversation she overheard and the payment we intercepted. And we know he received an email from Nate Battleford within a close timeframe. But we don't actually know if the two are related. We also don't have proof that anyone coerced George into quitting. And so on. Then we can do a gap analysis, factoring in what is essential to prove in order to meet our objective."

"Got it," Evan replied.

"Renee, you're with me. I want to look over the physical evidence from all of the threats Kaylee's received. The visit to the office, the break-in, the voicemail message and attack in Virginia. Then the car bomb. Something has to tie back to Fleming or whoever is running the show." Renee nodded. "Let's meet back here at about four o'clock this afternoon to regroup. But let's connect immediately if anything urgent is uncovered."

The team broke up to get focused on their individual tasks. Kaylee reached for her cell phone, presumably to call Antonoli in Paris. Sam approached Evan.

"Do you have a minute?" he asked his friend.

"Yeah, what's up?"

"We need to talk in private."

Evan raised his eyebrows, but followed Sam into the small den.

"What's going on?"

Sam closed the door and took a position in the middle of the room, arms straight along his side. "You were correct yesterday, when you said there's tension between Kaylee and I," he started.

"Yeah, I figured that. As you can see, she's pretty stubborn when she sets her mind on something, so—"

"No, Evan. That's not it," Sam interrupted, determined to spit out the words needed. "You know that I had met her, four years ago. I helped her home after she had hurt her ankle. We got to know each other a bit, just for a couple days."

Evan straightened up and crossed his arms firmly across his chest. "Okay."

"I didn't know Clement's daughter worked at the paper, so I didn't make the connection between the name she gave me and your . . . fiancée," continued Sam, eyes fixed firmly on his friend's face. "We got close."

Evan leaned forward, his expression more chilly. "How close exactly?"

"Intimate close."

Sam waited for the reaction that was sure to come. Evan's eyes narrowed, and his face looked carved from ice.

"You and Mikayla. While she was engaged to me."

"I didn't know that, but yes. She didn't know who I was either, not until I confronted her," Sam explained, keeping his tone calm and factual.

"And when was that exactly?"

"The day you arrived back from overseas, after you had spoken to Clement about his retirement," he explained. "That's when I knew. I stopped it immediately."

Evan blinked a few times. "She broke the engagement and ended our relationship the next day."

Sam remained silent, not wanting to give excuses and explanations when none would be satisfactory.

The punch was swift and hard, a right hook straight to the jaw. Sam's head snapped back from the blow, and he felt his lip split as it smashed against his teeth. He shook his head, trying to clear his vision in case there was another one coming.

"What the fuck, Sam!" Evan yelled. "You slept with my fiancée and you didn't tell me? You and I weren't tight or anything back then, but shit, man! I had a right to know."

Sam wiped away the trickle of blood from his mouth.

"I know that. You're right, mate. I should have told you. But I didn't, and I regret it. So I'm telling you now."

"That's why she wanted you on this case," Evan said as other things started to become clear. "Have you guys been together all these years?"

"Nay! Of course not," Sam shot back. "We have had no contact since the day I found out who she was. Not until she showed up at Fortis last Friday."

Evan watched him hard as though seeing Sam for the first time.

"But now things between Kaylee and I are . . . complicated," Sam finally acknowledged.

"Complicated?" Evan shouted with a rude snort. "You're screwing each other, aren't you? Jesus Christ, Sam. What the fuck!"

Sam clenched his jaw hard, resenting the crude depiction of what was happening between him and Kaylee.

"It's not like that." He took a deep breath, shoving his hands in his pockets. "I think there could be something more between us."

Evan scoffed, then laughed bitterly. He gave Sam a scathing look and stormed out of the room.

CHAPTER 18

The first calls Kaylee made that morning were to Annie and Paul, to prepare them for the damage to the front of the office building and to let them know she would be working from home at least for the day. She then called Terry in Paris to let him know what had happened yesterday and the decisions that had been made since. Not surprisingly, he was angry and concerned, but also relieved. They worked out how to submit the formal withdrawal from consideration for the new government building in Paterson, New Jersey.

"So, it is over, Kaylee? Have you achieved what you set out to do?" Terry finally asked.

She didn't have a concrete answer for him.

"I wouldn't say it's over. But, now that I have some professional help, I think the end is in sight," she explained.

"Good. Sam Mackenzie seems very capable, and I would imagine his whole team is the same. I'm sure they will do everything they can to uncover the truth."

"Yeah, I know."

"Have you put any thought into what will happen with Antonoli Properties when this is well and truly over?" he asked.

"I don't know, to be honest. I imagined we would just shut it down. Or if it proved profitable, you would take it over and buy me out."

"Yes, we did discuss those options at the onset. But I think you have enjoyed building the business, even if it was with ulterior motives, no?"

"I think you're right, Terry. If I stop and think only about the business plan, and the early vendor proposals, then winning the two Brooklyn projects, and working on them now, it has been fun," Kaylee mused.

"Well, it sounds like you have decisions to make, my friend."

"Thank you for everything you've done, Terry. I know you didn't think any of this was a good idea, but you still supported me. I really appreciate that."

They spoke for a few more minutes; then Kaylee slowly walked back to the living area. Raymond, Renee, and Sam were at the table working away at computers.

"Where's Evan?" she asked as she approached.

Sam stood up and took Kaylee gently by the arm, steering her away from the others. But not before she caught a glimpse of his busted lip. Her heart started pounding.

"He's out on the terrace," explained Sam in a soft voice. "I told him. Everything."

Kaylee took in a shaky breath and looked down.

She could only nod, knowing this moment was inevitable. Sam held her back as she tried to walk away.

"You might want to give him a few minutes to cool off," he added. His expression was stoic, but she could see that his emotions were buried just below the surface.

"No, it's fine," she insisted. He cleared his throat and released her arm.

Kaylee walked out onto the terrace, where Evan was leaning against the glass railing, looking out at the city skyline. She stood beside him silently for a couple of minutes.

"I never thought you were a liar, Mikayla," he finally said. "Or should I call you Kaylee?"

She didn't respond, knowing that he was lashing out from feelings of betrayal and anger.

"You told me that something was missing in our relationship, that you loved me as a friend, but it wasn't enough for a marriage," he added.

"That wasn't a lie, Evan," she said sadly. "You know it's true. You must know that we never had a strong passion between us. We were apart for weeks at a time, with you working overseas, only talking occasionally. I was fine with it—it worked for us at the time. I understood your work schedule, and I was busy at school, then with my career. I didn't need anything else."

Evan looked down at her, and she could tell he was confused and waiting for her to say it all.

"I didn't want more. Until I did," Kaylee finally admitted. "That's how it happened, just a random thing. Some guy who came out of nowhere, and made me feel . . . Suddenly I knew that I wanted more from a marriage than a comfortable routine and good friendship."

"Why didn't you tell me that, Mikayla?" Evan demanded. "I would have been mad, hurt, but at least I would know the whole truth. He was my partner, for Christ sakes!"

"That's why, Evan!" she replied. "It was bad enough that I broke up our engagement, hurting you, disappointing our parents. What good would it do to damage your business relationship with Sam? He hadn't done anything wrong—I had. So I couldn't live with that too."

He looked away and swore slowly under his breath.

"I'm sorry, Evan. Maybe we should have told you at the time, but it wouldn't have changed anything. Not really, and you know that," she continued. "I've seen you with Nia, remember. The way you look at her. That's what things should be like, right? That's what matters in the end."

"Are you in love with him?" Evan finally asked, his tone slightly warmer.

Kaylee sighed deeply. "I don't know. Love at first sight seems like a ridiculous fantasy. But whatever I felt for Sam when I met him is still there, even now. But it feels more like slow torture, to be honest."

"Good, you deserve it," Evan said, but there was a wry smile on his face. She elbowed him in the side, and he yelled out in protest.

"Will things be okay between you and Sam?" she finally asked.

Evan looked down, shoving his hands in his pockets. "I don't know. I have to wrap my head around this whole thing. He's the most straight-forward guy I know, that's all."

"Evan, he had no clue who I was. When he found out, he was so angry. About the impact to you." Evan swore again. "I don't know why he didn't tell you, but I know it's weighed on him. So please try not to make it into something bigger than it needs to be."

He ran a hand over his low-cropped wavy hair. "Let's get back inside. We have work to do."

Kaylee followed Evan, and they joined the others at the dining table, setting up one end to review the stack of documents she had amassed over the last couple of years. She was very aware of the cold barrier between the two partners, but the others seemed unaware.

Sam and Renee left later in the afternoon to have a closer look at the destroyed BMW, which was now sitting in a scrap yard. They returned a few hours later and went back to work at their computers. The housekeeper arrived around noon, as was her usual schedule. Kaylee told Silvia that she had hired a few consultants for work and they'd be at the apartment for a few days. Silvia quickly made them lunch and took Niko out for his afternoon walk. She completed her cleaning chores and made a big pasta dish for dinner before leaving in the late afternoon.

"Okay, let's regroup," Sam said once Silvia had left. "Raymond, where are we with the information we have from Clement Media?"

They all surrounded his large panel screen while he opened up a few documents.

"I've reviewed the files we had collected on Holt four years ago. Here is the email from Battleford, dated Friday, May eleventh, at two-thirty in the afternoon," Raymond explained as he opened the communication.

"*Someone will be in touch*," Sam read out loud. "Pretty cryptic. Any other communication between them? Phone calls or text messages?"

"Yup." He moved between files on the screen. "There was a call the day before between Holt's cell phone and a landline number connected to Groveland Development. It was over twelve minutes long. But no way to say exactly who he spoke to. And I couldn't find any calls between Holt and someone at city hall that week, either by cell phone or through a work line."

"He had told me the complaint came from the comptroller," Kaylee recalled. "It was a lie."

"It appears so," Raymond concluded.

"Is there anything on his cell phone after he was fired that Monday? So after May fourteenth?" Evan asked.

"I checked that, but his mobile number became inactive after that, then canceled a few days later. Tried to find if he'd gotten another number registered to him through his cell phone carrier, but the records have been archived. Will take me a little more time to access the data."

"What about the annual audits from Clement Media?" Sam asked.

"We've completed security checks for all employees at the twenty-one papers and publications under the Clement umbrella. A few cases of the usual drug usage, inappropriate relationship, a couple of DUIs, but none have triggered a red flag for signs of bribes, exerting influence, or other corruption."

"Okay. So we have pretty compelling evidence that Anthony Fleming directed Battleford to bribe Holt," Sam said. "Let's see if we can prove Fleming also had him killed and got to George."

"I'll dig up all the police records and any media coverage from the car explosion, and access George's phone records from that time. Maybe we'll get lucky."

"What was the name of the chief editor at the *Journal*?" Sam asked.

"Mark McMann," Kaylee provided.

"We should talk to him," added Sam. "If I remember correctly, George had McMann fire Holt, and question him on who was involved in the bribe. Maybe Holt gave up some information."

"And maybe that information got Holt killed and George caught up in the mess?" Evan suggested. "It makes sense. Explains why George was so insistent that Fortis should back down."

"Renee, let's see what McMann is up to these days and set up a conversation," directed Sam.

"I should do it," Kaylee interjected. "I could say that I'm ready to return to journalism, and want to meet him to talk about job opportunities."

"No, it's too risky," Sam said immediately.

"Hold on, that's not a bad idea," interrupted Evan. Sam gave him an annoyed look.

"I can ask questions as part of an innocent conversation, or allow him to think my dad told me whatever Jason knew."

"McMann is still in Baltimore, but he left the *Journal* and the newspaper business entirely a couple of months after George retired," Raymond added as he pulled up information in a Web browser. "He's the VP of media relations at a company called Quinten."

"That's even better," said Kaylee. "I'll ask him about an opportunity in corporate communications, similar to my role at the Clement Foundation."

"It's a good plan, Sam," Evan insisted quietly.

Sam planted his hands on his hips and looked hard down at Kaylee. "Okay, but if we can set a meeting, I'm going with you."

Kaylee let out a slow, deep breath, trying to hold back her excitement. This could be it. The missing piece to the whole puzzle.

"Is there anything more we know about the connection between Groveland and Ross Construction?" Sam continued, looking at Evan.

"No more than Mikayla already told us," Evan replied. "There's no doubt Ross is a front. It's registered in Delaware, and has no assets or employees on record anywhere."

"Why Delaware?" Kaylee asked.

"One of the easiest states to create a ghost company with very little scrutiny or information required," Sam explained.

"I looked into their banking records, and it's exactly what you'd expect," Evan continued. "They have a sweeper account that funnels cash from the U.S. on a set schedule to another one in the Caymans that is untraceable."

"So how are they doing the work on the city contracts they win?" Renee asked.

"Through subcontractors and cash labor," Kaylee explained. "They set up an office on the build site and hire only the skilled workers they need. I'd bet they keep enough money in the bank to pay the expenses while the profits are quickly sent offshore."

"But there has to be some way for Fleming to direct these businesses," Renee suggested. "Someone has to be in charge at Ross, or there's an agent of some kind from Groveland."

"That's the person we need to talk to," agreed Sam. "Evan, can you create a plan to stake out any of the current Ross building sites in the area?"

"They have three projects right now in New Jersey," Kaylee confirmed.

"We can check with Lucas to see if any of our agents are free for a few days, bring in a couple of DaCosta consultants from the New York office, like David Ferguson," Sam continued.

"Got it," Evan acknowledged. "Do we have a list of Groveland employees that we can cross-reference?"

"Yup. Here is everyone on the payroll, starting with owner, Anthony Fleming." Raymond opened a folder and tiled a series of photos across the screen, starting with the head of the company, who looked well dressed, wealthy, and powerful. "Looks like Battleford manages operations. He spends most of his time with suppliers and vendor relationships. Then we have a few managers for design, engineering, and construction."

"Okay, send me everything you have," Evan requested. "Any luck with the physical evidence?"

Sam nodded while he walked over to his laptop.

"The explosion yesterday was from a small bomb attached to the engine," Renee told them while they all moved over to look at the information Sam was pulling up. "It had a remote-controlled detonator."

There were several images on the screen. Some were pictures; others were diagrams.

"I took these pictures right after the explosion," Sam explained. "This wasn't your typical car bomb that's triggered from the vibrations of a moving car. This one was meant to go off at a precise moment. As a very loud and impressive message."

"They were watching," Evan said.

"Absolutely. Kaylee and I weren't on a schedule, and Junior was late meeting us at the office. So there was no way they would know to trigger the explosion as we left the building unless they had eyes on us."

Kaylee felt a shiver of fear trickle down her spine.

"I did some research for any similar devices using a few possible schematics," Renee continued, pointing to a few other images and technical drawings. "They're very popular in Mexico, Greece, and almost every conflict-ridden country in Africa and the Middle East. Much less popular in the United States, but I found five reports over the last few years."

"One in particular caught my attention. From last year, in Rockville, Maryland," Sam explained as he pulled up pictures from an online news report. "The car blew up in the parking lot in front of a post office, and belonged to a woman that worked there. But the post office is right across the street from one of the city planning offices."

The group around the table was silent for a few seconds.

"Another message," Raymond finally said.

"Looks like we have a plan for the next few days," Sam declared as he stepped back to stand in front of the Fortis team and Kaylee. "Raymond will continue looking through any information from four years ago. Kaylee will arrange a meeting with Mark McMann. Evan and I will set up surveillance at the Ross sites. Renee, can you review our security footage again to see if we can identify who triggered the explosive or when they planted it on the car?"

Everyone nodded, then went back to working at their computers. Kaylee went into the living area and sat down on the sofa with her cell phone to catch up on some work for Antonoli. Despite the efforts to go after the people responsible for the threats against her and her dad, there was still a business to run. Annie and Paul were dedicated employees, as were many of the tradespeople working at the two building sites in Brooklyn. Kaylee had a responsibility to them until other arrangements were made.

At around seven o'clock, the team took a break. Sam took Niko out for a walk again, and then he sat with Renee and Raymond at the kitchen table for dinner. Evan took his plate back to the dining table to eat in front of his computer. Kaylee returned to the sofa and ate while watching the news. But her stomach churned from the obvious rift between Sam and Evan, ruining her appetite.

Evan, Renee, and Raymond stayed for another couple of hours, doing a little more work and sharing information, then went back to their hotel rooms for the night. Sam continued working in the kitchen so Kaylee went to her room for some much-needed rest. But as she lay in bed under the covers, she kept hoping for a knock at her door. In her imagination, it would be Sam, feeling as relieved as she was to have all their secrets out in the open. There would be no barriers between them, and new possibilities.

But of course, it didn't happen. She fell asleep alone with her wishful thinking.

CHAPTER 19

"What're you wearing?" Evan asked in a husky voice.

It was Sunday night, and he was in his hotel talking to his girlfriend, Nia, through a video chat application. Nia smiled seductively. He could see that she was lying back in their bed, with a couple of down pillows behind her head.

"Right now? Let me see." She kept the camera on her copper-brown face but was looking down at her body. "I'm wearing those pink panties you really like. The see-through ones, and . . ."

"And?" he prompted, loving how much she teased him.

"And nothing else." Evan groaned. "Would you like to see what I mean?"

"I think I would," he replied with an appreciative smile.

"Okay, but under one condition."

"And what's that?"

"You tell me what's going on with you."

"What?" he asked, confused. "I don't know what you're talking about."

"Yes, you do, Evan. You've been acting weird ever since you got to New York. So tell me what's going on, and maybe I'll reward you."

Evan sighed. Nia James was very sharp and she knew him very well.

"Maybe?"

"It depends on how long it takes for you to stop pretending it's nothing," she explained with absolutely no remorse. "Is it Mikayla?"

"Yeah. No. I don't know," he replied, obviously conflicted.

It had been three days since he had learned about Sam and Mikayla, and Evan was still struggling with the knowledge. While his blinding anger had faded somewhat, the idea of his friend sleeping with his fiancée remained an uncomfortable fact. It was also aggravating trying to figure out why it mattered at all four years later.

"What does that mean?" Nia asked when he didn't explain his convoluted answer.

"Yes, it has to do with Mikayla, but not just her," he said, certain it wouldn't satisfy her.

"Are things okay there on the assignment? I thought you said she was safe now."

"She is. There's no immediate danger. Most of our leads have hit a dead end, but we're focusing on detailed surveillance now," Evan told her. "In fact, I've just spent another fifteen hours in a car or hiding behind dusty equipment. For the second day in a row."

"Poor sweetheart, I'm sure you could use a little help relaxing," Nia suggested.

"I'm pretty tense."

"Well, I'm happy to help. Once you tell me what's bothering you," she persisted. "Is it about Mikayla or not?"

Evan sighed, wishing she were more easily distracted.

"Yes, but not the mission."

"Baby, you're starting to lose credits here. In fact, I'm starting to feel a little sleepy."

"Okay, okay," Evan conceded, amused despite his internal turmoil. Then he told her a very simplified version of the facts.

"Wow, I did not see that one coming," she said afterward. "Though it does explain a few things."

"Really? Like what?" he asked, wondering how anything about it could provide clarity.

"Sam," Nia said, as though there were something obvious Evan should know. "He's always seemed a little . . . lonely to me."

"What?" Evan demanded with a loud snort. "Lonely how? He's not exactly a choirboy, Nia. The man gets plenty of action, trust me. Not as much as Lucas, of course. That is, before Lucas met Alex in the spring and lost his mind. But you get my point."

"I'm not talking about how many women he dates, Evan. I've met a few of them, remember? I'm just saying that Sam always seemed distant or distracted even while out with some very beautiful women. Like there was a part of him that was unreachable."

"I think you're reading too much into it, Nia.

Sam's not exactly the life of the party. He's a sarcastic smart-ass on a good day."

"Well, the more I think about it, the more it makes sense."

"Nothing about this makes sense, Nia."

There was silence, and Evan watched her full lips turn into a frown.

"Are you jealous? Is that what's going on?"

"Jesus, Nia. You know how I feel about Mikayla. And about you. I'm not jealous," he said with frustration. "But I think I have a right to be pissed off."

"Maybe, four years ago. Or if you were still in love with her and hadn't moved on with your life a long time ago," Nia said with some reproach. "But you don't and you have, right? So what exactly is so upsetting about your ex-fiancée and one of your best friends being together?"

He sighed with frustration. "It's the fact that they both kept a pretty big secret from me."

"Or is it some stupid guy thing that I don't understand? Like, any woman you've been with belongs to you even if you don't want her anymore?"

"Okay, now you're just being ridiculous," he snapped.

"You're right. It is ridiculous."

They were both silent and annoyed with each other.

"Did you tell Mikayla why you wanted to marry her?"

"Christ, woman, what are you going on about now?"

"Don't patronize me, Evan," she scolded softly, and he knew he had crossed a line. "You've told me

on more than one occasion that you were with
Mikayla because the relationship didn't interrupt
your work, that it would have been a comfortable
marriage but without any passion."

"Those weren't my exact words," he mumbled,
still embarrassed about his juvenile thinking not
that long ago.

"Whatever. Did you tell her that?"

He was silent. Of course he hadn't. And he was
starting to see Nia's point, unfortunately.

"No, of course you didn't. You let her and Sam
admit their mistakes and regrets, and you stood
there like a victim, inexcusably wronged by his
close friends, and completely innocent of all wrong-
doing," she said with brutal honesty. "When, really,
Mikayla just saw the truth before you did, and she
had the balls to call you on it. You should be thank-
ing her for it, not brooding about your bruised ego.
So who's been keeping secrets?"

"Okay, I think you're being a little harsh."

Nia rolled her eyes through the video app.

"Maybe, but you're really stubborn. And what is
wrong with Sam and Mikayla finding happiness together?" she asked, in a softer tone. "Why shouldn't
they have what we have?"

He looked away, easily remembering the many
veiled and guarded looks Sam would give Mikayla
when he thought no one would notice. And she
wasn't much better. *Shit.* Evan hated it when Nia
made perfect sense.

"I'll answer you after I get a peek of those pink
panties," he teased, feeling measurably better.

"Mmmm. You've changed the subject. Which

means you know I'm right," Nia noted with a cheeky grin. "I know how difficult that is for you, so maybe you've earned a reward."

"How big is the reward?"

"How much time do you have?"

As Evan had told Nia, the leads that Fortis was pursuing for the New York mission had dried up pretty quickly. Raymond could not find any relevant information connecting George Clement and Jason Holt from four years ago. Renee was unable to identify the person, or persons, who had planted the explosive device and detonated it on Wednesday evening. Kaylee was still waiting for a reply from Mark McMann to set up a meeting. By Saturday morning, Sam determined that they should focus their effort on local surveillance of Ross operations, in hopes of identifying someone with information connecting Ross and Groveland.

Evan's plan had him, Sam, and Renee positioned at each of the three Ross construction sites from six o'clock in the morning until eleven o'clock at night. They rented three nondescript vehicles and loaded them up with digital cameras, binoculars, a small cache of concealable weapons, and enough water and quick meals to keep them fueled. For hours, they noted the operations and movement of people and equipment, and took digital pictures of anyone who looked to be in a leadership role. Raymond remained at the apartment with Kaylee, and provided central communication and support through connected earpieces. They also hired David Ferguson to stay with Kaylee as backup.

On Monday, they were on their third day of stakeouts.

"Boys, I think we have something," Raymond announced.

"What is it?" Sam asked. He was in Clifton, about twenty miles to the northwest.

"I've been tracking Fleming, Battleford, and some of the other managers at Groveland, just in case one of them oversees the Ross projects," Raymond explained with excitement. "According to credit card records, Nate Battleford has just bought water and mints at the Newark airport."

"Shit," Evan swore. "He's headed to one of the Ross build sites."

"Yup, it would seem so," Raymond confirmed. "I'm searching through the security footage to get eyes on him, maybe track wherever he's headed."

"I think we have to assume it's either the Newark or Jersey City build," Sam suggested as he put away his digital camera and started up the budget rental car. "They're both equally close to the airport. I'm going to head back south to be closer to either."

"Okay, I got him," Raymond announced about ten minutes later. "He's in a limousine. There are two men with him, and they look like professionals. I'm logged into a traffic camera and they're on Interstate ninety-five. They're headed into Jersey City."

That was Renee's position.

"Evan, how long will it take to get there?" asked

Sam, who was now on the highway, driving toward the target site at a high rate of speed.

"Twenty minutes, tops."

"Renee, maintain your position until Evan and I get there," Sam instructed firmly. "Raymond, once Battleford is at the build site, find us positions that will give us access to him with little resistance."

"You got it," Raymond acknowledged.

"What's the play here, Sam?" Evan asked.

"I'm hoping to find a private spot to have an intimate conversation with him, see what he can tell us about Groveland and bribes to city officials, with a little persuasion. You and Renee will offer cover in case the two bodyguards he's with have skills."

The building site in Jersey City was the renovation of a public school located near the suburbs. Renee's rental car was parked on the street across from the school, in front of an auto body shop. For the next fifteen minutes, Raymond provided updates on Battleford's approach, and outlined several options for the team to converge on the target. When the limo finally arrived and drove into the construction zone, Renee casually got out of the car and walked around the block to a secluded spot at the corner of the unfinished building. She had a clear line of sight to the trailer near the entrance of the closed-off area, which was being used as a makeshift construction office.

Evan arrived first, and Raymond directed him to another location, where he could creep onto the building site undetected, and with an open view of the office. They both watched with weapons drawn as Battleford exited the limo with his two bodyguards and talked to several men who approached.

"I'm parked at the far side, near the park," Sam announced a few minutes later. "How are we doing?"

"I have eyes on the target," Renee confirmed.

"Ditto," added Evan.

"How many men are with him?" Sam asked as he ran casually toward the action.

"I see six including the two bodyguards," said Renee. "There should be one woman inside the construction office, doing administrative stuff."

"Okay, let's see if he goes inside—then I'll join him for our chat. If not, we move to plan B."

"And plan B is . . . ?" Raymond asked.

"I'll grab him before he gets back in the car," Sam replied as he found a secure position from which to watch the target. "It's a little messier."

The team held their breath as Battleford slowly made his way around to the side door of the trailer, opened it, and stepped inside. The two bodyguards and other workers remained out front, casually talking. Sam quickly ran from his position to the back of the trailer; then he crept along until he could look around the corner and scope out the access entrance.

"You have company, Sam," Renee whispered into the earpiece. "One of the supervisors is entering the office."

"What about the others?" he asked, completely relying on his colleagues to provide accurate visual intelligence.

"The bodyguards and other guys are out of visual range. You're clear," Evan confirmed.

Sam withdrew his Beretta, released the safety, and made his move. With a quick run, he reached the doors of the trailer and swung them open. The woman was the first to notice him. She was at the very back of the large space, standing beside a desk with a thick folder in her hands. It took her a second to realize he was a stranger with a gun. Battleford was in the middle of the floor with his back to the door, and the second man was just inside. She let out a strangled scream, just as Battleford turned around to find Sam's gun pointed directly at him. The other man immediately stepped back and raised his hands in the air.

"Nate Battleford, you and I need to have a chat," Sam said calmly.

Battleford spread his hands wide by his side, suggesting he was unarmed. "You could have made an appointment."

"Perhaps, but I'm not known for my politeness," replied Sam. "You are?" The question was directed to the man standing just a couple of feet away.

"Nigel," he replied briefly, swallowing loudly.

"Okay, Nigel. I'm only here to talk to your boss. So why don't you go stand beside that lovely lass in the back?"

Nigel nodded and moved sideways and backwards until he was next to the administrator. She now clutched the folder to her chest like a protective shield. Sam holstered his gun in the clip at his waist.

"Who are you, and what do you want?" Battleford asked, clenching his jaw.

"I'm a concerned citizen who has very concrete

evidence of Ross Construction doing business with force and intimidation. All things that would put the man in charge in jail for a very long time," Sam detailed with a steady gaze on the target. "I also know that Groveland Development owns Ross. And you, mate, are now the only connection between Groveland and Ross. That makes you the man in charge, doesn't it? Unless you know something I don't."

Sam watched as Battleford started blinking from nervousness. His original arrogant stance transformed to one more crestfallen and vulnerable.

"I don't know what you're talking about," he claimed, glancing behind him at the other two people.

"Oh, I think you do, Nate. I think you know exactly what I need to know about who is really in charge of this operation," Sam insisted. "Otherwise, you can do the time on their behalf."

"Look, maybe we can work something out," Battleford said, leaning closer to Sam and lowering his voice to just above a whisper. "I'm sure we can agree on something that will make this whole thing go away. Just name your price."

"Wrong answer, Nate," Sam replied, putting a hand on the butt of his Beretta, looking even more menacing than before. "Are you the man? Or are you going to tell me who is?"

"I can't tell you anything!"

"Sam, things are starting to get warm outside," Renee warned through the earpiece. "Looks like the bodyguards are heading your way."

"Nate, I'm not a patient man," Sam continued.

"So let's cut right to the chase. Four years ago, you bribed Jason Holt at the *Baltimore Journal* to bury a story on corruption by Groveland. Is that another crime you're willing to go down for instead of your boss?"

"Look, I can't help you, man. You're wasting your time."

"I can see that, Nate. So maybe the FBI will have more luck with this discussion."

Sam stepped forward, ready to take Battleford into custody.

"Wait, wait!" he shouted in panic. "Just wait a second!"

"Sorry, mate, you're out of time," Sam said, now close enough to grab Battleford by the arm and pull it behind his back. "I am detaining you for delivery to police custody under the suspicion of bribery and coercion."

"I'll tell you what I know," Battleford whispered as he leaned closer to Sam. "Just get me out of here!"

Sam paused for a second. Until he caught a flash of sudden movement from behind Battleford and turned quickly to the man named Nigel, who was now holding a pistol pointed at him. The woman screamed, throwing the folder in the air and dropping to the floor to crawl behind her desk. Sam drew his weapon just as Nigel fired, and the sound of two gunshots in rapid succession ricocheted through the small trailer. Sam felt one bullet hit him square in the chest, making him stagger on his feet, but he managed to duck instinctively while firing back. His shot hit Nigel in the right shoulder, and the man jerked back, falling against the rear wall and dropping his gun. Sam slammed back against the side wall of the trailer, clutching at the area near his heart, gritting his teeth against the sharp, intense pain and trying to catch his breath. To his right was the body of Nate Battleford on the floor, with a black hole between his eyes.

CHAPTER 20

"Sam, you good?" Evan shouted through the earpiece.

There were a few short bursts of gunshots outside.

"Aye, I'm good," Sam replied, trying to keep his voice even. "The trailer is secure, but I have Nate Battleford down. The other guy is injured."

"Okay, Renee and I have the two bodyguards pinned down near the limo. You're clear to exit," added Evan.

"The police are on their way, ETA three minutes," Raymond confirmed.

"Okay, give me sixty seconds with this guy in here. He took out Battleford, and I want to know why."

After a few more seconds, the pain in his chest had subsided to a pounding throb. Sam pulled up his black cotton top to undo the large, thick Velcro tabs on each side of his ballistic vest. His breathing became marginally better. He crouched down in front of Nigel. The assailant was breathing deep against the pain in his shoulder, and blood covered his arm down to the elbow.

"Who do you work for?" asked Sam, skipping the preliminaries. "Is it Anthony Fleming?"

Nigel just looked at him with defiance.

"Why did you take out Battleford?" No response.

Sam sighed and did an efficient search of the injured man, quickly locating a wallet and cell phone. He pulled out his own cell phone and took pictures of each piece of ID, then quickly turned on the phone. It was locked.

"I don't suppose you'll give me your passcode." No response.

Sam took a tool out of his pocket and used one of the very sharp ends to pry open the SIM card holder on the side of Nigel's phone and removed the tiny chip.

"We can hear the sirens, Sam," Evan interrupted. "Time to go."

"Aye, I'm done here."

When Sam cautiously stepped outside, the police cars were turning onto the street in front of the Ross building project. Battleford's security detail and the other construction employees were more concerned with the impending arrival of city law enforcement to care about the Fortis team, allowing for a trouble-free retreat out the back side of the construction site.

Thirty minutes later, Sam, Evan, and Renee walked into Kaylee's apartment, dusty but determined.

As they strode through to the dining room, all

three immediately started removing the small collection of guns and knives strapped in strategic places on their bodies. Each weapon clanged loudly on the wooden surface as the agents laid them out for cleaning, then eventually storage. Still acting in practiced unison, they pulled off their dark outer-layer tops, then the protective vests underneath, leaving them in black undershirts.

Sam looked over at Kaylee as she walked into the area from the hall to her bedroom. Her eyes were wide and unblinking as she caught his gaze. He felt an immediate sense of relief.

"Okay, what do we have, Raymond?" Sam demanded, quickly refocusing on the mission.

"The shooter is Nigel Dobson, and he has a very interesting background," replied Raymond. "On paper, he's a subcontractor, billing Ross as a construction supervisor for the last three years. A very well-paid supervisor making about two hundred and fifty thousand dollars a year."

"Clearly, he's being compensated for his other skills," Renee said.

"That's because he was a detective with the New Jersey State Police up until three years ago," added Raymond.

Evan whistled. Things had just gotten a bit more complicated.

Sam took a wide stance and crossed his arms across his chest to think.

"We went into this surveillance assuming that Battleford was in charge of the Ross projects, but looks to me like someone else was pulling the strings," he suggested, rubbing the sore spot on his chest absently. "Based on what went down in the trailer, it looks like Battleford was a pawn instead. He wanted to talk but couldn't in front of Dobson."

"So Fleming has more than one person of authority doing his dirty work for Ross," Evan concluded.

"It makes sense," Renee added. "An operation like this requires that as few people as possible know all the connections, but that knowledge also makes them a threat to Fleming. It would be necessary to have eyes on someone like Battleford as much as possible."

"Aye, it seems there really is no honor among thieves," Sam agreed. "Makes you wonder if those bodyguards were protection or escorts."

"Lucas is now online by video," Raymond interrupted to inform them.

Sam and the others moved so they could see the third Fortis owner on the computer screen. Kaylee and David Ferguson joined them.

"I'm mobilizing a team here in Virginia to make contact with Anthony Fleming as soon as possible," Lucas announced. "Michael will take the lead, with Tony and Lance for support. They have the details on the key evidence we have connecting Ross to Groveland and Battleford to Holt."

Lucas had been patched into the communications link as the field team drove from Jersey City to Lower Manhattan and was up to speed on the new developments.

"Do we know where Fleming is?" Sam asked.

"The last position I have from him was at the

Groveland bridge project outside Bethesda," Raymond noted. "That was about an hour ago. I'm still trying to track him down."

"It's almost four o'clock now, so we're watching both his office and his house in Arlington," Lucas said.

"We have to find him before he learns about Battleford and the activity in Jersey City. It might spook him into going underground, and Battleford is our only leverage right now," Renee said.

"And before Dobson can tell anyone about my questions to Battleford," Sam added. "I took his SIM card, so that should buy us some time. It also gives us access to his phone contents."

He tossed the microchip into the air, and Raymond caught it.

"Okay, let's see where this leads us." The former NSA agent took out a card reader and loaded in Dobson's SIM. "I'll start cross-referencing the data with Fleming and the Groveland information we already have."

The team watched Raymond do his magic, waiting for some actionable intel that could help plan their next move.

"There's nothing there," Raymond confirmed about ten minutes later. "Dobson uses his cell phone mostly for communication with other Ross employees and several vendors. There are a couple of personal contacts, like a girlfriend in Jersey City and a few friends. But whatever instructions Dobson was following, he didn't get them through this phone."

"We got Fleming," Lucas suddenly announced through video. "Michael has eyes on him now entering the Groveland office building. Our team is preparing to go in."

"Good. Have them prepare for significant resistance," Sam instructed. "I guarantee Fleming's security team is well trained. We now have enough hard evidence to ensure Fleming is arrested and faces a long federal investigation, so let's use it and Battleford as leverage to confirm he ordered the actions against Holt. But we cannot mention George Clement. It's too risky."

"You got it," Lucas confirmed.

"I have us connected to the voice communications between Michael and the team," Raymond told them.

"Put it on the speakers," Sam instructed, and the group around the dining table started listening to the action for about twenty tense, nerve-racking minutes.

The first half of that time was filled with silence and static, suggesting Michael Thorpe was leading Tony Donellio and Lance Campbell through the building, toward the target. The small ground team had elite training and exceptional skills from the FBI, Interpol, and the U.S. Army Rangers, respectively. They were stealthy and efficient, reaching what they would soon confirm as Fleming's office on the top floor of the eight-story building in less than ten minutes. There were sounds of scuffling, a few groans and gasps, labored breathing.

"The security team has been disarmed. We're

approaching Fleming alone in his office," Michael whispered before speaking more loudly in a firm, authoritative voice a few seconds later. "Anthony Fleming, please remain seated behind your desk and you will not be harmed."

"Who are you? What do you want?" Fleming demanded, his voice only faintly heard through the voice transmission.

"We're here to obtain information in a private investigation."

"What? You can't just barge in here and attack my people!"

"Mr. Fleming, we have proof of federal crimes being orchestrated from these offices under your authority, so it will be in your best interest to cooperate with our investigation," Michael continued evenly.

"This is outrageous!"

"Mr. Fleming, we have concrete evidence that one of your employees, Nate Battleford, has been engaged in intimidation, coercion, and bribery while executing his responsibilities in your company. Was he acting under your orders?"

"Nate? What evidence? I've never asked him to do anything like that."

"Four years ago, Jason Holt with the *Baltimore Journal* was paid fifty thousand dollars in cash to kill a story on Groveland bribing city officials in exchange for building contracts. Then he was murdered to cover it up," Michael persisted. "Was that done under your direction?"

"I don't know what you're talking about. I have

nothing to do with anyone being killed!" Fleming's tone becoming increasingly desperate and frantic.

"I repeat, Mr. Fleming, we already have the evidence on Nate Battleford and Groveland's illegal business practices. We will be handing them over to the FBI today. To be clear, the only interest of our private investigation is the truth about the murder of Jason Holt. If you give us the information we need on Holt, there will be no need to add a murder investigation to your charges."

"What do you want?" Fleming finally demanded, starting to feel the corner he was squeezed into.

"Did you bribe Holt and then have him killed four years ago?"

"No! I had nothing to do with it."

"Then who did? Battleford works for you, and Holt was killed to protect Groveland business interests. Who else would profit from the cover-up, Mr. Fleming?"

There was a brief silence.

"We only need the truth, or you will soon be under investigation for murder on top of everything else," Michael pressed.

"You have no idea what you're involved in here," Fleming finally stated so softly that the Fortis team around the dining table in Manhattan almost didn't hear it. "You're scratching at a door you do not want to open."

"Last chance," Michael insisted.

"I had nothing to do with that Holt incident. And I have nothing further to add."

"Then you can plead your innocence with the feds," stated Michael.

The team listened for another minute or so as the agents on the ground left Anthony Fleming alone in his office and made a quick retreat from the Groveland building.

"Dammit!" Sam muttered, slamming his fist on the desk.

There was a long silence.

"Michael and the others are now returning to headquarters," Lucas confirmed. "I'll give you guys a call back after I've debriefed them."

"Thanks, Lucas," Sam replied before they disconnected. "Raymond, can you connect us with the FBI field office in Maryland? We need to turn over what we know and get this guy and his people off the street as soon as possible."

"But he didn't tell us anything," Kaylee protested, finally speaking up for the first time. "How will we learn what he knows?"

"Don't worry. We have a pretty good relationship with the Bureau," Sam told her in a solemn voice. "It's a bit of a barter system. They share all the information on the cases we bring forward to them, and in return we continue to bring them cases with the evidence all tied up nicely in a bow."

"I'll see if they'll allow Michael to sit in on Fleming's questioning once he's brought in. The feds still tolerate him for some reason," Raymond added, teasing the friend he'd worked with on many cases over the last few years.

"So, what now?" Kaylee asked, with her arms around her.

Sam took a deep breath and the others stepped

back from the table, each coming to terms with such a swift end to the intense operations through the afternoon.

"I think we celebrate a few victories," he said, looking around at each member of his team. "By the end of this, Groveland Development and Ross Construction will be under federal investigation. And your evidence, Kaylee, will ensure they are shut down and prosecuted."

He looked down at Kaylee intently from a few steps away.

"You, *doolally* lass, have managed to take down a major criminal organization."

"What?" Kaylee asked, not sure if it was a good thing or not.

"He said you were crazy," Renee explained with a shake of her head. "But what he really means is that you're brilliant. Right, old man?"

Sam smiled and then chuckled, as did the others around them. Evan walked forward and pulled Kaylee into a big hug. It was clearly brotherly, but Sam turned away, annoyed by how jealous he was that his friend was free to hug her so openly.

"I could do with a celebration," Raymond said. "Good food, some wine, music. It is the Fourth of July, in case everyone has forgotten."

Renee snorted. "You've been here eating catered homemade food this whole time, you bastard. We're the ones who need something besides energy bars and warm water."

"That's not my fault. Blame Ice. He's the one who planned the operation," Raymond protested.

Sam watched their banter and agreed that they could all use a little relaxation.

"Aye, let's order some food from somewhere nice," he replied. "But we're still on lockdown until tomorrow. I want to make sure Fleming is firmly in custody before we consider this mission completed."

Raymond didn't need any further encouragement, and got busy sourcing a restaurant that would deliver anything from steak to lobster to sushi. Sam, Evan, and Renee got busy cleaning their weapons, then locking them up in one of the custom trunks they had arrived in. Sam remained busy, but his attention was occasionally drawn to Kaylee. She was sitting on the living room sofa, occasionally looking at her phone but mostly just deep in thought. As badly as he wanted to go over to see how she was doing, Sam continued to maintain a professional distance.

A short while later, he went into the den to change out of his work clothes and finally have a look at the damage to his chest.

"That looks like it's going to hurt for a bit," Evan said as he walked into the open door and found Sam standing in the middle of the room with his chest bare. There was a red, welted spot just right of his heart. From experience, he knew it would soon darken to a spectacular shade of purple, then black and blue over the next couple of days.

"I've had worse," Sam replied. He turned away and grabbed another one of his shirts, which were now washed by Silvia every few days. There was an awkward pause while he pulled it on.

"Look, I've been thinking about things," Evan finally added. "I think I reacted badly to what you told me. About you and Mikayla."

Sam turned back to his friend, hiding his relief under a stoic expression.

"Someone very smart reminded me that Mikayla made the right decision to end our relationship. So it's a little foolish to be mad about what may have caused that decision," Evan continued with his hands in his pockets. "She was brave when I wasn't."

Sam nodded and cleared his throat.

"You made the right decision, Sam, not to tell me about it four years ago," continued Evan, causing Sam to blink in surprise. "I would not have seen things so clearly back then, and I didn't know you as well. So there's a good chance I would have let my ego ruin a good partnership. Fortis may not be what it is today if you hadn't made the right call."

Sam cleared his throat again, rocking back on his heels. Evan tapped him on the back of the shoulder with what came close to being affection.

"If you think there is something between you and Mikayla, don't let any of this stuff stand in your way."

CHAPTER 21

The team enjoyed a big meal with beer and wine from Kaylee's collection. Then they sat around talking for a couple of hours, telling stories about experiences with their various agencies prior to joining Fortis. Kaylee could only listen with an open mouth and wide eyes at what these people did on a regular basis. Even the usually silent David Ferguson shared a little bit about his work with DaCosta Solutions as a logistic support specialist in a few different conflict-ridden zones.

The only person who didn't talk was Evan, and Kaylee had a growing suspicion about why. When he had first arrived in New York almost a week ago, she'd assumed it was as a close friend and as Sam's partner in their security firm. But Kaylee had done her research over the last few years and knew that Fortis was very specialized and highly skilled in the security field. They also had very little public information about them, despite the fancy website that came up in a browser search. What she couldn't figure out was why Evan had joined their ranks.

After his father died suddenly last year, Evan had been appointed as interim CEO of DaCosta Solutions, and everyone had just assumed he would take the role permanently. After all, his father had built the company, and Evan had worked there since he graduated college. Kaylee had been as surprised as anyone to learn that he had stepped down from the role, preferring a seat on the board of directors.

There was no doubt that Evan had the experience to run a firm like Fortis, but how did a corporate executive who had been born into wealth and privilege operate at the same level as the other agents around him? If Kaylee hadn't seen it in real life over the last few days, she wouldn't have believed it. And now his silence within the boisterous group discussion spoke volumes about how little she knew about the real Evan DaCosta.

It seemed like everyone had their secrets, and it made Kaylee feel a little better about things between them.

"What are you smiling to yourself about?" Evan asked as he sat beside her around the dining table. It now had much less equipment on it as the team pared down their support. He handed her a bottle of beer.

"Nothing. I was just thinking about the very large collection of handmade Italian shoes you had," she told him.

He laughed. "I still have it. Though I think Nia has been slowly giving them away to charity."

"One day, you'll have to tell me how running the international operations for DaCosta gave you the skills needed to carry a small arsenal of weapons into a field of bad guys," she told him smoothly. "I don't think it would have been listed in the roles and responsibilities."

Evan chuckled, obviously not surprised by her statement. "Maybe one day. But, for now, let's just say I've picked them up over the years."

"No worries, I won't ask any more questions. I wouldn't want you to have to kill me."

He burst out laughing at the old cliché, and Kaylee giggled beside him. It felt good to recapture a little of the easygoing friendship they had started out with.

"How does it feel to have this whole thing finally come to an end?" he asked, after taking a long sip from his bottle.

"Surreal is probably the best word," she replied with a sigh and drank down some of the cold draft. "I didn't imagine it would go down like this, at all."

"No, I don't imagine you did," Evan agreed. "Sam's not one for the subtle approach, that's for sure."

She smiled, looking over at the man he'd referenced, appreciating how relaxed Sam looked standing between Renee and Raymond, patiently tolerating their teasing.

"I am thrilled that we got Anthony Fleming, but he didn't exactly admit to bribing Jason Holt, right?" she said. "Which means we still don't know for sure that he's the one threatening my father."

"Sure, it would have been fantastic to hear Fleming admit his involvement, but it's hardly surprising that he didn't, Mikayla," Evan told her. "From what we heard, there is no doubt he knew about Holt. So if he's responsible, it will come out soon enough."

"That's the thing. What if he isn't?"

The words hung between them, dampening the celebratory mood a little.

"Perhaps it's time that we talk to your father, together?" he suggested.

"I can't. Not if there is any chance it wasn't Fleming. It would completely send him over the edge, and I'm not sure he's that far away from it now," she whispered.

"Well, time will tell, right?" said Evan. "The news about Fleming will be in the media soon enough. Let's see how he responds."

"Yeah, you're right," Kaylee agreed, trying to pull herself out of the pessimistic mindset. "I'm making plans to return home later this week. I want to be there with him when it comes out."

"What about Antonoli Properties? What are you going to do with it?"

"Continue to run it for now. I have to finish the two projects under way," she insisted. "I'll just have to do it a little more remotely. Maybe hire a couple more people to work on site."

Evan nodded, swallowing back a mouthful of beer.

"Well, for what it's worth, you did good." He bumped her shoulder with his. "Crazy, but good."

"Gee, thanks. Now you sound like Sam," she mumbled, but pleased by his statement.

"The Scotsman sometimes gets things right." They both looked over at Sam, who rubbed at a spot on his chest and winced noticeably. "And don't worry about any injury from the gunshot. There'll be bruising and tenderness for a few days, but he was wearing a vest so there's no real damage."

Kaylee could only blink at his words, processing what they meant. Sam had been shot? During the operation at the Ross construction site? She was about to ask for more details, but Evan bumped her shoulder again and stood up, ready to pack it up for the night. She stayed silent, deep in thought, while everyone worked together to clean up the dishes and leftovers. Then David and the Fortis team left just before midnight.

Renee went to the front door and called Niko for his last walk, like she'd done before the stakeouts.

The terrier ran to her, but Sam took the leash out of her hands. "I'll take him out. I could do with some fresh air."

"Suit yourself," she replied with a shrug. "I'll stay with Kaylee until you get back."

"Good."

Sam and Niko watched her head to the hall bathroom, then heard the door close. Kaylee and Sam looked at each other, then away and back again.

"I won't be long," he said.

"Okay," Kaylee replied softly as he walked out of the apartment and closed the door behind him.

She stood there for about five minutes, not sure what that exchange had meant or what she should do. Did he want her to wait here for him? Why? Or was he just being polite? She paced a little in front of the door. Feeling foolish, she then went into the living room, thinking she could pretend to watch television. But it was after midnight, and that would just look contrived. Kaylee walked back to the front door again. A minute later, she sighed and went to her room. Sam Mackenzie knew where she was if he wanted to see her.

After wasting some time straightening up a few things, Kaylee finally changed into loose pajamas, then washed up in the bathroom. About thirty minutes later, she was lying in bed with a reading light still on, feeling a crushing weight of disappointment. It wasn't that she had any specific expectation from Sam. It had been a long, eventful day following several other long days, so it was not surprising that he'd want to get some sleep. But Kaylee had expected . . . something.

Finally, fighting tears, she turned off the light and lay back. Kaylee had just closed her eyes when there was a soft knock at her door. She sat up, uncertain if it was her imagination, then jumped out of the bed to check, just in case. It was quiet as she padded across the large room softly in the dark and opened the door. Sam stood there, silhouetted by the soft light filtering from down the hall, and filling the opening with his size.

Kaylee stood in front of him, unable to see his face, but feeling his eyes on her, hot and intense. For a few moments, she didn't know what to do or to say. Finally, she stepped backward, and he followed. She did so again; so did Sam. Then he closed the door softly behind him. They stood there in the dark, only about a foot apart, still and just breathing. The tension mounted until Kaylee thought she would scream from it. It felt like so long since she had touched him, felt his hands on her, that she was afraid to make the first move. If he rejected her again, she wouldn't know how to recover.

She must have swayed forward, pulled by her need for him. Sam inhaled a breath and wrapped an arm around her waist and pulled her up against his hard frame. He didn't kiss her right away. Instead, he held her tight, stroking her back with long caresses. Kaylee raised up on her toes and wrapped her arms around his neck. His chest was bare, and she could press her cheek against the silky, warm flesh. He smelled so good, like soap and raw masculinity.

Sam gripped her hips and lifted her off the floor, walking toward her bed to lay her back on it and follow her down onto the surface. Their bodies were fused again, and he completely surrounded her with his substantial size. She ran her hands slowly down his neck and along the top of his shoulders, loving the feel of warm flesh over rock-solid muscle. Her fingers trailed down his arms, gripping the biceps, biting her lips as they bulged against her touch. He was so deliciously strong. Kaylee pressed her lips on the top of his cheek, then scraped the skin with her teeth. Sam shuddered against her. She licked the spot and he sighed loudly. In the darkness, every touch, taste, and smell seemed sweeter and more intense.

Sam pressed his hips gently against hers, and she spread her legs for him, wrapping them around his waist so his male contours could nestle boldly against her core. He flexed against her, repeatedly rubbing against her sweet spot through two layers of clothing. She was soon wet with arousal and shuddering with need. But still he only held her close, controlling their pace and limiting their movements. His thick, rigid erection pressed hot and heavy against her belly.

His slow, sensual movements soon became torturous, creating an urgent need for more of him. Kaylee gradually started to suck on his skin harder, gripping his shoulders tighter, grinding her hips against his faster. But Sam wouldn't change his pace. He just held her close and continued that muted rub at her through their clothes until she wanted to hit him.

"Please," she finally panted, digging her nails into the skin on his back. "Sam, please."

"What?" he asked in a low growl as his body went still.

She squeezed her eyes shut, biting her lips, trying to hold back the words out of spite. But she couldn't. She was too hot, too needy, for pride.

"I need you," she finally gasped. "I need you."

Sam loosened his grip to rise up on his knees. They worked together to remove her pajamas by feel until she was finally naked. She felt him move off, and then back to the bed as he removed his pants. There was the tearing sound of a condom packet. Then Sam was back on his knees in front of her, only visible through shadows. He gripped her legs under the knees and gently lifted them up off the bed until they were straight in the air and draped them over his shoulders. Her bum was lifted off the bed. Sam took her hips and pulled her toward him, filling her with one long, strong stroke. Lightbulbs went off behind her eyes from the intensity of the contact. He held her firm and stroked smooth, hitting that magic button within her.

Kaylee was soon a panting, moaning mess. Every thick penetration was so insanely good, she cried out over and over again, completely lost in his control. The orgasm built fast, pulled her high, and just when she struggled to crest, Sam stilled within her. The pause lasted a few seconds with his hard cock still buried deep. Kaylee flopped back on the bed, struggling to catch her breath while his sweat dripped onto her stomach. *Jesus*, she was going to die from wanting him.

Slowly, Sam caressed his hands over her legs, then gripped her thighs, lowered them to his side so she could wrap them around his waist, with all the time in the world. Kaylee could barely breathe in anticipation of what would come next. He finally lifted her into the air and tightly into his arms until their naked torsos completely meshed. He kissed her forehead, her cheek, tucked his face into the curve of her neck. Then he started thrusting into her again, faster, surer. Kaylee wrapped her arms around his neck and held on. Their bodies became slick with sweat as he gave her all she wanted and more.

Sam came first, silently with his body clenched from the force. Yet he continued to stroke and stroke until she gripped his hair and moaned deep in a long, shuddering orgasm. He held her in that position for some time, allowing their bodies to relax and cool. Then Sam laid her back on the bed, covering her with the sheets. She listened as he went into the bathroom and came back to pull her into his arms.

"Why didn't you tell me you had been shot today?" she asked in a quiet and tight voice, stroking gently over his chest, near his heart. "You could have been killed."

He covered her hand with his.

"I'm fine. It's nothing," he sleepily replied. "That's why we wear vests."

She closed her eyes, fighting back tears and sharp feelings of guilt and doubt while Sam's breathing became slow and deep with sleep. It wasn't until she woke up in the morning alone that she thought about how few words they had exchanged.

The Fortis team was already at work when Kaylee joined them at the dining table. It was only eight-thirty. Sam was sharing an update from the local and federal arrests the night before. He then gave instructions on the wrap-up of the mission, including the follow-ups needed with the various police departments. Anthony Fleming was out on bail, but officially charged with a laundry list of crimes, including the murder of Jason Holt. The news media hadn't picked up the story yet, but it was only a matter of time.

Kaylee was only half listening to his words as she watched him talk. Her thoughts were still on last night, what it had meant and where they could go from there. Her heart still raced at the thought of Sam, shot while on a mission she had set up. She looked around at them, all putting their lives on the line for her and her family, and she could not be more grateful for their help.

And now that it was over, it was time to make decisions about things in New York so she could spend some time in McLean with her family as soon as possible. Annie and Paul could definitely hold down the fort for a few days, but eventually a long-term solution would be needed. She was about to call Annie to have an impromptu meeting when her phone buzzed with a new email. From her personal account. Kaylee opened the message from Mark McMann and read his response to her note from over four days ago. He had been traveling and was back in town, happy to meet to discuss opportunities for her.

She looked over at Sam, and wondered if he would still support the plan. Battleford was dead and Fleming had been arrested. Wasn't that enough? Kaylee walked out of the great room and into the hallway, calling Junior as she went. They had only spoken briefly over the last couple of days.

"Hey," she said.

"Hey."

"Are you still mad at me?"

"Annoyed, yes, but I don't want to strangle you anymore," he replied.

"Well, that's something, I guess. I have news," she offered, then filled him in on the main points of what had happened over the last few days.

"Have you spoken to Dad yet?" Junior asked at the end of it.

"No," Kaylee admitted. "Have you?"

"Yeah, on Sunday. He was the same. I told him I had seen you while I was in New York, but he didn't say anything or ask any questions."

She closed her eyes. What if it was too late for him? What if he'd fallen too far to bounce back?

"What about Mom?" she asked. "I'm going to call her today and see if she'll come home this weekend. We can have a barbecue at the house or something."

"Yeah, maybe," her brother said. "Look, Mikayla, it's really good that you've taken down Groveland for their corruption, but it might not have any impact on Dad."

She was silent, knowing what he was going to say.

"His behavior may have nothing to do with bribes and threats. He might have just gone through some mid-life crisis and never come out of it. It happens all the time."

Kaylee let out a deep breath. "I know, Junior. You're right, but I still had to try."

"Okay. Well, tell me what Mom says, and I'll plan to be around this weekend."

"Thanks. I'll talk to you later."

She tapped her phone against her chin, deep in thought, until Sam approached her.

"Is everything okay?" he asked. His rich Scottish burr sounded softer, more soothing.

Kaylee took a deep breath and went for it. "Mark McMann agreed to see me, and I still want to go ahead with the meeting."

CHAPTER 22

Sam looked down into Kaylee's beguiling eyes. They sparkled with anticipation but still had smudges of sadness underneath. He fought the urge to pull her up against him and agree to anything she wanted. That was the hold she had on him, and he was finding it harder and harder to resist.

"Let's do it," he told her, and she blinked in surprise.

"I don't know, Sam," she said immediately. "Maybe it's time to just let the police handle it from here. What if someone gets seriously hurt next time? I just can't be responsible for that."

"Kaylee, that is what I do, what my team does."

She looked away, clearly still unconvinced.

"Look, your objective was to identify who was exerting influence on your father, right?" Sam continued, and she nodded. "Fleming might be our guy, but we can't confirm it yet. So let's continue to look until we know for certain."

Kaylee looked away but not before he saw a glimmer of tears in her eyes. Damn it, she was twisting him up inside.

"You know I'm right, Kaylee. You've come so far to find the truth, and now we can help you finish it."

"Okay," she finally replied with a soft, hesitant smile. "Just promise me that you guys won't take any unnecessary risks, okay? It's bad enough that Junior thinks all this is just wishful thinking. That Dad may have just gone through a mid-life crisis that we can't do anything about."

"Kaylee, I don't know your father very well. I've only met him once. But if you and Evan believe there is even a remote chance that he needs help, then we will do what we can to help," he told her firmly. "I will not let you do anything on your own anymore. You have Fortis working for you now, and we always deliver, with the right plan and resources."

Sam's biggest fear was that she would go off on her own again, acting on some crazy idea. The thought of all the trouble she had put herself in, with the best of intentions, still gave him a headache.

"Thank you, Sam. That's more than I had hoped for."

He nodded and crossed his arms. "So, when is McMann available for a meeting?" he asked.

"I'm going to suggest later this week. Maybe Thursday?"

"That could work. Evan and the others are heading back tonight."

"What about you?"

He knew what she was asking, but Sam didn't

know how to answer. His plan was to return to Alexandria tomorrow, maybe Thursday, depending on Kaylee's activities and how secure he felt things were in her day-to-day life. But what he wanted was to be where she was, at least for a little while longer, until he figured out what was going on in his heart. Other parts of his body were very obvious about their needs.

"I have some flexibility this week. If you're going to meet McMann on Thursday, let's fly in tomorrow," he suggested.

"Okay, I can make that happen."

"Do you have somewhere to stay?"

"Oh," she muttered. "Good point. I've been traveling as Kaylee Stone for the last year so I've always stayed in a hotel just in case."

"Will you stay with your parents this time?" Sam asked.

"No, I'm sure my dad's not ready for that yet. I'll just book a hotel again."

"Stay with me." Sam hadn't been planning to make the suggestion; the words just slipped out of his mouth before he could stop them. "It's only for a night or two, right? And it will make it easier for us to coordinate the meet with McMann."

She opened her mouth, but didn't reply for a few seconds. They ticked by really loudly.

"That's really nice of you to offer, but it's not necessary—"

"Kaylee, it's no big deal. It's just for convenience. And pack your running shoes."

She looked away for a moment, then back at him, now with a pleasant smile on her face.

"Okay, thanks."

"With that settled, I'm sure you have a lot to get done before tomorrow. So I'll leave you to it." He walked away, feeling like an idiot.

As planned, Evan, Renee, and Raymond flew home Tuesday evening. He and Kaylee had a late dinner in awkward silence, and then she went to her room to pack for their flight the next day. At about eleven o'clock, Niko ran across the room and sat near the front hall, ready for his walk. Sam considered taking him out now, leaving Kaylee here to continue packing. The surveillance system in the apartment was still up and running; the threats against her had effectively been neutralized. But Sam faced an irrational concern about leaving her alone.

"He's all ready to head out, isn't he?" Kaylee said as she walked toward them.

"Aye, I was just about to take him out, but I thought we should go together."

"Sure, I wouldn't mind a walk."

She slipped on flip-flops, and they headed downstairs. It was a warm, fragrant night, and they walked slowly and quietly around the usual path. Niko did his regular routine of investigating every rock and leaf that he came across before finally taking care of business.

"Is it okay that I bring Niko with me tomorrow?" she finally asked when they were on the way back to the building.

"Of course. I assumed you would. What else would you do with him?"

"I could ask Silvia to take him until I'm back."

"No, it's fine. I like dogs."

They walked in silence a little longer.

"Can I ask you something?" she continued.

Sam swallowed, knowing it was not going to be something easy or flippant.

"Aye, but I can't promise I'll answer."

"Evan seemed less tense today. Did you guys come to an understanding about . . . things?"

"We did. It was not pleasant at first, I'll tell you that. But I think we'll be fine," Sam told her honestly.

"Good. You guys make a great team. I would hate it if anything I did came between that."

They rounded the corner to the front entrance.

"Do you think you could ever forgive me?" she asked softly.

Sam clenched his jaw and frowned. "It's not about forgiveness, Kaylee. It's about trust."

"Meaning you don't trust me." Her words were heavy with sadness, and Sam hated it.

"I don't know. Maybe I don't trust what's going on between us. And I don't trust myself when I'm with you."

It was much more than he had intended to say, but it was the truth.

Kaylee didn't reply. In the apartment, she took his hand and they walked to her bedroom. With the lights off, they removed their clothes and climbed into the middle of the bed. She straddled his lap and nestled his lengthening cock into the warmth between her thighs. Like always, Sam was flooded with such urgent need, it left him light-headed.

He ran his hands over her back, adoring the firm

lines and silky feel of her skin. He cupped the round curves of her ass, squeezing its fullness. She gasped and his heart skipped. Her smell was still the same. Chanel, he remembered. Except Sam knew for a fact that it didn't smell as good on any other woman. He kissed her neck, licking at the skin, savoring her flavor.

Kaylee sat, and he could feel her eyes studying him in the dark.

"Can we be honest here, in bed?" she asked softly. "Can you trust this, for as long as it lasts?"

She reached down and wrapped a delicate hand around the base of his cock. Sam bit back a moan. Did she realize that she could have anything in the world when she was holding him like that? Then Kaylee stroked him with tight fingers and he couldn't think straight. She brushed his manhood along her dewy seam, and he suddenly understood what she wanted. His heart was pounding loudly in his ears, and the primal need to be with her, inside her, completely unfettered, was so strong he broke into a sweat.

"Are you on protection?" he managed to ask with the last of his working brain cells.

"Yes," she whispered, rising up on her knees and sliding down on his shaft until he was sheathed tightly in her satin grip.

They made love slowly and quietly, first with her riding him and at a steady rhythm, then with her beneath him, legs spread wide to receive his thrust. There was a third and a fourth position before Sam couldn't hold back the rush of pure ecstasy that she always inspired. She joined him in climax, gripping his length in her body and prolonging the intensity of his orgasm. Then, as their breathing slowed, there came the same realization that always did. This could be the last time he ever felt this perfect unison with a woman. Kaylee would walk out of his life again eventually, and he'd never experience anything like her again.

His stomach churned sickeningly at the thought. Like a pointless ritual, just before he fell asleep, Sam told himself to put an end to things, now. But of course, he wouldn't.

They returned to Virginia on Wednesday afternoon, then took a car straight to his house just south of Alexandria. Sam gave Kaylee a quick tour of the three-bedroom, mid-century modern bungalow. He put her bag in his bedroom, and they both worked quietly in his living room for the remainder of the day. Sam grilled steaks for dinner with a salad, and they watched television afterward. At bedtime, they walked Niko through his neighborhood. Back home, they went to bed and indulged in the same slow, intimate lovemaking that was quickly becoming his weakness.

"Tell me again how you will ask about Jason Holt," Sam said. They were eating lunch at a small restaurant near Mark McMann's office in downtown Baltimore. Her meeting was in twenty minutes, at two o'clock.

"I'll spend the first half talking about the job I want, referring to the communications job Quinten Laboratories currently has posted," Kaylee explained as she sipped her sparkling water. "Then, when the formal interview is over, I'll ask about when he left the newspaper. Then about Jason, and say how shocked I was. I'll leave it open for him to give details. If he doesn't, I'll ask specifically what he thought about what Jason told him."

"That's good. Just remember to say as little as possible. And don't fill in any silences—let him. That's when people talk the most."

"Thank you for the tips, but I have done this before you know," she told him, crossing her arms. "Being a journalist is all about getting people to tell you things, and communications is mostly about listening."

"All right, don't get cheeky about it," he replied with a tolerant smile. "Quinten is on the fourth floor of the building so I'll ride up the elevator with you, then stay close until you're done."

"I could just go alone and meet you at the car," she suggested.

"Aye, you could. But you won't. Now come on, let's get you to your interview on time."

Kaylee stood up, wearing a blush-pink suit with a tied belt around the waist, a narrow skirt and dark chocolate-brown shoes as high as usual. Her hair waved softly around her face and brushed her shoulders, and her makeup was light and pretty, highlighting her features. She looked as beautiful and sophisticated as always. Sam paid the check, and they walked together across the street and up to the Quinten offices. When they entered, the walls were lined with large framed pictures of research labs and testing equipment. According to their website, they were a development and testing company for the industrial use of mineral and sediment.

Kaylee introduced herself to the receptionist while Sam just said he was meeting a friend for coffee.

Mark McMann came out to greet Kaylee with a big smile on his face. Sam had seen his photos from their research in advance, and he looked as expected—tall, slender, and mid-forties, with dark hair and brown eyes and an unnatural tan on his pale skin.

"Mikayla, it's so good to see you," he said.

"Same to you, Mark. Thanks so much for making time to see me," she replied, shaking his hand with a wide smile of her own.

"My pleasure of course. You look lovely, as always."

Kaylee gave him a sweet grin, revealing her twin dimples, and then they walked away, presumably to his office. Sam remained in the waiting room, working on his phone and maintaining the look of someone who was about to be stood up for a coffee break. Kaylee returned about forty minutes later by herself, said bye to the receptionist, then got into the elevator. Sam waited a few more minutes, then mumbled something appropriate and took the stairs down. They met in front of the restaurant again, as planned.

"It's the mayor," she whispered loudly, looking around. "Mark all but said it."

"What?" Sam demanded, completely caught off guard. "Let's get to the car. Then you can tell me the details while we drive."

She followed his direction until they were leaving Baltimore and on the way back to Virginia.

"Start from the beginning," he instructed.

"It's a pretty short story," she said. "Everything went as planned. I asked him about leaving the paper. He just said it was time and the opportunity at Quinten came along. I asked about Jason and his sudden leave, and the conversation became pretty stilted at that point."

"Why?" Sam asked.

"I don't know. He seemed really surprised that I brought it up, and he became pretty stiff and formal. I said I was shocked about what he had done, just like we had planned."

"And what did he say?" he probed.

"Nothing. We both sat there for at least a half a minute, but I just looked at him." Sam smiled. "Then he said: 'Yes, it was shocking. It's unaccept-able that businessmen and city officials should try to manipulate the media for their own gain.' I said, 'I know, I was very disappointed. I hope they got what they deserved.' And he said, 'Unfortunately, some people in high places are untouchable.' And that was it."

Sam was silent, driving and thinking for a few moments. "You think he was talking about Lyle Gordon, the mayor of Baltimore."

"Absolutely," she declared passionately. "Who else is a city official in a high place and untouch-able?"

"He could have meant a businessman."

"But think about it. Didn't you say that Fortis had identified the bribes from two small companies? So the only unknown was the last one. So why would Mark specifically mention city officials unless it was for the one you couldn't confirm? And the other two were hardly in high positions, right?"

Sam thought quietly again. She made a lot a sense, but something about the information just seemed inconsistent with the facts they had already confirmed.

"So, are you thinking the message from Battleford was unrelated? Or was he working for the mayor?" he asked.

"I don't know. It could be either, really. But if Jason told Mark that it was someone high up at city hall, that's what my dad found out. And that would have been the knowledge that got him into this mess," she concluded. "Does it really matter if Battleford was involved or not?"

"Kaylee, the facts always matter, especially when they are inconvenient."

She looked away, and Sam could feel her frustration at him, as though he were holding her back from finally discovering the truth. And he understood exactly why she would feel that way. But he had promised to keep her safe, and that was what he had to do at all costs.

"Look, the FBI is still talking to Fleming. Why don't we see what comes of it over the next few days before we draw any conclusions?"

Kaylee sighed and rested her head back in the car seat. "Okay."

They drove the rest of the way in silence until they were going through D.C.

"Are you still going to your parents' house for the evening?" he asked.

"Yes, if that's okay," she replied, looking out the passenger-side window. "Only my dad is home, but Junior said he'll stop by later."

"No problem. We should be there just after four o'clock."

She nodded, and went back to thinking. Soon, she was directing him through a very upscale neighborhood, though Sam was already familiar with the streets, since Evan's family home was not far from hers. Both were equally massive and elaborate in design. He pulled his Jaguar into the circular driveway.

"Can you stay?" Kaylee asked before they got out of the car. "You don't have to. It will probably be awkward. But you can if you want to."

Those smudges were back under her eyes.

"Sure, I can stay."

CHAPTER 23

Ida opened the door as soon as Kaylee rang the doorbell. It didn't seem appropriate to use her key when she didn't live there anymore.

"Ms. Mikayla, so good to see you!" the older woman exclaimed, pulling Kaylee into a hug.

"Hi, Ida. You too. This is a friend of mine, Samuel Mackenzie," she said as they broke apart, and the three of them walked farther into the house.

"Nice to meet you, Mr. Mackenzie," Ida replied politely.

"It's Sam, please. Nice to meet you also."

"Where's Dad?" Kaylee asked. The house was eerily quiet and they continued past the front rooms through to the kitchen at the back of the house.

"Last I saw, he was in his study watching the news," Ida replied. "Can I bring you both anything to eat or drink?"

"No, we're fine, thank you."

Kaylee continued on with Sam silently beside her until they reached the study. She knocked. There was a muffled response so she opened the door, only to find her fifty-one-year-old father with his pants around his ankles and his naked butt squeezed as he worked on the woman bent over the desk in front of him. Sam had the fastest response, gripping Kaylee's arm and pulling her back. It took a couple of seconds for her to grasp what she was seeing, and it was impossible to hold in her scream.

"Dad!"

George Clement whipped his head around in surprise, as did the woman bent over the desk equally as bare assed. She just happened to be Kaylee's mom. There was more screaming, before Sam finally pulled Kaylee away and firmly shut the door. He kept a hold on her arm until they reached the kitchen and he settled her down into one of the counter stools like a child.

"Breathe," he encouraged, rubbing his hands up and down her arms. "Just breathe."

"Oh my god, oh my god, oh my god," she panted, now waving her hands in front of her. "I can't stop seeing it. Ewww, ewww, ewww!"

She felt his laughter before the boom sound came out of his chest. Then Kaylee watched as Sam doubled over uncontrollably. She thought back to the image of her parents, who were always so polished and proper, going at it like kids. Even well into his cups, and yelling about something at the slightest provocation, George Clement was more dignified than most men. So to see him with his pants dropped in the middle of the day . . .

Kaylee snorted; then it turned into a giggle as she covered her face with burning embarrassment. Sam was still laughing uncontrollably. She would look up and scrub at her eyes, and he would look at her and double over again. After a few tries, he managed to speak.

"That's not what I expected when you said your dad was not doing well. He looked pretty good to me."

Then they both realized what he'd said and started laughing hysterically again. Kaylee's stomach started to hurt, and tears were now trickling down her cheeks.

"Please stop," she begged.

"That's not what she said."

Kaylee hit him; then they were out of control all over again.

"Blimey, Kaylee, I hope that was your maw."

She grinned up at him, then put her head down on the counter and covered it with her hands. "We have to go," she mumbled.

"What?"

"We have to go," she repeated louder. "I don't want to see them. What would I say? Oh god, this is horrible."

"Don't be daft. It will be fine."

Kaylee sat up and studied his relaxed expression. He sounded so cute when he reverted to funny-sounding Scottish words, though almost all seemed to be insults. She was pretty sure "daft" meant stupid.

"Too late anyway. Here they come."

She bowed her head in defeat and turned toward her parents as they walked into the kitchen. They looked comfortable and relaxed now that they were fully clothed, though her mom's hair wasn't quite as neat as usual.

"Hi, sweetheart. We had expected you a little later," Elaine said without any sign of embarrassment.

Kaylee hopped off the stool and gave her mom a dutiful hug.

"Hi, Mom. I didn't mean to barge in like that."

"Just forget about it," Elaine suggested, and Kaylee really hoped that she could. The sparkle in Sam's eyes suggested he might not let her anytime soon.

"Hi, Dad," Kaylee said, then hesitated before giving him a hug also. He held on for a little longer than she'd anticipated, then rubbed her back. She blinked back the tears that swelled up.

"Hi, baby. It's good to see you."

"And who is this, Mikayla?" At her mother's prompting, they all turned to face Sam.

"Mr. Clement, I'm Samuel Mackenzie with Fortis. We met a few years ago."

"Yes, of course," her dad replied in a booming voice. "Evan's partner."

"That's right. And Mrs. Clement, it's a pleasure to meet you."

Noting the questioning look on her parents' faces, Kaylee added more of an explanation. "Sam and I were out together this afternoon, and he offered to give me a ride here."

"Any friend of Evan's is a friend of ours," her mom replied, though her eyes still sparkled with speculation.

And that started a very enjoyable evening. As promised, Junior showed up at around six o'clock for dinner, and they ate together in the dining room. Afterward, they moved outside to relax and enjoy the beautiful weather by the pool. Kaylee watched her parents interact, and was confused by how connected they seemed. There had been several times in the last year where her mom had seemed at the end of her rope dealing with her dad, so their current interaction was an unexpected relief. George still drank a few glasses of scotch, and wasn't quite sober by the end of the night. There was some quiet brooding, but no dramatic moodiness or outburst.

"I like your Sam," her mom said later as things were winding down.

"He's not really mine," Kaylee protested, looking over at the topic of their gossip. He was talking with her dad and brother, then looked back at her and grinned.

"Sure, he is," Elaine said knowingly.

"Mom, how are things with Dad? And I don't mean what I saw earlier!" Kaylee quickly protested slapping a hand over her forehead. "Oh god!"

"Don't be silly, sweetheart. You're a grown woman so you have to understand these things."

"What does that mean, Mom? I know Dad hasn't been himself for a long time."

"Oh, he has his moments. Yes, he's not the same as he was for most of our marriage, but sometimes that happens. I'm just learning to take advantage of things when it's good."

"Is he still drinking too much?" Kaylee asked.

"Yes, I won't deny that. But until he wants to do something about it, I can't help him. And neither can you or Junior," her mom explained. "I know that's hard to hear, but that's the truth, Mikayla. The sooner you learn that, the less stress you'll have in your life."

Kaylee bit at her lip.

"Is he still angry with me for moving away?"

"Not angry. More disappointed and overly protective. But he'll get over it, okay? He has to. You can't live with us forever, afraid to upset your father."

Kaylee leaned into her mom, and the two women shared a loose embrace for a few moments.

They left her parents' house at almost ten o'clock and drove back to Sam's secluded cottage. Niko was waiting patiently for his walk so they quickly took him around the block. In the bedroom, they quietly got naked before Sam picked her up high under the bum and lay her back at the edge of the bed as he stroked deep. There were no preliminaries, no words, and only one position.

Friday morning, Sam woke her up early for a run. They went four miles at a steady pace. She came back a sweaty, gasping mess, and he looked like he had gone to get the mail. They ate toast and coffee in his small but modern kitchen. Kaylee's mind was off concocting plots when he interrupted by clearing his throat.

"I have a confession."

She sipped her coffee and looked back at him. Her confessions lately had been pretty massive, so it seemed fair that he could have one or two of his own. She held her breath and waited.

"I lied to you about taking you and Antonoli as a client."

Her brows furrowed with puzzlement.

"What do you mean?"

"It means I'm not actually working for you. Like, there is no official assignment here."

Kaylee smiled, shaking her head and feeling a little like *Alice in Wonderland*.

"Okay, you're going to have to explain that one to me. I've just seen you and a bunch of your employees put in a lot of hours in the last two weeks. So how is that not working for me?"

"I'm on vacation," he added as though that would somehow make it clearer.

"What?" she said, laughing. "You really have to find something fun to do in your downtime."

"Funny. That's what Renee said." Then he cleared his throat. "You won't be billed for the work because I did it on my own time."

"You mean you're literally on vacation. Right now?" He nodded, looking a little sheepish. "Why? Because we're sleeping together? Is that some kind of violation to the company code of conduct?"

Sam sat back in his chair.

"I've never read the company code, to be honest. And that would have been a good reason. But I wasn't charging you from the beginning."

"Why?" Kaylee asked. She wasn't mad, just perplexed.

"You wanted complete confidentiality or you would get someone else, and I couldn't do that. So I pretended to agree to your terms like you were the client. But that was just so I could help you without argument."

"Hmmm, clever," she mumbled and sipped at her coffee.

"I don't lie to my partners, Kaylee. Not intentionally. And one secret was enough to last a lifetime."

"I get it, Sam. I insulted your integrity," she said quietly. "Why did you help me then, on your vacation?"

"Don't ask me that. You knew I couldn't walk away from you even if I tried," he said in a heated voice. "That's why you came to me in the first place, Kaylee. I just wasn't going to do it under your terms."

Kaylee had known they had unresolved things between them. How could they not, after everything that had happened? But it didn't make it any easier to face them, knowing they were her doing.

"I don't know what to say. Thank you seemed inadequate."

He looked away. "You don't need to thank me, lass."

"Can I at least cover the cost of the team and the equipment? The expenses you've incurred?" she suggested, starting to feel really guilty about the trouble she had caused. "Please? It wasn't my intent to put your people at risk, impact your business or take advantage of our . . . relationship."

"The team is always well compensated so the matter is settled," he said, chopping his hand through the air.

"So why are you telling me?"

"Well, I could hardly hide it from you once a bill is due, now could I? And I want you to understand that I have not been following your direction through this situation. I've been directing it. I will continue to do so."

She looked at him, trying to figure out what he was saying. Finally he looked back with his sky-blue eyes sharp and direct.

"You want to go after the mayor, Kaylee. And I won't let you do it alone. So if we do, it's with a plan that I approve."

They studied each other for a bit until Sam raised an eyebrow and Kaylee sighed.

"Fine. But I won't sit on the sidelines, Sam. I won't be tucked away while you and your band of warriors go to battle."

"Why would I do that? I might need your ninja skills."

Kaylee couldn't resist a small exasperated smile.

"Now, today is my last official day of vacation and I've been told I need to do something fun. So let's go find something."

They went golfing, something they both loved and hadn't done in years. Sam had a set of clubs that he'd brought over from the U.K., and they made a quick stop at her parents' house to get hers out of storage. The country club her family belonged to was booked weeks in advance so after some research, they found a small nine-hole course outside the city. While the round started out casual and fun, it quickly became competitive. He was good. Powerful and accurate, but Kaylee was better. It turned out that Samuel Mackenzie was a big, bad-ass motherfucker, except when he was losing to a girl. Then he was just grumpy, volatile, and downright emotional. Kaylee hadn't had so much fun in years.

Afterward, they returned to his place to shower, then walked to a nearby pub that Sam often frequented.

"We can't go at him with threats," Kaylee determined, talking about how to shut down the mayor's involvement in widespread corruption in Baltimore. "He's too connected with many unsavory people who want to keep him in power. It has to be more surgical and controlled."

"Like, go after what matters to him most?"

"Exactly. What would matter to a politician who's been in power for over seven years? Something more important than money?"

"More power? His health? Family?"

"Hmmm, maybe," Kaylee pondered. "I have a friend who still works in his offices. I haven't spoken to her in a few years, but she might have some insights into what he's like personally, besides what's in the papers. But there has to be something we can use to apply pressure."

"You mean, like coercion?" he asked with a

straight face. "I'm starting to see that you would make a brilliant criminal mastermind."

"Hmmm. Maybe that will be my next career move." He flashed her a smile.

"What is it that we'll be asking him to do? Stop taking brides? I can't imagine he's the only one, Kaylee. He might just be the tip of the iceberg."

"I know that, but if he's the one controlling my dad, then he's the only one we need to take out of the game."

"Unless we can get him to use his powers for good instead of evil."

Now Kaylee smiled at his silly teasing. "How?"

"If we have to find out what motivates him the most, and we agree it can't be money, then we have to convince him that he can have more of it without corruption than with."

Kaylee tapped her finger on the pub table, feeling a tingling of excitement.

"That's going to require a lot of plotting," she suggested.

"I've seen your skills, ninja. I think it's worth a shot. And if that doesn't work, we'll use a club instead of a scalpel. I'll just take a team and go in to have a chat with him."

CHAPTER 24

Sam asked Renee over on Saturday to get her insights on a few things. Namely, the information from Mark McMann that seemed to incriminate the mayor of Baltimore in bribing Jason Holt, then forcing George Clement out of running Clement Media, and the ideas he and Kaylee were throwing around to address it. But Sam also needed an impartial perspective on the situation, and Renee would provide that. They had similar years of experience at MI5, the British secret service, investigating all sorts of plots and criminal enterprises, some involving high-level government officials. She would have a good handle on whether their plan had merit.

And, quite frankly, Sam was no longer certain of his own objectivity when it came to helping Kaylee.

Unfortunately, Kaylee thought Evan would have some ideas, and Evan brought along Nia to meet Kaylee again. And Evan invited Lucas in case they needed to hack into something quickly, and Lucas couldn't stay away from his new girlfriend, Alex, while she was in town. Noting that it was a party of seven, Kaylee invited Junior over to join them, making it eight.

At two o'clock, Sam looked around his rear yard, backing onto the river, and gave up on the idea of a private discussion with anyone. While Evan and Lucas's girlfriends chatted among themselves and played with Niko, everyone else was in the middle of a giant debate.

"I think we find the evidence we need and give it to the police," Lucas said, handing out a cold beer bottle to anyone who raised a hand. "There is always a data trail."

"Maybe, but we haven't found one yet. And we don't have enough leads to know which direction to go next, right?" Evan reasoned. "Seems to me that our best sources of accurate information are Holt, McMann, and George. It's in the best interest of everyone else involved to not tell us anything. Fleming, for instance. If that's true, let's look at what those sources have provided so far. We know from Holt that someone from city hall was likely involved. We can't talk to George directly, but we've gone through all the communication and records we can access from four years ago. They don't tell us much about who's influencing him, except it has to be someone powerful and connected. Now, we have the lead on Mayor Gordon from McMann, and it finally connects a few dots. So it seems to me that we either act on intel we have, or back down."

"I say we back down," Junior mumbled. "This is all too crazy for me. You can't just take down a city mayor—particularly one that we all think is well connected to who knows what kinds of organized crime."

"It's no different from a senator. Three actually, but who's counting?" Lucas stated blandly.

"A czar and a prime minister," added Evan. "Under DaCosta operations of course."

"A few judges and a bishop," Renee topped up.

They all looked at Sam for his contribution.

"A prince. But we were only fifteen and he was a wanker," he told them with a big smile.

Everyone laughed.

"All right," Junior conceded, throwing up his hands in defeat. "You guys are obviously the experts."

"So, we agree? We'll look for a way to get to the mayor?" Kaylee asked.

"Until we have more evidence," Lucas said.

"Agreed, let's do it," Evan added.

Kaylee looked up at Sam, and he nodded with his support.

"Okay! I was going to call a friend of mine who works in the mayor's office, but I don't like the idea of getting anyone else involved. She's the one who gave me the lead on contract overspend four years ago. Thank God I kept her name out of it then," Kaylee explained, leaning forward. "So I did a lot a research this morning and, from what I can remember, Lyle Gordon likes to think he's a bit of a celebrity. He throws big parties, and his wife is very social. He loves to be on the front page of major papers and thinks nothing of having his kids there with him. And from what I've pulled up, he hasn't changed at all in his second term."

"He has an ego," Sam concluded.

"Yes," Kaylee agreed. "Maybe that's his motivation. He obviously loves being mayor and being the man in charge. But another election is around the corner, and there's a city councilman who's been eyeing the job for years now. Emeril Marchesi has persistently hinted at city corruption under Gordon's leadership. In fact, Marchesi is the one who started to make noise about city budget mismanagement back when I was writing for the *Journal.* No one really paid attention to his accusations from what I remember, but it was enough to mark him as an adversarial opponent. It looks like Marchesi lost to Gordon by only a slim margin in the last election. So what if Mayor Gordon believes hard evidence of city corruption will go to Marchesi before the next election? I bet he'd do anything to prevent that."

"Anything like what?" Junior asked, drawn back into the planning out of curiosity.

"Like declare his own stance on stopping city corruption, and using the evidence to start a public inquiry."

The five people around her were silent for about a minute. Then Renee grinned.

"It's brilliant, actually."

"Yeah," Lucas added. "It sounds like something the CIA would do."

"It does, actually," Evan mumbled, looking at Kaylee with new eyes.

"But the mayor is corrupt, so why would he go along with this? Stop the corruption that he's profiting from?" Junior asked, clearly baffled.

"Because the evidence is going to come out

anyway. This way, he can control it and use it to his advantage. Be a hero, the one to clean up a dirty city."

"Okay, but why not just give the evidence to Marchesi and let him use it. Then get a good man into the office."

"It's an option," Sam noted. "But we don't know he's a good man. And we don't have any leverage to use on him, so no control over how he uses the information."

"The evil you know, and all that," said Evan.

"Lastly, that won't necessarily remove any influence that Dad's under, Junior. At least not right away," added Kaylee.

There was more silent contemplation.

"Like I said, you guys are the experts in this kind of thing," Junior told them. "But to me this sounds like a massive game of chess where we're intimidating the criminals."

"Exactly!" Renee agreed. "It's bloody brilliant!"

Junior just shook his head and went back to listening. The others leaned forward so they were surrounding Kaylee in a tight circle.

"So how do we approach Gordon?" Lucas asked. "We can't just knock on his door with a proposition."

"And it has to come from someone he thinks has clout in his social circles, right?" Kaylee reminded them. "I mean, the family is in the paper and local magazines every week at a charity event, or expensive social function. His wife is on two charitable boards, heads the Scottish Society and the PTA. It has to be someone from these types of circles."

"What about you, Evan?" Lucas asked. "You're still on the board at DaCosta. That has to carry some influence."

Evan shrugged. "Maybe—"

"Wait," interrupted Renee. "What was that, Kaylee? His wife is head of the what?"

"The PTA?"

"No," Renee said, shaking her head and pulling out her cell phone to type in something. "You said head of the Scottish Society. The Scottish Heritage Society of Maryland, to be exact, and one of the largest organizations of its kind in the United States according to their website. And that's going to be our in."

Renee looked at Sam as he sighed dramatically. The others looked between them, waiting for an explanation.

"Are you going to tell them, or should I?" she finally demanded. "Fine, I'll do it."

Renee stood up and stepped just in front of Sam then bowed, backing away.

"May I present to you," she stated in an overly formal, proper English accent, "Samuel Mackenzie, Viscount Andri and the future Earl of Seaforth."

Lucas was the first to snort; then Evan was laughing also. Sam rolled his eyes, and Renee had a big grin on her face. Kaylee smiled up at Sam.

"That's useful, having our own resident Scotsman who could pretend to be titled. It would definitely impress them," Kaylee mused. "But do you think we'd get away with it?"

"You all think I'm taking a piss?" Renee replied

with an even bigger laugh. "I'm dead serious. Sam's dad is the current Earl of Seaforth."

Sam shoved his hands deep into the front pockets of his jeans and shook his head. He had not seen this coming. He shot Renee a dark look that he hoped demonstrated how annoyed he was. His family title wasn't a secret exactly, but it wasn't something that he ever talked about. Certainly not in America.

"Are you kidding me?" Lucas asked with eyes squinted. "How did I not know this?"

"Wow," Evan added. "Now I've heard everything."

"Okay, let's all calm down. It's hardly a big deal. Viscount isn't even a real title, it's just a courtesy, really," he mumbled. But his friends continued to look at him like he had grown another head.

Kaylee cocked a brow at him and Sam shrugged.

"So what do you think?" Renee continued. "Will his majesty here be impressive enough to get the mayor's attention?"

"Yeah," Kaylee replied. "I think he'll do."

Renee went back to her phone to do more research on the mayor's wife, Emma Gordon, and her Scottish Society activities. Evan, Lucas, and even Junior started to pepper Sam with a bunch of random silly questions about the peerage in Great Britain. Sam answered a couple but ignored most. Kaylee just listened. Her eyes connected with his every once in a while, but Sam couldn't tell what she was thinking.

"I think I've found the perfect occasion," Renee announced, holding up her phone in victory.

"What?" Kaylee asked.

"There's a fancy dinner coming up next Saturday in support of a Celtic kids' summer camp. Looks like the Scottish Society is a big sponsor."

"Next week? That's really soon," Kaylee said, biting her lip. "Won't tickets for something like that be sold out? Maybe we should go for something a little further out so we have time to get ready."

"It's either now or never," Renee advised. "I don't see anything posted that would work in August. So, if we don't act now, we'll have to see what comes up after that. And it has to be something that the mayor will attend, not just his wife."

"What do you guys think?" Kaylee asked the group.

"If we're going to do this, now's as good a time as any," Lucas said, and Evan nodded.

"Sam?" Kaylee finally asked, turning to face him.

"A week is plenty of time in our business, so let's do it," he told her.

Kaylee looked around again. "Okay, it looks like we have a plan for a plan."

The party broke up soon after, and by early evening, Sam and Kaylee were alone eating a meal of leftovers from lunch.

"So, the future Earl of . . . what again?" she finally asked.

"Seaforth," Sam provided. He'd known the topic was going to come up again with Kaylee. She had been too quiet about it in the afternoon.

"Right."

"What?" he demanded when she just looked at him, assessing.

"Nothing. I'm just thinking about how little I know about you."

"I'm a pretty simple man. There's not much to know."

She snorted rather rudely. "I'll assume you're being extremely sarcastic."

Sam shrugged. But it did raise a good point. So much of their interactions up to now had been focused on Kaylee's family, her relationship with Evan, her situation with Antonoli. And all with a great deal of scrutiny. It seemed a little unfair that she did not have the same insights into his life other than whatever small comments he may have made when they first met.

"What do you want to know?" he asked.

She started with the easy stuff, about his family and life near Inverness, Scotland, while growing up. Sam was an only child. His mom ran a small luxury inn on the family property, Seaforth Manor, while his dad dabbled in farming on the surrounding land.

"What did you do before you joined Fortis?" she asked.

"I worked for MI5 as a security advisor in London."

Her mouth fell open.

"MI5? As in the British spy agency? Like Sean Connery and James Bond?"

"No, that's MI6," Sam corrected with a tolerant smile. "MI5 is our secret service. That's how I met Lucas actually. We worked on a project together with Interpol."

"So you weren't a spy?" she persisted, looking at him closely as though to test for the truth.

"Definitely not." There was no need to tell her that up until a year ago, her very own Evan Da-Costa had actually been a spy for the CIA, code name "Ice."

"Huh, British secret service," she echoed. "I can see what you mean about being a simple man."

He chuckled.

"So, what else? Any marriages, children? Other lovers?"

"Nope, none of the above."

Sam felt as though there was another question on her mind, but Kaylee didn't put it forward.

"Well, that's all I can think of right now," she finally conceded. "Except, do you own a kilt?"

"Aye, of course! Two actually. And before you ask, no self-respecting Scotsman wears pants under his kilt."

"Good to know," she replied, laughing. "Now, all we have to do is get the future Lord of Seaforth invited to a party next weekend. But I'm sure I can take care of that."

"I'm back in the office on Monday, but let me know the particulars as soon as possible. It sounds like a small mission, but I'll pull together the plan and the required team."

"I need to be back in New York this week," she said after a pause.

"When are you leaving?"

"Tomorrow evening."

Sam knew that she had planned to be in Virginia for only a few days, to meet with McMann and see her family. But he was still surprised by her sudden announcement.

"I'll help with the planning for the dinner with the mayor from there. Then I'll come back here on Friday," she added.

He must have made some kind of appropriate gesture of acknowledgment because Kaylee stood up and started clearing their dishes from the table. Sam joined her and they worked in silence, but his thoughts were far away. She was going back to New York alone, without anyone there for her security. Yes, he reminded himself, there was now a state-of-the-art digital surveillance up at both her apartment and office, but was that enough? What if people from Ross suspected she had provided information about their threats to her?

He took a deep breath, knowing he was over-reacting, trying to remind himself that Kaylee was very smart and capable of taking care of herself. A ninja. The thought almost made him smile to himself. Or maybe he had since, at that moment, Kaylee looked at him funny. He went back to stacking even more leftovers into the fridge, and trying to figure out why the thought of her leaving was creating a giant crater in the base of his stomach.

It was only because they'd spent every day together for the last two weeks. Two very dramatic weeks. That's all. He got used to her company. Once she was gone for a few days, everything would go back to normal, and he'd have a few good memories out of it.

A few good memories? Yer stowed oot o'jobby!

His inside voice was right, he was full of shit. Sam slammed the fridge door harder than necessary.

"I'm going to take Niko for a walk," he said,

standing. The terrier came running up to him as though on cue.

"Okay, I can come along if you'd like," Kaylee offered, but Sam was already through the front doorway.

"No need. I'll be back in a few minutes," he explained politely. If only it would help to figure out what the hell was eating at him.

CHAPTER 25

It was surprisingly easy to get a titled Scotsman into a sold-out society dinner just days away. By Monday afternoon, Kaylee had secured four tickets to the event, with two seats at the mayor's table.

She wondered briefly who had been bumped to accommodate someone thought to be higher up on the food chain and shook her head at the silly things that matter to people. The same petty, inconsequential things that had been an everyday part of running the Clement charity with her mom. They did such good work for the improvement of literacy in the D.C. area, but lots of the "society" women involved treated it like a popularity contest in a college sorority.

Once the tickets were secured, Kaylee called Sam with an update. By Tuesday afternoon, she was on a video call with him, Evan, Renee, and Raymond to iron out the details of the very simple plan.

"Kaylee and I will sit at the mayor's table, while Evan and Renee use the extra tickets," Sam explained. "We'll be suited for any issues, but mostly,

Evan DaCosta is there with a date as a show of strength. Raymond will be connected to provide communication and logistics support, if needed. At some point during the dinner, I will have a private chat with the mayor, ideally in front of his wife, making it clear that I have evidence of city corruption and that his only option is to publicly announce that he is starting a public inquiry."

"What evidence are we going to hint at?" Evan asked.

"Fleming and the Groveland contracts," Sam said.

"From four years ago," Kaylee added. "The feds are looking at Groveland using Ross as a front and the corruption in New Jersey. Only we know they used a different shell company to do the same thing in Baltimore four years ago."

"Exactly," concluded Sam. "It's enough to show I have real information and I'm serious about giving it to Marchesi if necessary."

"So we make sure he gives the speech that night, and Bob's your uncle," Renee said.

"I think we have to make sure it gets as much media coverage as possible," Kaylee suggested. "Send tweets, post a video of the speech on YouTube, and push the story to as many mainstream media outlets as possible."

"Good plan," agreed Raymond. "I'll create an online profile that can do that from the event. Maybe for you Kaylee, since you're known in Baltimore as Kaylee Stone?"

"Am I going as Kaylee Stone, or under my real name?" she asked through the video link on her computer, not sure what made the most sense at this point.

"It should be Kaylee Stone. Mikayla Stone-Clement is too close to George Clement for my liking," Sam said.

"Okay, I'm fine with that."

Sam continued for a few more minutes to review the more technical aspects of the small assignment. Kaylee was still a little surprised that the Fortis team was so willing to support her.

"When are you returning to Virginia, Kaylee?" Sam asked.

"Friday morning," she confirmed.

"The event starts with cocktails at six o'clock on Saturday. Let's meet in Baltimore at four o'clock so we can scope things out a bit in advance. So we'll meet at headquarters first."

Kaylee could see the agreements around the room. That was it, the plan was happening.

"Are you okay?" Sam asked when everyone had walked away from the large video monitor. He was standing near the middle of the room he was in, so she saw the top half of his body. But it still felt strange not to be there with him.

"I'm fine, just thinking about what to wear," she lied with a smile. "And how to get an emergency visit with my hair stylist by Thursday."

"You hardly need it, lass."

Kaylee smiled, pleased by the suggestion.

"There's been no sign of trouble there, right? No one from Ross Construction?" he asked.

"Nope. Everything has been pretty quiet over the last two days," she told him.

"How's Niko doing?"

"Good. He's pretty easygoing so he went right back to his schedule before all this craziness began," she explained. "I went for a run this morning. Not as far and not as fast, but I did okay."

"I did too," he replied, relaxing in his stance with his hands on his hips.

"I bet you went much farther and faster without me holding you back," she teased. It felt so good to talk to him, even for a little bit.

He shrugged. "It's not important."

They looked at each other for a few moments.

"What time do you arrive on Friday?" Sam finally asked.

"Around eleven o'clock."

"Okay, I might be able to pick you up at the airport."

"That's not necessary. I'll just take a car."

"You're welcome to stay with me again while you're here."

Kaylee smiled since she had hoped that was the case. "Okay, I'll do that."

"I'll send you the security code for the back door so you can let yourself in."

"Sure, that works."

Sam cleared his throat.

"I have to get to another meeting," Kaylee told him, sitting up in her chair to show some urgency. "I'll talk to you soon?"

"Sure, whenever."

They both said bye and she disconnected the link. The truth was, there was no meeting. Kaylee just didn't want Sam to know she was perfectly happy just looking at him by video even if there was nothing to say. Pretty pathetic. She sat back in her office chair to indulge in another few minutes of deep thought. Ever since she had returned to New York alone, Kaylee had felt a little lost. Like Niko, she had fallen back into her routine pretty easily and did all the same things as before the threats had started. Except, back then, she'd had a purpose. There had been a reason for living in New York, building a small company, and living with one of her really good friends.

Then, suddenly, after two weeks of what could only be described as crazy drama, her purpose was gone. Problem (almost) solved. And now, when she went to sleep at night in her Manhattan apartment, Kaylee no longer had a reason to be there. And it didn't help that where she really wanted to be was with Sam. And there were no easy answers for that problem since Sam clearly wasn't certain that he wanted her.

Her five minutes of time wasting were up, and Kaylee got on with her day. Wednesday and Thursday were much the same, except she and Sam didn't talk, text, email, or communicate in any way. She tried not to dwell on it or give it any significance, but by the time she flew back to Virginia, Kaylee was tired of the uncertainty in her current situation. So she made a commitment. One way or another, by the end of the weekend, she would have a plan for what came next in her life, with or without Samuel Mackenzie.

She was walking through the airport when her phone vibrated with a message from Sam with the security code to his back door, noting that he would join her there shortly after five o'clock that afternoon.

It was a very hot day, and Kaylee sat out in his backyard in shorts and a tank top, working on invoice payments to the various Antonoli suppliers and subcontractors. Niko barked just as Sam came out of the house.

"How was your flight?" he asked, stopping by her chair.

"Good," Kaylee replied, looking up at him, then back down to her work.

"It looks like it's going to be a pretty big storm," he added.

She looked around, noticing the darkening skies for the first time. There had been perfect blue skies just about thirty minutes ago.

"I should take Niko out for a long walk now. Just in case he hasn't done anything yet. He hates going in the rain."

Kaylee jumped up and grabbed her laptop and other things to bring them into the house. Sam followed her.

"Give me a second to change and I'll go with you," he suggested. "There's a trail along the back that he liked last weekend."

It took a few laps along the shoreline between Sam's property and that of a few neighbors before Niko put some effort into doing his business. They were just about to cut through the deep backyard to the rear entrance of the house when the sky opened up and poured buckets of rain down on them.

Kaylee screamed in surprise, frozen in place. The

sheet of water was so heavy that she could hardly
see in front of her. She felt Sam take hold of her
hand and they started running across the grass.
Niko was way ahead of them, already cowering
under the roof line with his head bent in fear, and
shaking off as much water as possible. They stopped
at a dry spot on the deck, pausing for a moment to
look around at the downpour with amazement.
Thunder boomed, followed by several bolts of
lightning that seemed to hit too close for comfort.
Kaylee jumped a foot in the air with another sharp
yelp, and Sam started laughing.

She looked to him, then down at herself. They
were both completely drenched from head to foot,
and Kaylee started laughing also. Another deafen-
ing thunderclap made her grab his arm. Sam
pulled her close until their soggy clothes slapped
together.

"Not to worry, lass. I'll protect you."

The rain should have felt cold against their skin,
but the evening was so hot and muggy that it was a
welcome relief. Kaylee looked up at Sam, and he
leaned in and brushed her lips with his. They
shivered from the electricity between them. He
coaxed her mouth open gently so he could stroke
his tongue deep within. She gasped at how good it
was, knowing it had been so long since they had
kissed like this. His hold around her waist quickly
became more firm as he pulled her closer against
his length.

"Kaylee," he whispered when their lips separated
for a brief moment.

"Yes," she answered.

Suddenly, the heat outside and from his touch was unbearable. She pulled out of his embrace to strip off her wet clothes quickly until she was standing naked in front of him. Sam looked down at her. His blue eyes were now as dark and stormy as the sky, and they ran over her body like a hot caress. Kaylee reached out and took hold of his T-shirt and pulled the fabric up to reveal his rippled abdomen. Sam caught on pretty quickly, tearing off his top and shorts in record time. He was proudly aroused and so mouthwateringly masculine that she wanted to lick her lips in anticipation. His eyes fell to her lips, and Kaylee realized she had done just that.

Inspired by the weather and the week since they had last been together, she held out her hand to him, then walked backward into the storm, now measurably calmer. Sam quickly pulled her into his arms as the warm summer rain showered down on their bare bodies with a massaging force. It was the most erotic thing she had ever felt.

"Blimey, lass. Ye'r driving me mad," he growled before they were kissing again with even more wet intensity.

God, Kaylee felt so alive, so powerful and in charge. She stroked her hands over every part of his body that she could reach, memorizing all the hard slab, contoured ripples and shallow valleys. Reaching between their bodies, she took hold of his jutting cock, using a tight grip to stroke down its wet length. He shuddered against her, so she did it again until Sam was moaning into her ear.

Sam picked her up as he liked to do, carrying her over to a lounge chair nearby. He put her down, turning her so she faced the back and surrounded her with his size, effectively shielding her from the steady spray. Pulling her tight against his body with his arms wrapped around her waist, he pressed up with the power of his thighs to take her deep. . . . Wow, it was incredible. Kaylee cried with satisfaction, then arched her back to beg for more.

"Ah, Kaylee. Sweet lass," he groaned, then whispered her name over and over again with every long thrust. The rain flowed relentlessly over them, adding both slickness and friction to their every touch. They didn't last long, coming one after the other with loud cries of completion that were muffled by the storm.

They were still breathless, and Sam lifted her into his arms and sprinted back into his house. A very relieved white terrier ran in behind him.

"Let's get you warmed up." He put her down in the bedroom, then dashed into the bathroom to grab a stack of towels.

"I'm fine," Kaylee insisted. But he ignored her, covering her head with one, then using another to dry down her body.

"That was just mad," he mumbled, finally wrapping the fluffy cotton around her body and tucking it in like a sarong.

She rubbed at her hair, watching as he dried himself down.

"It was fun," she insisted with a teasing smile that showed off her dimples. "Wasn't it?"

He stopped, letting go of his towel so it fell heavily to the floor. With both hands cupping her face, he looked down into her eyes.

"Of course it was fun. You're fun." He kissed her gently, stroking her lips as though trying to discover every inch. "I missed you."

"You did?"

"Aye, very much."

Sam took one of the damp, plush cloths off of her and guided her backward, maneuvering her body until they were both in the middle of the bed. With deliberate movements, he unwrapped the second towel around her like a present, then tossed it on the floor with the other.

"Did you miss me?" he asked, taking hold of both her feet and planting them wide so her knees were bent.

"Aye," Kaylee whispered with another cheeky grin.

He slid his hands down the inside of her thighs and rubbed his thumbs in massaging circles right at the apex. Her breath caught sharply as she watched his every move.

"For years, I've slept comfortably alone. And now suddenly I'm wide awake at all hours because something is missing."

"Were you lonely?" she asked, trying to maintain the light, teasing tone.

Sam stopped and looked down for a second, fixing his steady gaze on hers again. "I was." He stroked one of his thumbs along the tender ridge of her wetness, before delving into the slippery valley. Kaylee moaned and bit at her bottom lip. "I don't know what to do with you, Kaylee. I want you so much, it's making me mad."

Her hips bucked when he buried his middle

finger into her tight canal with shallow thrusts. His thumb twirled over her clit in the tiny little circle he knew she loved.

"Sam," she panted. Her back arched from the impending climax. "Sam, please."

"Wait for me, lass," he asked, quickly pulling her hips toward him, covering her with his body and plunging into her depths. "I want to feel you coming around me."

With every stroke, he seemed to pull her closer, tighter, until it felt like their bodies were indistinguishable. Their shouts of pleasure mingled in the air until Sam came hard, crying out her name, and Kaylee followed soon after.

They lay in bed awake for some time, listening to the rain under the sheets. He was on his back, and she was draped along his side with her head on his chest.

"That felt like how it was that first time," she whispered at some point.

"Every time feels like that to me," he replied.

"I mean, you've been . . . silent. Every time since," she tried to explain.

"I didn't know what to say."

"And you do now?"

He took a while to respond. "I'm working on it."

"Okay. I can wait," she promised with a yawn.

CHAPTER 26

"Okay, show time," Sam mumbled quietly.

He and Kaylee stood up as Lyle Gordon, the mayor of the city of Baltimore, and his wife, Emma, got up from the table.

It was Saturday evening, and the Celtic charity dinner was going as planned so far. Kaylee and the team had arrived in Baltimore early. Sam had booked a hotel room for them a couple of blocks away. They'd dropped Kaylee there, and then he, Evan, and Renee had completed a reconnaissance trip in and around the venue for the dinner, mapping out anticipated traffic flow, exits, and potential hazards. By five-thirty, they were back at the hotel room getting dressed for the night.

Sam looked down at Kaylee, who was stunning in a full-length cream gown with a sexy plunging neckline. The soft color made her darker skin glow. Her hair was up in a simple bun, and a delicate sparkle of jewelry hung from her earlobes and draped her neck. He was pretty sure they were real diamonds.

She smiled up at him, her eyes dark and smoky, and her lips painted a deep, sexy red.

Like Sam, all the Scotsmen there were in full kilt outfits, including clan tartans, black military-cut jackets, hose, and a pouch called a sporran.

"We should make the rounds and socialize a bit. You're quite a hit tonight, Viscount Andri," Kaylee teased as she eyed his formal attire with appreciation, and not for the first time.

Sam tried not to react, but he seemed to have a little more swagger in his step tonight. It wasn't just his stroked ego that had him walking taller. His body was still humming from the night before. Just when he didn't think things could get hotter between them, that Kaylee could be any sexier, she dragged him into the rain, naked.

"Sam?"

He turned his head sharply to find Renee staring at him.

"What's wrong with you? You've been acting weird all week," she said with her brows still folded.

Sam ignored her, looking around the room until he spotted Kaylee talking with Evan and another couple.

"She's the one, isn't she?"

"Who?" he asked, still focused on Kaylee, though she would be completely safe with Evan.

"Don't play dumb with me, old man. She's the one you've been waiting for."

He looked back at his friend, now standing near six feet in her heels and looking even more attractive than usual. But Sam was focused only on the truth in her words.

"I wasn't waiting for anyone."

"Yeah, you were. But maybe you just didn't realize it," she retorted. "Now stop daydreaming and find the mayor for your little chat."

Annoyed by her chastising, he quickly got back into character and walked the room. Kaylee had been correct; many of the other guests seemed overly interested in him, wanting to chat and find out everything they could about his Scottish peerage. Though neither he nor his parents had ever put much emphasis on it, Sam had been raised to respect the military history and highland traditions of Clan Mackenzie and Mackenzie of Seaforth. So he had plenty of irrelevant facts and authentic details to share. By halfway through the night, he was nauseated with himself. The smirks from Evan and Renee didn't help. The sooner he approached the mayor and got this mission done, the sooner he could drop the obnoxious posturing.

Lyle Gordon was an easy man to find in a crowd since his laugh was usually the loudest. His round shape and pink shiny skin suited the sound. Sam gradually made his way in that direction until the two men were adjacent to each other in separate conversations.

"Viscount Andri, right?" Gordon asked, and Sam turned to face him with a polite look on his face. "Thank you for joining us on this evening. It's a real honor and a surprising treat for many of the guests here tonight."

"Mayor Gordon, please just call me Sam. I keep telling everyone that the viscount title is a silly courtesy. Certainly not necessary so far away from home. Did you enjoy your dinner?"

"I did—it was very good."

"Good," Sam echoed, subtly steering the shorter man toward the side entrance to the rented hall they were in. He knew it led to a small vestibule, perfect for a very private conversation. "I wonder if I could have a word with you for a moment about some very private matters?"

"Sure. I'd be happy to help in any way possible," Gordon said.

Sam smiled down at him blandly and opened the exit door. Just as he ushered the mayor through, he did a quick scan of the room until his eyes quickly found Kaylee. She was talking to a tall, lean man whom he immediately recognized as Mark McMann. Surprised and a little alarmed, Sam looked around again and found that Evan was just a couple of people away from her and Renee was within line of sight. His shoulders relaxed slightly, and he followed Gordon into the small hallway to make his proposal, leaving the two other agents to manage any risk from McMann's unexpected presence.

Kaylee watched Sam lead the mayor toward an exit door and felt a bubble of excitement in her stomach. This was it, almost at the end of the line, she thought to herself.

"Mikayla? I thought that was you." She looked behind her to see Mark McMann approaching. "What are you doing here?"

They shook hands, and she put a big smile on her face.

"I'm here with a friend," she replied.

"Yes, that's right. A lord or count or something?"

"Something like that. Are you a member of the society?"

"Yes, just for the last few years. It's great for network and business contacts." She nodded and looked around, trying to locate either Renee or Evan. "Speaking of which, there's someone I'd like to introduce you to. A friend of mine who's always looking for great talent to join his team. I'm sure he'd like to discuss your experience."

"Oh, okay," Kaylee replied, swallowing through her nervousness. But their plan had been to continue socializing while Sam spoke to the mayor, so what harm could there be in meeting a referral from Mark? She walked with him across the hall until they reached a corner near the bathrooms.

"He was here a moment ago. Why don't you wait here and I'll try to find him?"

Kaylee nodded as he turned away, then sighed, hoping this detour wouldn't affect their plan.

In a blink of an eye, a big man was up behind her with a firm arm around her waist. He twisted her around and slapped his hand over her mouth before she even thought to scream, then shoved her through the door in front of them. His grip was so tight that she was quickly struggling to breathe.

"Quiet or I'll snap your neck right here," the man growled in her ear.

She put her efforts into cooperating and saving her energy. Her survival instincts were starting to come alive, and she hoped a passive approach would make him complacent in securing her. Quickly, he forced her through a service hallway behind the bathrooms, then out a heavy door to the outside. Kaylee felt panic rising again, knowing that her chances of surviving this dropped dramatically if he managed to get her away from the building.

The man easily took each of her wrists until they were both held tightly behind her back with one of his hands, and he slowly removed his hand from her mouth.

"Make one sound and I'll pull your arms out of their sockets. Do you understand?"

She nodded, grateful to have a full lungful of air.

He took out his phone and made a very short call. "I have her. Behind the hall."

"What do you want with me?" Kaylee asked the second he hung up, the device still in his hand.

"Shut up!" he snapped, pulling hard on her wrist, and she bit back a scream of pain.

"Don't pull my arm and I won't scream," she muttered against her better judgment.

"Oh, you're a mouthy one. Let's see how much lip you have when I get you alone."

Kaylee clenched her teeth to prevent any other comments. They waited there for another few minutes until she could feel him getting anxious. As subtly as possible, she looked around the area to find anything that would help her situation. There was nothing. It was a small side street that was dark and deserted on a Saturday night. She bit back a curse when a car came toward them from the left and stopped right in front with the driver side at the curb. The man used his hold behind her back to shove her toward the vehicle.

Kaylee panicked and started yelling. "No! Let go of me!"

He shoved his phone away and slapped a sweaty hand back over her mouth, blocking her nose. She struggled against his grip, then screamed against his palms in pain when he twisted her arms unnaturally.

"Next time, I'll break them."

Still, she resisted, kicking back at his shins, trying to stomp down on his foot with her tall heels. Nothing worked. Tears of frustration were pooling in her eyes. They were at the car door, and he pulled on the handle to open it. Then there was a loud bang behind them, and her attacker swung her around with him as he turned with alarm. Sam was running toward them with his gun drawn and pointed at his target behind her.

"Let her go," he demanded in a deadly calm voice.

Suddenly, a shot rang out from right next to Kaylee, and the bullet struck the wall beside them. The driver in the car had a gun. Sam ducked to take cover but couldn't fire back with her in the path. As scared and panicky as she felt, Kaylee could see it all so clearly, as though everything had slowed down. Her captor removed his hand from her mouth and reached into his jacket for his own weapon. Seizing the moment, Kaylee bent her head forward, then shoved it back fast and hard, praying she'd do some damage. The back of her head made contact against the bridge of his nose with a satisfying crack. He cried out in pain, letting go of her wrists.

Slightly dizzy from the painful impact, Kaylee

twisted away from him and out of his reach. There were several more shots fired. She covered her head and ran, not stopping to look at what was happening behind her. Sam would want her to get out of reach so she wasn't a pawn in the situation, so she planned to keep going until there was a secure spot to hide.

In a long, tight dress and very high sandals, she made it only a block down the street when she heard a car approaching. More shots fired toward Sam.

"Kaylee! Run!" Sam yelled.

She tried, really hard, but there was nowhere to go and the car was too fast. It halted to a stop just ahead of her; then the driver jumped out of the car. She skidded to a stop, and tried to evade his grasp. But he easily grabbed her brutally by the upper arm and punched her in the side of the head with a right hook. She crumpled like a deflated balloon and was out by the time he threw her in the backseat.

"Kaylee!" Sam screamed again, even though he knew she couldn't hear him.

Another bullet whizzed by him as the driver took a shot before driving away. Sam was running at breakneck speed, his arms and legs pumping hard in unison trying to defy the laws of physics to reach the car before it turned down the next street and out of sight. Desperate, he slowed enough to shoot at one of the tires, trying to slow it down. His aim was true. The tire popped. The car skidded but kept going. He took another shot just as it made a wild right turn. *Fuck!*

"I have eyes on the car, Sam," Raymond said into the earpiece. "They're on South Paca Street, approaching Redwood, but they're about to hit some traffic."

"I'm on it," Evan confirmed. "I'm at the Redwood exit of the building so I'll head them off."

"I'm right behind you," added Sam, still running at full speed, unhindered by his kilt. "I got one of their rear tires so that will slow them down. Renee, stay on McMann. Don't let him out of your sight."

"Got it," she confirmed.

"Evan, she's knocked out and in the back seat. One assailant, the driver. I took out the second guy by the back door."

"The Baltimore police are now on their way," added Raymond.

Finally, Sam reached the corner to the next street and had eyes on the car moving slowly in a line of traffic. For another minute or so, there was only the sound of heavy breathing as Sam and Evan sprinted to converge on the vehicle. The sounds of police sirens were now audible.

"I'm a few cars back," Evan advised, and Sam could now see him in front, gaining on the car. As though in unison, both agents veered to the left, moving off the sidewalk, through the traffic, until they were running along the median in the road. A line-up of drivers watched, open mouthed, as they passed with impressive speed and endurance. Many did a double take at Sam and his bare legs flashing beneath billowing pleats.

The driver holding Kaylee must have been spooked by either the approaching police cars or a glimpse of the men chasing him down. Sam watched in frustration as the vehicle squealed while doing a U-turn in the middle of the two-lane street, dangerously cutting off several cars going the other direction. Sam and Evan slowed their pace, measured the distance of the car now coming toward them, and took careful aim, very mindful of the crowded street. They had only seconds to make the right move, or there could be disastrous consequences. Sam noted every detail as the driver pointed his gun out the window and pulled the trigger.

Sam fired, very sure of his moving target, but, out of the corner of his eye, he saw Evan go down. Sam's shot had blown out a second tire. The getaway car swerved wildly and the driver tried to maintain control with only two functioning tires.

"Evan!" yelled Sam into the communication device, even as he was still running toward the car. "Evan!"

"I'm okay," came his response, finally. "It was a close one."

Sam didn't have time to be relieved. He watched as the vehicle swerved again to the right and climbed the curb until it rammed into a fire hydrant and finally stopped. Sam didn't stop running until he had eyes on the driver. The guy was now pinned behind the airbags, and had a gash on his forehead. He seemed disoriented until Sam approached the window, at which point he swung open the passenger door, catching Sam in the torso and throwing him off balance. The assailant was a big guy, a couple of inches shorter but almost equal in mass. He slid out of the car, just in time for Sam to grab his shirt and plant a straight jab into his mouth, then another. The guy bent forward in pain, then rammed his shoulder into Sam's stomach, plowing him backward with sheer power.

Sam stayed nimble on his feet so he wouldn't go down, then clasped both hands together and pounded them into the middle of the guy's back. It broke his hold, enough for Sam to snap a knee up under his chin. The big guy wobbled. Sam swung his elbow into his temple twice, and the thug fell to the ground, hitting the sidewalk with a thud.

Breathing heavy with exertion and relief, Sam stepped over the dead weight and ran back to the crashed car. Evan had caught up by then, and they were together when Sam opened the back door, desperate to believe she was now safe with minimal harm.

The back seat was empty, and his heart dropped to the floor.

CHAPTER 27

Kaylee's head was pounding and she felt sick. Slowly gaining consciousness, she knew pretty quickly that she was lying across the back seat of a car. She blinked with confusion, looking around and trying to figure out where she was. It hurt to turn her head, and her stomach lurched in protest, but she couldn't tell if the nausea was from the pain in her head or the wild swaying of the vehicle. Within another minute, Kaylee could remember what had happened.

Someone had grabbed her from the charity dinner, and her last memory was of Sam yelling her name.

Sam!

They had shot at him. Two men, several times. She looked around the confined space but saw only the head of the driver. The car swerved hard, throwing her prone body forward and back quickly. She reached out to brace herself, and realized that she wasn't restrained. Testing her limbs for any signs of injury, Kaylee became more and more aware of her surroundings.

She pushed herself up onto an elbow, very careful not to draw any attention. But then screamed when two gunshots popped loudly right near her. Right after that, there was another bang that sounded like an explosion and sent the car skidding to the side. The driver swore. Kaylee rolled forward on the seat until she was over the edge and sandwiched behind the two front seats. She was trying to push herself out when the driver swore again, even louder, and the car rammed hard into a solid object and jerked violently to a dramatic stop.

Kaylee must have screamed with her eyes squeezed tight, but she couldn't recall. Her next thought was that she was still alive. She took a breath, blinked, and listened. There were sirens, a hissing sound, and heavy breathing from the driver. Or was that her? Tentatively, she wiggled her right arm so that her hand was pressed to the floor of the car and slowly pushed herself up. Her shoulder burned right inside the socket. Inch by inch, she squeezed out from the space behind the front seats and rolled back onto the back bench, resting there for a few deep breaths.

The driver started pushing at the firm plastic airbag that had deployed and filled the space between his body and the steering wheel. Kaylee knew she had to get out of there now, before he got free and was able to resume his abduction. Still lying down, and hoping to remain unseen, she looked to the passenger-side rear door, reaching for the handle. Finally, she pulled on the metal, but the door didn't budge. It was locked. Desperate, she pulled again and gasped with relief when the latch released and the door opened. The driver's-side door opened just as Kaylee was crawling out of the car and onto the flooded pavement.

The car was wedged up on a fire hydrant, and the water was flowing steadily onto the street in a hard spray. The loud sound muffled everything else around her, adding to her confusion. The only thing she could think of was to run. She waited for a few seconds, trying to figure out where the driver was and if she could get away without being seen. The sirens were now almost louder than the gushing water. Kaylee squeezed her eyes tight and made a decision. Staying low with the body of the car to block her from view, she quickly crept away toward another car parked just after the collision site, then to the one after that, until she was sitting on its front bumper. She paused there, holding the bottom of her dress, ignoring the painful squeeze of her stiletto sandals.

"Kaylee?"

Sam? Was that his voice above the noisy commotion? Kaylee swallowed, looked around, then raised up just enough to look over the top of the car.

"Sam," she whispered.

He was standing in the middle of the street, gun in hand and looking around. The body of the driver was laid out on the ground behind him. She stood up and whimpered.

"Sam!" yelled Kaylee as she stepped out from between the two cars.

Kaylee started walking toward him in a slow,

painful gait just as three police cars pulled up around them with tires squealing. There were shouts, confusion, and guns drawn as everyone reacted to the situation. But she just kept walking as fast as her bruised feet would allow her. Sam put his gun away at his waist, shouted something, and started running toward her. Evan was there, yelling as he approached one of the officers, but all she could see was Sam until he was close enough to catch her.

"I got you," he told her with a thick burr, scooping her up into his arms and pulling her close to his chest.

Over the next hour, he hardly let go of her. Evan was very effective at de-escalating the immediate situation and calming the officers on site. He soon had the crime scene under control. A fire truck and ambulance arrived a short time later, and Kaylee was efficiently examined for any injuries. Her arms hurt and her head had a lump near the left temple where the driver had knocked her out. Sam and the paramedic wanted her taken to the local hospital, but she refused. Kaylee just wanted to go home.

At some point, Evan drove up to the scene in the truck they had driven from Alexandria to Baltimore earlier that day. Sam gently carried Kaylee into the back seat, and they drove away.

"Where are we going?" she asked, looking around. They had been driving for about ten minutes before she realized they weren't going back to the hotel just a few blocks from the accident. The painkillers she had been given were kicking in, and she was getting a little fuzzy around the edges.

"I'm taking you back to Alexandria," he told her.
"What about Renee?"

"She and Evan will stay here in Baltimore to help coordinate with the local police," he explained softly.

"But Evan's driving, isn't he?" she asked, maybe too quietly for Sam to hear.

The car stopped a few minutes later, and Kaylee looked around, recognizing the area.

"I used to live here," she said with confusion as Sam lifted her out of the truck. He might have responded, but she was slowly fading into a deep sleep.

At one point, about ten minutes later, she blinked a little, and looked around. Sam was holding her close to his side with her head resting on his chest. They were somehow up above the city, flying with the sun setting on the horizon. Her eyes fell again, and she marveled at the power of strong painkillers.

It was several hours before Kaylee woke again. She moaned against the pain in her head.

"Shhh," Sam soothed her.

She opened her eyes, and they were lying together in his bed. The room was dark.

"Do you want something to drink? More pain relievers?" he whispered.

"Please," she managed to mumble. "What happened? Is everyone okay?"

"Everything is fine. Go back to sleep—we'll talk in the morning," he suggested, pulling her close. "You did really well, lass."

The next time she woke up, it was bright outside

and Sam was gone. Kaylee rolled onto her back. His spot was no longer warm. She paused there for another minute, staring up at the ceiling and recalling the series of events from the evening before. Someone had grabbed her, attempted to take her away for God knew what reason. But why? And why now?

Other questions slowly filled her thoughts. What happened after Sam had taken her away? Who were those two men? What happened with the mayor and Sam's proposition? Kaylee slowly scooted her bum to the edge of the mattress and sat up. There was still a headache and soreness, but it wasn't horrible. Her mouth was dry and her stomach growled with hunger. There was a bottle of water on the side table, and she gratefully swallowed several mouthfuls.

Feeling a little wobbly, Kaylee went into Sam's bathroom to brush her teeth and wash her face. Looking in the mirror, she noticed what she was wearing for the first time. It was a blue T-shirt with a crest on the chest and the name MACKENZIE embroidered along the bottom. She was naked underneath.

In the large mirror above the sink, she looked at herself and acknowledged that she looked like a hot mess. There was a purple smudge on the side of her face, just above her left cheekbone. It was tender to the touch. Kaylee combed out her hair and put it up into a high ponytail. In the bedroom, she pulled on underwear and a pair of yoga pants, then went to find Sam.

He was sitting at the kitchen counter with Niko by his feet, and he stood up as she approached.

"What are you doing out of bed?" he demanded with disapproval.

"Hello to you too," she teased. His frown softened a bit as he bent down to kiss her softly, lingering for a couple of seconds to play gently with her lips.

"You should be resting," he continued when they parted.

She did feel really tired and still a little groggy.

"I'll rest out here," she conceded. He helped her over to the sofa in the living room until she was reclined back against the arm with a cushion nestled in her lower back.

"Is there anything to eat?" she asked. "I'm starving for some reason."

"That's a good sign. Anything in particular? Coffee also?"

"Yes, please." It smelled fantastic. "Maybe just toast."

He brought both over and placed the plate and cup on a coffee table before sitting down at the other end of the couch, lifting her feet into his lap.

"What time is it?" she asked while chewing on the warm, buttered bread.

"Almost one o'clock."

"What? I can't believe I slept that late."

"It's the medication. You were restless through the night," he explained.

She ate a few more bites, drank half of her coffee.

"So? Are you going to tell me what happened, or do I have to pry it out of you?" she finally demanded. "What happened with the mayor?"

He began massaging one of her feet by gently rubbing his thumbs over the balls. How had he known they were so tender?

"Nothing," he said simply.

"What do you mean? I saw you walk out of the room with him just like we had planned," she insisted, sitting up a little higher.

"Aye, I did. But he's one to chat a bit about nothing," he explained, shaking his head. "I was just introducing the topic when Renee said you had disappeared from the room."

"So you didn't tell him about the evidence we have?"

"No, I had to go find you, now didn't I?" he insisted making her feel a little ungrateful for his effort. "But it hardly matters now."

"Why not? Who were those men that grabbed me?" she asked.

"We've confirmed their identities, but they're just local, hired thugs," he explained. "The driver is known as Lucky, but his real name is Frank Pacini. He's a known associate to Nicolas Francesco. That's the guy who attacked you in the hotel."

He added the last detail when it was clear that she didn't recognize the name.

"But that doesn't make any sense. I thought he was sent because of the threats from Ross Construction and the bid in Paterson?" Kaylee questioned. "He said he was there to prove that they were serious."

"Well, there's definitely a connection. Lucas sent me a note just before you woke up to say he has an update for me," he explained. "Do you feel up to listening in?"

"Yes, I'm fine."

"Okay, I'll see if he's ready now to meet."

She lowered her feet and sat up straight, wincing only a little. Sam typed a few things into his phone, then turned on the giant panel-screen television mounted on the wall across from the couch. The image on the screen changed a few times until there was a clear view of a live video stream of a boardroom. Lucas Johnson appeared on the screen, and Kaylee realized they were connected to the Fortis headquarters.

"Are Evan and Renee back from Baltimore yet?" she asked while Sam configured the video connection a little more.

"They arrived this morning, and they're at the office now. They'll join the call also."

She let out a deep breath and waited as patiently as possible for some information.

"Sam?" Lucas asked, looking at them through the television as though they were in the same room.

"Aye, we can see you."

The door behind him opened as Evan and Renee walked into the room wearing their customary black cotton clothing. They flanked Lucas on either side.

"How are you feeling, Mikayla?" Evan asked with concern creasing his strong features.

"I'll be fine," she assured him, and he smiled.

"Okay, let's get started," Sam said. "Renee, can you fill us in on McMann?"

"Mark?" Kaylee interrupted with surprise. "Why?"

"Listen," Sam urged softly.

"He was standing on the opposite side of the room from the bathrooms when I noticed that Kaylee was gone," Renee explained. "He seemed normal, talked to a few people, and had a drink. But he checked his phone regularly. I also noticed that he stayed well away from the mayor over the next half hour or so."

"How long did he stay?" Sam asked.

"For a good hour after the crash. We could hear the sirens, but it was very faint, so few people noticed. But I'm pretty sure he did," she continued. "He checked his phone for a bit, then stopped. Nothing much after that."

"Renee and I followed him from the dinner to the outskirts of the city until he drove inside the Central Cement plant," added Evan. "There was a pretty strong security setup out front, so we stayed under cover until he came out about forty minutes later. Then he went home."

"Where is he now?" Sam asked. Kaylee listened quietly, still trying to understand where it was going.

"He was home until about ten-thirty this morning, but he's now at his office," Lucas explained as he pressed a couple of buttons on the tablet he held.

The video display divided, and a still picture appeared on the screen of Mark McMann in an underground garage. It was clearly from some kind of public surveillance equipment.

"So, what else do we know about him now that we didn't before?" Sam asked. "What was he doing there last night?"

"He's a member of the Scottish Society," Kaylee said. "That's what he told me when we spoke."

"What else did he tell you?" Sam asked softly.

"Nothing, really. He was more surprised to see me there," she recalled. "Then he said he wanted me to meet someone about a job."

As she said the words out loud, it became very obvious that Mark McMann had set her up for the abduction. She had willingly followed him to the exact spot where that animal could grab her. It was likely the stress that had followed and the powerful pain medication that had prevented her from connecting the dots sooner.

"What else?" Sam urged.

"Nothing that I can think of," Kaylee admitted.

"Well, we managed to find plenty of interesting things about McMann," Lucas declared. "Raymond and I did a little fact-checking last night after Evan's update to us. The company he works for now, Quinten Laboratories, describes itself as a research and development company that develops and tests new uses for minerals and other ground materials. What they don't advertise is that they have only four clients for these new discoveries. All four companies are cement manufacturers across the eastern seaboard."

Lucas put up four pictures, with Central Cement being the first.

"It appears that Quinten is a new-age racketeering operation," he explained. "They get federal government funding for independent industrial research. That research discovers that new forms of cement products are better. These four companies are the only manufacturers of the new and better products, which they sell back to the government. What's even better is that all four cement manufacturers are owned by the same man, Patrick O'Toole."

His image went up on the screen, showing a small man in his early sixties with wrinkled ivory skin, pale blue eyes, and a small patch of gray hair.

"If you look deep enough, it turns out that Patrick O'Toole also owns Quinten Laboratories."

"I recognize him," Sam stated suddenly. "I've seen a photo of him standing with Kaylee and her mother about three years ago."

"Where?" asked Kaylee, looking hard at the professional headshot, trying to remember the man.

"It was a charity event of some sort," Sam explained. "The picture was in the paper.

"Interesting," Evan mumbled.

"That's just the beginning, my friends," Lucas replied. "What is one of the biggest uses for cement in the United States?"

"Construction," Kaylee answered, sitting up straighter.

"You got it," confirmed Lucas.

"So Mark McMann leaves the newspaper business

to take an executive job in what turns out to be a major supplier to construction sites," Sam surmised.

"Seemed obvious that something was up, and I had Raymond go through all the data we had collected on Jason Holt and George Clement, then all the information on the Antonoli assignment. We added McMann to the mix, and there was one common denominator, Nate Battleford."

The picture of the now-dead Groveland employee came up.

"Battleford is the only one who communicated with Holt during the bribe at the *Baltimore Journal*. He worked for Fleming at Groveland for over six years, and he was taken down at the Ross building site."

There was now a map of pictures displayed on the screen with process flow arrows to highlight the connections.

"How does that connect McMann to anything other than firing Holt four years ago?" Kaylee asked.

"We have Sam to thank for that. Battleford's SIM card was a wealth of information once we knew what we were looking for," Lucas explained. "We already knew he emailed Holt to arrange the bribe. We now know that he also communicated directly with McMann just before McMann left the paper and got the job at Quinten."

"He's a fixer," Evan stated.

"It looks that way," Lucas confirmed. "Battleford had a pretty impressive list of contacts for various means, including our new friend Lucky. No surprise since the guy who attacked Kaylee was sent by Lucky from Baltimore. But this time, Lucky was working for McMann directly."

"Why did he suggest that the mayor was responsible for bribing Holt, and then have me grabbed by those goons?" Kaylee asked.

"We won't know for sure until we talk to him. But I suspect he lied when you asked about Holt in your meeting, then saw you sitting at the mayor's table at the charity dinner just a week later and panicked," Renee guessed. "He must have had Lucky's contact information from other situations."

"But who did Battleford work for? Who was pulling his strings?" Sam asked. "I don't think it was Fleming. If he was telling the truth, Fleming had nothing to do with Holt's bribe. So who did?"

"Like I said, all roads lead to Battleford," Lucas said as a final picture reappeared at the top of the image map. "Raymond found several direct communications between Patrick O'Toole and our fixer over the last five years. And the cherry on top? O'Toole is the chairman of the board for Clement Media."

CHAPTER 28

Sam managed to hold Kaylee back from seeing her parents for a full day. But by Monday evening, her patience was all gone. He was either going to have to drive her to their house in McLean or there was an Uber driver only five minutes away. She had checked.

They arrived at the Clement home at a few minutes to seven o'clock. He looked over at her as they walked up the front steps. She seemed nervous and excited, but also worried, and Sam was pretty certain why. For months, all her efforts had been centered on saving her father from some unknown threat that had changed him for the worse. Now that she'd accomplished that goal, what if it was too late to go back?

The housekeeper greeted them with the same warm welcome, and they found George and Elaine eating dinner at the table with another woman. Sam recognized the guest right away.

"Mikayla! Sweetheart, how are you?" asked Cecile DaCosta as she jumped up from her chair. It was clear where her son Evan got some of his strong features. The two women hugged, and Sam could easily see the affection between them.

"Hi, Miss Cece. You look great!" Kaylee said with a bright grin.

"Well, I do try." Cecile then looked up at Sam with recognition. "Evan's friend, right?"

"Hi, Mrs. DaCosta. It's nice to see you again."

"How are you, young man? The last time I saw you was at Santos's funeral. You gave me that beautiful pot of orchids," she remembered, tapping him on the cheek. "They lasted for months and all my friends were so jealous."

Cecile gave Elaine Clement a knowing look, and Elaine rolled her eyes.

Sam grinned roguishly. "I'm glad you liked them. Orchids are my favorite."

"Now, I have to get going," Cecile told everyone. "Talk to you tomorrow, Elaine."

After she left the room, Kaylee kissed her mom and dad. They both said friendly hellos to Sam.

"What was so urgent that you had to see us tonight, Mikayla? Is everything okay?" Elaine asked.

Kaylee looked up at Sam, and he gave her a small smile of encouragement.

"I have something really important to tell you," she began, sitting in the chair next to her mom. "But now that I'm here, I don't even know where to begin."

"Baby," her mom said in a patient tone. "If you're pregnant, just come out and tell us."

Kaylee shook her head and let out a small laugh.

She looked up at Sam, embarrassed. Sam shrugged, casually. The idea was not that upsetting.

"No, Mom, I'm not pregnant," she confirmed. "It's about New York and what I've been working on for the last year."

Kaylee must have been practicing the story because she gave George and Elaine a succinct summary about Nate Battleford and Anthony Fleming running Ross Construction and Groveland Development, how Battleford had bribed Jason Holt then likely had him killed, then been involved with Mark McMann's new job at Quinten Laboratories. But she was clearly working her way up to the rest of the story, likely worried about her dad's reaction.

"Kaylee, what were you thinking? It was reckless and stupid to put yourself in that kind of danger!" Elaine yelled. "I understand your need to learn the truth, but no story is worth that kind of risk."

"I didn't do it for a story, Mom," Kaylee finally said.

"Then why? I don't understand," insisted her mother with a hand over her forehead.

"She did it because of me and Clement Media," George acknowledged, then knocked back the two fingers of scotch at the bottom of his glass.

"What?" Elaine demanded, looking between her husband and her daughter.

"Dad?" Kaylee whispered as her eyes locked with her father's, noting his calm resolve and pained awareness. "You know about Patrick O'Toole?"

She sat back in her chair, and Sam pressed a comforting hand on her shoulder.

"I've known for a long time," confirmed George. His face had fallen and looked very tired.

"What about Patrick, George?" Elaine asked. "I don't understand any of this!"

"Tell us, Dad. Please!" pleaded Kaylee. "It's time."

"Patrick and I have known each other for years. We started up a small magazine back in the day, as partners. We were still in college. But Patrick didn't see the potential and we had different ideas about how we should move forward. So, after college, he went to work in the cement business and let me run the paper. The more I expanded and increased profits, the less he was willing to take a buy-out for his share. Finally, he was willing to negotiate. He had an investment he wanted to make. So we made a fair deal, but he kept five-percent ownership and the role of chairman of the board."

"I know all that, George," Elaine reminded him. "We talked about it at the time."

"That part was fine, Elaine. And we worked well together for some time," George admitted. "Until I discovered he had set up companies like Quinten. Companies that were supposed to be independent researchers. But the whole purpose was to convince the government and other builders that newer cement products were better. And since Patrick's cement companies made this superior type of cement or concrete, he'd win more contracts than his competitor and at higher costs."

"I don't understand. If he's better, what's the problem?" Elaine asked, looking at the others.

"Mom, it's like your doctor telling you that you need a specific kind of medicine or you'll get sick,"

Kaylee explained using an analogy. "You trust your doctor so you buy the medicine from the pharmaceutical company that makes it. But the pharmaceutical company pays the doctor to tell everyone they'll get sick. They're manipulating the marketplace to create a demand for something only they can provide. It's very deceptive or, in some cases, illegal."

"How long have you known about this, Mr. Clement?" Sam asked.

"About twelve years. I didn't approve, but I didn't think it concerned me," he reflected. "Patrick knew how I felt and we didn't talk about it. Until a reporter from one of my papers questioned Patrick openly about his affiliation with one of these research companies and Patrick asked me to make sure the story never went to print. It seemed harmless. The business was much smaller then, and I couldn't afford to make any enemies. Patrick said it was win-win since I was protecting my own reputation. So I did it. Maybe he was right."

George paused and looked down into his empty glass as though he wished there were more in there to drink.

"Patrick never let me forget it, but he never asked again. He didn't need to since he had become really good at greasing all the right wheels."

"Until Kaylee's story about spending at city hall got killed," Sam concluded.

George nodded. "I knew it was him behind it because it had Patrick's approach written all over it, even if he was too big to get his hands dirty anymore. I thought firing Jason Holt would fix the problem, but a few days later, Patrick came to see me. He knew that you were the one who wanted to write the story, Mikayla, under your pen name."

"Oh, Dad," Kaylee gasped, covering her mouth.

"So, basically, he expected me to just stand back and let him use my company to further his interests. Of course, I refused and he threatened to destroy me if I didn't cooperate. I threatened to go to the police with everything I knew about his operation. But I knew he had no limits and I couldn't take the risk that he would hurt my family."

"What did you do, George?" asked Elaine. Her eyes were filled with shock and sorrow, but she grabbed her husband's hand tightly in hers.

"I made a deal with him. I wouldn't go to the police if he didn't use my papers for his corrupt practices."

"But you also stepped down from the CEO role at that time, Mr. Clement. Was that part of the deal?" Sam asked.

"No, I made that decision on my own," he whispered, still looking down. "I started that first magazine as a voice for the truth, and I built a whole media business based on that. How could I continue to run it if I was complicit in criminal activities and cover-ups? I couldn't do that on top of everything else. So I stepped down. But I stayed on the board because I wanted Patrick to know I was watching him. I might not be CEO, but Clement Media still had my name on the door. I was not going to let it all go to shit."

The room was quiet for a minute or so after his last statement. Sam felt sorry for the older man, but he was more concerned about Kaylee. She had pursued this whole thing to save her father from some unknown coercive wrongdoer. And now she was seeing that he didn't need saving, except from his own conscience.

"Dad, we think Jason Holt told Mark McMann everything he knew about the bribe he'd been offered, and then McMann told Patrick O'Toole. Is that what happened?" Kaylee asked. It was the one thing she and Fortis had not yet been able to confirm.

George nodded as he struggled with his emotions.

"Why? Mark had worked with you for years. Why would he do that?" she asked.

"Yes, Mark and I have known each other for a long time," George agreed. "He started as an eager reporter, always ready to follow a good story. And he was the one who interviewed Patrick about his relationship with research and development companies."

"It was Mark's story that you buried," Kaylee whispered.

"He didn't know why at first, but I think he figured it out over time. As Patrick's reach expanded, so did his criminal activities, and I suspect Mark tracked it all," George speculated. "I think I tried to make up for it over the years, giving Mark bigger positions in the company. But I guess the situation with Jason presented an opportunity, and he took advantage of it."

"Do you know why he went to O'Toole with what he knew about Holt and Kaylee? Why not Anthony Fleming? Those contracts that Kaylee was asking about were billed by Groveland, not any of the cement companies that O'Toole owns," Sam asked.

George finally looked up.

"Because Mark knew that Patrick also owned Groveland."

Sam rocked back on his heels. It was the last piece of information that they needed to round up everyone responsible in this criminal enterprise and close out the mission.

"What happens now?" Elaine finally asked after a deep breath. "Kaylee, you said all those other people at those building companies are now under investigation. Will that include Patrick and Mark McMann?"

"It depends on what we can prove, Mom," Kaylee explained. "These people are very good at burying their activities under layers of fake companies and aliases. So, I don't really know."

"The good news is that Fortis has a pretty big collection of data on all of them. We just didn't know exactly how to put it all together. But with the information you've just provided, George, we do now," Sam added. "We've seen bigger criminals than Patrick O'Toole fall from much higher positions. Are you willing to go on record with what you've told us?"

"Yes, I am."

"Is George in trouble, here?" Elaine finally asked, stammering to get the words out.

"I don't think so, Mom," Kaylee tried to assure her, but then looked up at Sam for further assessment.

"I don't think so either," Sam agreed. "There's

no hiding that O'Toole was the chairman of the board for Clement, but I think the State Department and FBI will be much more interested in what you know than anything you may have done. And considering the threats that were made to Kaylee recently, no one would fault your actions."

George nodded. "I knew this day would come eventually. The truth always comes out. That's why I stepped down as CEO. That would have been the worst consequence to my actions. So as long as my family was safe from harm, it was worth the sacrifice, and I did it on my own terms."

Kaylee stood up and walked over to her dad, sitting in his lap like a little girl. Sam's stomach clenched at the compassion and understanding in her eyes.

"I'm sorry, Dad," she whispered, hugging him close.

"I'm the one who's sorry, baby girl. I will forever regret the danger you were in because of my cowardice."

Sam could tell that the family needed some time alone. He quietly slipped away from them, to the kitchen, where he called Evan to provide an update on what he had just learned. "I want the information against Patrick O'Toole to be as airtight as possible. Clement is willing to tell the authorities what he knows, so let's see if McMann will do the same."

Kaylee stayed with her parents for another thirty minutes or so; then she and Sam returned to his house. She was quiet during the drive, and Sam didn't want to interrupt her thoughts. Her father's story was a lot to absorb on top of everything else they had already discovered. She might not be ready to talk about it yet, but Sam thought she seemed more at peace.

It was after ten o'clock when they walked into his place. Niko ran up to the door, ready for his walk as always, and they went together around the block. Still, Kaylee did not talk, and her silence was starting to feel like a barrier between them.

In his bedroom, Sam sat on the edge of his bed and listened to her freshen up in the bathroom. *Maybe your usefulness is gone?* It was an ugly, insecure thought, and Sam didn't really believe it. Yes, she had been manipulative and deceitful with him in the beginning, but her reasons had been clear. But once that thought had been whispered by his inside voice, it became harder and harder to blindly dismiss.

"I know how difficult that must have been for you, Kaylee," he stated when she came back into the bedroom wearing his favorite CLAN MACKENZIE T-shirt. "Do you want to talk about it?"

She was standing still in the middle of the room, just out of his reach, rubbing the back of her hand over her eyes. Then her shoulders were shaking as her back curved forward in pain. The soft, whispering sobs followed. He immediately went to her and pulled her up against his chest. He could feel her pain deep in the pit of his stomach, and it hurt. Sam knew that if he could absorb it all for her, he would. He would do anything for her.

"Don't cry, lass," he pled, trying to swallow the giant knot growing in his throat.

He continued to hold her tight, running soothing caresses down her back until the worst seemed to be over. She wiped her face, but wouldn't look into his eyes. Sam knew she needed patience and understanding. He coaxed her into bed and under the covers, and pulled her close after turning out the lights. She sighed deeply while wrapping her legs over his and burying her face against his chest. He stroked her arm lightly until they fell asleep.

Kaylee slept in on Tuesday morning, and Sam decided to work from the house in case she needed anything. He was sitting in the living room on a call when she came out of the bedroom. She paused when she saw him as though surprised, and her professional clothing suggested she had somewhere to go.

Sam approached her in the kitchen when his call ended. She was making toast and a fresh pot of coffee.

"Did you sleep well?" he asked politely, leaning casually against the counter across from her.

"Too well, I guess," she replied. "You should have woken me."

"No harm done. Unless you have somewhere you need to be." His stomach tingled in warning.

She turned so her back was to him and poured a cup of coffee.

"I do, actually. I'm going back to New York today."

CHAPTER 29

He shouldn't have been surprised. Everything that Sam knew about Mikayla Stone-Clement suggested this moment was inevitable. Yet, he stood there without a plan for how to deal with it.

Kaylee sipped her black coffee before turning to look back at him squarely.

"Why?" he asked. There was no point in beating around the bush. He had nothing to lose.

"I have some things for the building company that I need to do in person," she explained.

"I mean why today? Why so quickly?" he insisted.

His tone was calm and even, despite the turmoil inside him. But it wasn't anger, just sharp disappointment.

"Today is as good a day as any," she said. "Things with my dad are out in the open, and there's nothing more I can do about it. Whatever happens now is completely out of my control, and that's fine. But, I can't live in limbo, living with no objective or purpose. So, I had to make some decisions. I have to move on."

She sounded firm in her stance, without any room for discussion. Like her decision had been made and he was not part of it.

"Move on from what exactly, Kaylee?"

"From everything," she said simply. "Everything about my life in the last four years has been about living up to my obligations and supporting my family. I'm not complaining about it. It hasn't been a hardship or anything. It gave me a clear purpose. But now I don't have to do it anymore. There are no expectations from anyone that should dictate how I live my life. That was exciting, until I realized I have no idea who I am or what I really want to do with my life going forward. But I have to figure it out. So I had to draw a line in the sand. Pick a day when my life stops being all about my family and starts being more about me again. That day is today."

"Does that mean that you're moving on from us, also?" he asked, needing to have complete clarity.

"I don't know how to answer that, Sam. I don't even know what 'us' is," she admitted.

"You could have asked. We could have talked about it," he retorted. "But you've gone off and made your decisions on your own."

Kaylee was about to respond but paused and looked away. Her defiant stance softened a bit.

"Then I'm asking now," she told him. "But I don't think you have any answers for me."

"You don't know that," Sam countered.

"I know that you don't trust me."

He couldn't respond truthfully because he didn't know what to say.

"I'm not leaving you, Sam. I'm leaving the situation," she explained. "I think this 'us' might be a part of the life I created to help my father. I'm not sure it can work once I move on."

"So I've served my purpose, then? Played my part in your scheme, and now you have no further use for me?"

She took a deep breath.

"Yes, I think that's the truth. But not because I see it that way, but because you do."

It took a moment for him to step back from his hurt and see what she was saying.

"I don't know what you want me to say, Sam. I know I created this situation between us. I accepted that a long time ago," Kaylee continued. "But, I've spent so much time believing that if we had met in a different time and place, it would have worked. You would be the man that I could share everything with. Life, children, love. I had a bar to measure every other man on, and none ever came close. So now that I'm reevaluating everything, I wonder if this time together might be about closing that chapter."

It took Sam some time after she had spoken to really understand her words. It was about that time in between now and when they had first met. A time that he preferred not to think about and had never considered discussing with Kaylee.

"Renee told me I was waiting for you," he told her. "I think she was right."

"See? We just needed to play it out. Now we can both move on without imagining some perfect relationship that really isn't realistic."

"Nay, that's not what I meant," countered Sam. "Some of what you said is true, for me also. I did find it hard to forget you, but I thought it was because you weren't real. The way I felt around you should not be possible so fast. That connection is supposed to build slowly over time, right? Love doesn't club you over the head one day. So, you could not be real."

Kaylee listened quietly, with her arms wrapped around her waist. Her eyes were sad, but she stood tall, as though ready for the truth, whatever it was.

"I always knew that if I saw you again, I would know for sure," Sam admitted. "But I didn't know which would be worse, finding out that love cannot happen that fast, or that it can. So I've been waiting to find out."

"What are you saying?" she asked.

He walked forward to stand in front of her, close enough to touch her, but he didn't.

"I'm saying you're right, I needed to close that chapter, also," he explained "You're real, Kaylee. More real than I ever imagined, and I knew it the moment I saw you again. It wasn't you that I didn't trust—it was my feelings. I just needed a little time to accept that I love you and I don't suspect it's going to change."

Kaylee gasped in surprise, and her eyes filled up. Sam wanted badly to pull her close and savor this moment, but there was so much still unsaid between them and he needed to know exactly where he stood.

"So when you get on that plane today, are you leaving me also?" he asked.

She shook her head, laughing a little.

"No, never. I've tried that once, and it didn't work out too well," she teased.

"For me either. So let's not do it again, lass."

Finally, he wrapped his arms around her body pulling her tight against him.

"I love you so much, Sam," she whispered into his ear. He swallowed around the large lump in his throat.

"You said you had to make decisions about your life," Sam finally stated. "You don't have to make them alone anymore. We can make them together."

He felt her sigh. "Well, the easy one is where to live. I want to come home, back to Virginia."

"That's a good start. I approve," he declared.

"The work thing is a little trickier, now that I've developed some new skills. There are lots of options to choose from." She pulled back to smile up at him, flashing her dimples. "I'm thinking professional ninja or join the CIA. Or maybe become a ninja-spy? Then I don't have to choose, right?"

Sam just chuckled and squeezed her tighter.

EPILOGUE

"I thought Evan and Nia were stopping by," Lucas said to Sam. It was Saturday afternoon over three weeks later, and the two men were standing by the barbecue in Sam's backyard keeping an eye on the baby-back ribs that were slowly grilling to tender perfection.

"Yeah, they should be here any minute," Sam confirmed. "Evan says he has some news."

"About what, a new case?"

"He didn't say," Sam replied as he carefully turned each slab of pork, testing the readiness of the meat.

"Things seem cool between you guys, now," Lucas added. "Right?"

Sam looked over at Kaylee, sitting by the pool talking to Lucas's girlfriend, Alex Cotts. Niko sat serenely in her lap, sleeping.

"Yeah, we're all good."

The friends were silent for a few minutes, drinking cold beer and listening to the sounds of summer along the Potomac River.

"Any updates on the case against Patrick O'Toole?" Lucas eventually asked.

Sam nodded. "I spoke to the head of the FBI investigation late yesterday."

He paused when Niko barked sharply, now with his head lifted and ears perked in alert. The small terrier then jumped off Kaylee's lap and ran to the back door of the house. A few moments later, Evan and Nia James stepped out into the backyard, holding hands. They said hello to the two other women. Then Evan left Nia with her new girlfriends to join his partners by the grill.

"Sam has a new update from the FBI on O'Toole," Lucas explained, while handing Evan an icy-cold bottle of beer from the cooler nearby.

"What are they saying?" Evan asked.

"We'd given them plenty of evidence that O'Toole was the head of an operation that was involved in everything from fraud to tax evasion to extortion," Sam reminded them. "Once George Clement told the feds everything he knew about O'Toole's business operations over the years, Anthony Fleming and Mark McMann quickly became very helpful, trading information for immunity on the most serious charges. But yesterday they finally got what they need to issue a warrant for O'Toole's arrest on two counts of murder."

"Really?" Evan exclaimed. "For Jason Holt? And who else?"

"Yup, Holt and Nate Battleford," confirmed Sam.

"What's the evidence?" asked Lucas. "Both Fleming and McMann were adamant that if Holt had in fact been murdered, they knew nothing about it."

"Turns out they were telling the truth. It was Nigel Dobson that finally talked," Sam told them, then clarified when both men looked unfamiliar with the name. "Dobson was the guy that shot Battleford at the Ross construction site, the former New Jersey State police detective. His former police chief finally gave the feds access to the archived data from Dobson's computer before he left the force, and they found an email exchange with Patrick O'Toole about a problem that needed to be taken care of in Maryland. It was dated one week before Holt died in the car explosion.

"That was enough to get Dobson to finally talk, and he stated on record that O'Toole hired him directly to take out Holt, then later to keep an eye on Battleford and eliminate him as a risk if needed."

The three friends were silent in thought for several seconds.

"What about George?" Evan finally asked. "I spoke to him last week, and he seemed to be doing okay. Looked more relaxed than I'd seen him in years."

"The worst is over for him," Sam confirmed. "The FBI and State Department have been happy with his cooperation and transparency. There's enough evidence to support his claim that O'Toole had threatened his family. I also provided our case files on the annual Clement Media security reviews that prove George was diligent about ensuring his papers weren't used to bury stories about the various construction, cement, and research companies under the O'Toole Empire."

"Kaylee must be relieved," Lucas said.

Sam nodded with agreement as they all looked over at the three women, now sitting together at an outdoor dining table and drinking white wine. Suddenly, Alex screamed with surprise, and gripped Nia's hand to look more closely at one of her fingers. The women then jumped up from their seats, hugging and kissing each other on the cheek with shouts of congratulations.

Lucas and Sam looked at each other with raised eyebrows, then over to Evan, who was looking at Nia with intense pride and adoration.

"Is there something you want to tell us, Ice?" Lucas finally asked.

"Nia and I are getting married," he confirmed, finally looking back at his best friends, beaming with a grin from ear to ear.

"That's fantastic!" shouted Lucas, slapping Evan on his back, enthusiastically.

"Well done, mate," Sam added with an approving smile.

"Have you set a date?" added Lucas.

"Not specifically, but it will be soon. We're thinking early fall," Evan explained while they looked back at the women they loved, who were chatting excitedly. "Nia wants to do something small, maybe a destination wedding."

"Any idea where?" Sam inquired.

"Not specifically. We talked about somewhere in Europe, maybe at a villa in Italy or Portugal," Evan explained.

"How about Scotland, at Seaforth Manor?" Lucas and Evan looked at Sam, and he shrugged. "My mum does weddings all the time and I'm sure she'd take care of everything, even on short notice."

"That's not a bad idea," Evan replied as they turned to watch the three women walk toward them, all smart, beautiful, and strong in their own unique ways. "It looks like we're going to Scotland."

Don't miss these other books in the Fortis series!

Turn the page for an excerpt from

Hard as Ice

On sale now wherever books and ebooks are sold!

CHAPTER 1

"How's your first assignment so far, Ice?"

The teasing question came through the video connection from one of the large-panel screen monitors set up around the room. It was from Lucas Johnson, his friend and business partner.

"Well, it's been twenty hours and I haven't been shot yet," Evan replied. "But it's still early."

Lucas laughed.

"Looks like you'll have to get used to the slower pace of civilian work. You might not be under fire for a few days in."

Evan shifted his stance and felt the pull of tight scar tissue in his thigh. The bullet wound was a souvenir from his final CIA mission in Azerbaijan eight months ago. It had been a long road to recovery, including an early retirement from government service. Now, he was a managing partner with Fortis, a full-solution security firm, along with his best friend, Lucas Johnson, and their third partner, Sam Mackenzie. They had a team of twenty-two specialized field agents, technicians, and operations analysts with experience from all branches of elite government service.

As Lucas mentioned, this Boston assignment was Evan's first with Fortis. He was leading a team of three agents on the ground to solve a multimillion-dollar jewelry heist, and recover the assets within a matter of weeks.

"I'll do my best not to get bored," Evan retorted with a hint of a smile.

"Looks like you guys are set up there?"

"Yeah. The additional surveillance is up and running through the building," Evan confirmed. "Michael and Raymond are on-site since early this morning to start the investigation," Evan replied, referring to two of the Fortis agents working on the ground for the mission.

Lucas nodded. His high-definition screen was so sharp, he could have been standing right next to Evan instead of over five hundred miles away in Virginia.

"Yup, we have the images from the Worthington building coming through here, now. When are you going in?" asked Lucas.

Evan checked the time. It was eleven forty-five in the morning. According to their client, Edward Worthington, the key subject usually took lunch at twelve-thirty each day, and had no appointments in her calendar for that afternoon.

"I'm headed to the auction house in a few minutes. I should make first contact before one o'clock," he confirmed.

"Okay. I've assigned two of our analysts here to do the preliminary research on the other employees.

I've sent you what we have so far on James," Lucas explained.

"Got it. I'll review on my cell phone, and give you an update later."

They ended the video call. Evan did a final check on the surveillance equipment. He and his team were based in two hotel suites in downtown Boston, several blocks from their client's offices. One suite served as Evan's temporary residence while in the city as part of his cover, and his three agents were staying in the connected room. In there, two powerful six-core CPUs were connected to four forty-two-inch LED flat-screen monitors set up around the living room, creating a control center. Evan looked around the various live feeds, all showing a different view of the Worthington business offices, the large art gallery in the front, and the warehouse in the back. It was a quiet day, with only four employees on the corporate floor, and three in the gallery and warehouse. His gaze landed on the image of Nia James, his target subject, as she sat behind her office desk reviewing several documents. He watched her for a few moments, until his cell phone rang.

"Yeah," he answered briskly, noting it was his third agent, Tony Donellio, assigned to local reconnaissance.

"Hey, Ice, I'm at her apartment." Evan clenched his jaw at the nickname. It was a remnant from his time in the CIA. Though he had left the agency, the Fortis team insisted on using it. That was mostly because Lucas chose to forget his real name.

"Good, do a full search and wire the place up so

we have eyes throughout. Then, you're searching the security guard's place, right?" Evan asked.

"Yeah," confirmed Tony. "His shift at Worthington doesn't start until six tonight, but our intel says he's usually at the gym by three o'clock in the afternoon. I'll be there by about one-thirty to have a look around the area."

"Good. He's the weak link. With nothing of use captured on the Worthington surveillance videos, and no signs of forced entry, there's no way he wasn't involved in the heist. Raymond and Michael are interviewing him tomorrow, but we need to find something on him to use as leverage. I'll meet you back at control later this afternoon."

"Got it," confirmed Tony.

Evan hung up and checked the time again. With one more hard glance at the subject, he checked the clip of his Glock and slid it smoothly in the small belt holster secured against the right side of his back. He added his suit jacket before leaving the hotel room.

In the lobby, the concierge gave him a friendly nod.

"How are you doing, Mr. DaCosta?" asked the middle-aged man, well dressed in a tailored suit.

"I'm good, Carlos. How are you?" Evan replied smoothly.

"Very good, sir. Shall I get your car for you?"

"Please."

Carlos waived at one of the valet attendants to request Evan's car to be brought around.

Worthington was an easy enough walk into the center of downtown, but Evan's cover required the image of wealth and prestige, and that didn't include a brisk walk in balmy May weather. His leased car, a sleek black Bentley, was brought to the front door within a few moments, and Evan smoothly made his way through the streets of Boston.

The Worthington Gallery and Auction House was a small chain owned by Edward Worthington. It had expanded from a single storefront operation based in Connecticut into a national player in the world of arts, jewelry, and estate auctioning over the last twenty years. They now had five locations across the country, a solid reputation, record sales, and plans to expand into Europe. All of that was now in jeopardy. Two nights ago, their Boston office was robbed in a meticulously executed jewelry heist. The thieves managed to enter the warehouse undetected and break into a digital safe, all while bypassing the state-of-the-art surveillance and security system.

The stolen jewelry included a white diamond necklace with a rare 13.16 carat pear-shaped red diamond in the center, known as the Crimson Amazon. The piece was scheduled to be exhibited around the world prior to the auction at the end of August. According to appraisals and expert opinion, that necklace alone should fetch over twenty-five million dollars. Along with a broader collection of rare and high-end jewelry pieces, the summer event was now anticipated to be one of the highest-value auctions in years, certainly the biggest in Worthington's history. It would put the company solidly on the map as a major North American player.

Within twelve hours of discovering the robbery,

Edward Worthington hired Fortis. Evan and his
team of highly trained protection and asset recovery specialists now had under six weeks to find the
thieves and recover the jewels intact. As with most
of Fortis's assignments, confidentiality and discre-
tion were critical. If Worthington's clients or
anyone in the industry discovered this massive
breach in security, the auction house would be
ruined. Which meant police involvement was not
the preferred option at this stage. Fortis had the
skills and resources in security, surveillance, inves-
tigations, and threat neutralization to quickly
and stealthily deliver services to their high-end
clients, all without the bureaucratic restrictions of
law enforcement.

Evan arrived at the Worthington offices at a few
minutes to one o'clock. He parked on the street in
a spot where he could see the storefront. With a
few moments to spare, he took out his phone to
review the file Lucas had sent. Most of it was old
information provided by the client in their initial
meeting. It confirmed that other than the owner,
only one employee knew when the Crimson Amazon
necklace had been delivered, and only one had the
combination to the safe: Nia James, the managing
director. The digital copy of her employee identification photo showed a young woman with a rectan-
gular face and sculpted cheekbones. Her hair was
pulled back into a sleek ponytail, accentuating the
feline angle of her dark eyes.

Evan scrolled through the other documents to
see if there was anything new or revealing about
her. Twenty-six years old, valid driver's license, no

passport. Born and raised in Detroit, moved to Boston eight years ago to attend college as a part-time student. Worked as a waitress, then graduated four years ago with a B.A. in Business. Senior sales manager at a jewelry store before being hired at Worthington eleven months ago. Clean criminal record, except for a sealed juvenile file.

A tire squeal and a honked horn caught Evan's attention. He looked up to assess the situation and it was easy to see the distraction to drivers nearby. The object of his surveillance was crossing the street at the intersection in front of his car. Nia James walked with a straight, proud posture, her chin held high with bold confidence. She wore a dark skirt-suit, tailored to fit her lithe body like a fine wool wrap. Her lean legs were coppery brown, naked and elongated by high-heeled shoes in a glossy burgundy leather. Their extravagant cost was evident in the telltale red soles. Half her face was covered with oversize sunglasses and her lips were coated in a rich ruby color that accentuated their shapely fullness.

The lunchtime traffic was pretty busy, yet cars slowed as the men driving them did double takes, or stared openly. Even guys walking nearby turned to appreciate the view of her figure, both coming and going. Evan would have found the show amusing, except it uncovered a complication he hadn't anticipated. Nia James was far more attractive in real life than her identification photos suggested. She walked with a smooth, sexy sway that told him she was very aware of her effect on men and was comfortable working it.

If his instincts were correct, and they usually were, he would have to adjust their plan accordingly.

Evan opened the driver's door to the black Bentley convertible just as she passed in front. He slowly unfurled his tall frame to exit the car, fully aware of the impression he made: rich, powerful, young. It was an image designed to capture the attention of an opportunist, and one he's used successfully many times as a covert operative. And like most women, Nia James responded. It was subtle, only with a slight tilt of her head in his direction, but it was enough. First goal accomplished.

She entered the premises, and Evan was only a few steps behind. The Worthington's offices occupied the first two floors of the historical building. He had the architectural specs well mapped in his head. On the first floor, there was an art gallery and antiquities dealership, selling a wide variety of valuable collectibles on consignment. The business offices were on the second level in an open loft space, accessed from the main floor by a wide, curving staircase. The warehouse and secure storage was in the rear of the building, with a delivery bay backing onto an alley.

Evan stepped through the front doors into the large gallery with twenty-two-foot-high ceilings. The walls were lined with framed art of various types and sizes. The center space had glass display cabinets and sleek tufted white leather benches. He could easily see Nia standing near the rear of the room, next to a reception counter that was manned by another employee. But he started a slow walk around the room, stopping occasionally to admire one of the many drawings, paintings, and photographs. He also knew the moment his target left the area through the door to the warehouse.

"Hi there?"

Evan turned to find a young girl walking toward him. She was twenty-one years old, with a bright smile and even brighter blond hair. And he already knew she was the gallery receptionist and office administrator, Emma Sterling.

"Is there anything I can help you with?" she continued, stopping next to him.

He smiled back.

"I hope so," he stated. "I would like to get some information about your auction services."

"No problem," she replied smoothly. "Are you looking to buy or sell?"

"Sell."

"All right. I'll introduce you to our managing director, Nia. She'll be able to evaluate your needs."

The young girl turned away a little, and pressed a button on a discreet earpiece. She spoke in soft tones for a few seconds before clicking it again and facing him again.

"Nia will be with us shortly. Can I get you something to drink?"

"Sure, some water would be great."

"Sparkling or flat?"

"Hmmm, flat is fine."

"No problem, Mr. . . . ?" She raised a brow and smiled even bigger.

"Evan. Evan DaCosta."

"Great, Mr. DaCosta. Nia will be here shortly."

He nodded and she walked away.

About a minute later, Evan watched Nia James cross the room with the same smooth, sensuous gait he witnessed earlier. He found himself anxious to see her up close, feel how potent her attractiveness was. Not that he would be affected, of course. He'd seen her type too many times over the years to be fooled by the artifice. And glammed-up women weren't really his type. He preferred the outdoorsy, active women who didn't take hours to get ready. The girl next door.

Yet as this woman, their prime suspect in a ballsy jewelry heist, stopped in front of him, Evan stopped breathing.

"Mr. DaCosta," she stated in a sultry voice, her hand extended. "I'm Nia James. I understand that you'd like to hear more about our auction services?"

She looked up to meet his eyes squarely. Hers were a warm brown, with speckles of copper and honey. Evan cleared his throat, matching her firm handshake. Tiny sparks sizzled up his forearm.

"Nice to meet you, Miss James. I was told Worthington would be able to help with an estate auction?"

They were interrupted before she could respond.

"Here you go, Mr. DaCosta," stated the receptionist as she handed him a chilled bottle of fancy imported spring water.

"Thank you. And it's Evan, please. Mr. DaCosta was my father."

Emma giggled, flipping back her silky blond hair. Evan thought he caught Nia roll her eyes, but it was the tiniest movement, and her pleasant, polite smile didn't waver.

"Thanks, Emma," added Nia. The young girl nodded and walked away.

"Yes, we handle estate sales," continued Nia smoothly. "Depending on what items are involved, we could provide support for an on-site event, as part of a larger auction, or here through our consignment sales. We've also done several successful online auctions if that's something you're interested in."

Evan nodded, taking a small sip of his drink.

"I haven't given it much thought, to be honest. My father died last year, and left me his collection."

"I'm very sorry to hear that," she immediately replied. Her eyes softened, causing Evan to pause. He wasn't expecting authentic empathy. *She's really good.*

"Why don't you come up to my office, and we can go over some of the details?"

He looked at his watch.

"I have a meeting shortly, so I can't stay now. But I can come by again later today. Is six o'clock too late?"

"I'm afraid it is. We close at five."

"That's unfortunate. I have to sort things out as soon as possible. I don't have much time available over the next few weeks before I head back home to Virginia, and Worthington comes very highly recommended."

"I'm sure we can arrange something," Nia offered.

"Good. If you don't mind meeting after hours, I'm staying at the Harbor Hotel. Why don't I make us dinner reservations tonight for six o'clock?"

It wasn't a question, and he could see that Nia was genuinely surprised.

"Mr. DaCosta—"

"Evan, please."

"Evan, that's not necessary."

"Sure it is. If you need to work late to meet me, the least I can do is feed you," he dismissed her qualms while pulling a business card out of his inside jacket pocket. "My cell phone number is on there, and my assistant's."

"But—"

Evan's phone rang, interrupting additional protests.

"Sorry, I have to take this. See you at six," he told her with a nod, then turned to walk briskly across the gallery floor. "Tony, what do you have?"

"The security guard is on the move," the agent stated. "He's on foot, carrying a duffel bag and looks pretty agitated."

"Did he make you?" Evan asked. He was now outside and getting into his car.

"Negative. I just arrived when he burst out of the back entrance of his building. Something spooked him and it wasn't me. I'd bet my paycheck that he's skipping town."

"Follow him," instructed Evan as he revved the engine. "I've got your location and I'm on my way."

He hung up the phone, then pulled the Bentley smoothly out into traffic, headed toward the Boston neighborhood of Dorchester.

Turn the page for an excerpt from Raven Scott's

Hard and Fast

On sale now wherever books and ebooks are sold!

CHAPTER 1

Lucas Johnson strode purposefully through the entrance of an apartment building in downtown Chicago. While he looked casual and relaxed in dark blue jeans and a lightweight charcoal blazer over a black shirt, his eyes were sharp and alert. A pretty, full-figured woman passed him in the lobby, giving him an open look of interest and appreciation. At six feet two inches tall with a lean, athletic build, he was hard to miss. Lucas flashed a wide, flirty grin and she winked back. His pretty face and disarming smile suggested a naughty playboy, not a brilliant and lethal former government agent.

"How far are you from the target?"

The question came from Raymond Blunt through the tiny earpiece in Lucas's ear. Raymond was an agent at Fortis, the full solution security and asset protection firm owned and managed by Lucas and his two best friends, Evan DaCosta and Sam Mackenzie. They had a team of twenty-two highly trained and uniquely skilled field specialists, technicians, and operations analysts with experience from all branches of elite government service.

Lucas had three men with him on the ground for this operation. Their objective was to shut down a small-time black hat hacker named Timothy Pratt who had tried to infiltrate their client's secure computer system with a sophisticated Trojan horse program.

"We're inside, heading into the stairwells," advised Lucas.

The other two Fortis agents were entering the building from different access points and linked into the connected earpieces.

"Okay, the signal is coming from the fifth floor," confirmed Raymond from his position providing surveillance support from their rented truck parked down the street. "According to the building schematics, you're looking for the third unit on your right from the west staircase."

Lucas was now at the base of the staircase closest to him.

"Ned, you take the east stairs," he instructed. "Lance, take the elevators and I will approach the target from my end. We'll converge on the apartment door. I'll make contact, with both of you as backup in the wings."

"Got it," confirmed Ned Bushby. Like Lucas, he was a former Secret Service agent.

"Confirmed," added Lance Campbell, an ex–Army Ranger.

Lucas ran up the staircase, two steps at a time. The hall on the fifth floor of the building was empty, except for Lance as he exited the elevator.

Ned came through the other exit door only seconds
later. The three men crept swiftly and quietly to
apartment 514. Ned and Lance took positions next
to the door, hands hovering near the grips of their
concealed pistols. Lucas gave them both a signal
with his hand and knocked.

There was no answer.

The men looked at each other. Lucas knocked
again.

"There's no answer, Raymond," Lucas stated in
the earpiece.

"Well, the system's on and running, so it may be
an automated program," Raymond replied. He
came to Fortis after twelve years with the NSA, and
next to Lucas, was their top systems and security
specialist.

"Do we have any activity from the target?" asked
Lucas in a whisper.

"Negative. No cellular phone usage since nine
forty-three a.m.," Raymond confirmed. "And the
phone's GPS signal is still in the apartment."

It was now almost eleven-fifteen on Friday morning. Lucas looked at his two men, putting up two
fingers to indicate their plan B. He then took out a
small, pointed tool from his back pocket, inserted it
into the door lock, and picked the standard resi-
dential lock in under twelve seconds. The deadbolt
took another ten seconds. The three men slipped
into the apartment silently, guns drawn and ready
for any situation. They quickly fanned out from the
front entrance into the small, messy studio apartment, checking in the closets and bathroom. The
abandoned food containers and discarded clothing

everywhere suggested the place was well occupied, but there was nobody home. A laptop was set up on the kitchen counter.

"Raymond, we're in," Lucas confirmed. "The computer is here."

"Boss," stated Lance from the living area. "He couldn't have gone far. His cell phone and wallet are on the coffee table."

Lucas nodded. He was already turning on the laptop to assess the tech.

"Let's be out of here in ten minutes," he told Ned and Lance. "You guys see if you can find any info that can identify his motives. I'll need at least seven minutes to clone the system and shut down the Trojan."

He did a quick inspection of the equipment, a standard, off-the-shelf laptop connected to a wireless modem. The operating system was another story. Lucas quickly bypassed the secure login and accessed the system administrative functions before connecting a small jump drive to one of the USB ports. It contained a highly complex program that he had designed, meant to wirelessly transmit a cloned version of the desktop, operating system, and hard drive of the target system. It also left behind a passive rootkit software that would allow Lucas and the Fortis team undetected access to the computer and connected networks.

"Raymond, I've started the clone," he advised.

"Yup, the data is coming through here," Raymond confirmed through the earpiece.

"Good, we're at forty percent transmission. It should be done in three minutes."

Lucas did a few more configurations to the programming code in the admin program, then backed out of the system, erasing all traces of his presence until not even the most elite intrusion detection specialist could sniff his activities. He put the computer back in sleep mode just as the data transfer was complete.

"Got it, Lucas," noted Raymond. "The info looks complete."

"Good. We'll be out of here in one minute." He turned to the other agents as they completed their careful search of the apartment. "Anything?"

"Nothing," Lance replied.

"I got this," added Ned, holding up a couple of empty, used bank envelopes. "Whatever Pratt's up to, he's being paid in cash."

The team did one final sweep to ensure everything was as they found it. Then they exited, locking the door behind them, and split up to meet with Raymond at their rented truck a block down the street. Ten minutes later, they were headed out of the city, back to the Fortis chopper grounded at a private heliport fifteen miles outside of the Chicago city limits.

"So, what are we dealing with here, Lucas?" asked Lance. "From what we saw, Pratt looks more like a messy college kid than a corporate hacker."

"He is a kid," added Raymond. "He just graduated from Johns Hopkins a year ago, with mediocre grades and an unremarkable college life. Up until January, he was doing tech support at Best Buy in Maryland."

"So what happened three months ago and why's

he in Chicago trying to break into the computer network at Magnus Motorsports in Toronto?" continued Lance.

"Hactivism maybe?" asked Ned.

"I don't think so," Lucas replied. "Magnus is a relatively small player in custom race car components. Their latest project is a high-performance, fuel-efficient hybrid engine. Not really something to upset any political or social groups."

"When Marco Passante hired us last year to set up a secure computer network and data backup system, was it just the timing of their new technology, or was he worried about a particular threat?" Raymond questioned, referring to the president and owner of Magnus.

"At the time, he suggested their technology had the potential to be revolutionary, and highly coveted in the auto industry," Lucas told them. "He talked about general concerns that his competitors would try to steal or destroy the work. Something that happens pretty often in the racing industry, apparently."

"Well, Pratt's not good enough to have built that Trojan we just shut down. He has no online portfolio or footprint to suggest he's an active hacker," Raymond added. "Looks to me like someone has set him up as a script kiddie for several months to go after information that has to be worth a big return on the investment. So either Passante had great foresight, or there is more to this client engagement than we thought."

"Raymond, my man, you've read my mind," Lucas concurred as they arrived back at the small airport in north suburban Chicago. "Once they've detected that we've shut down this attack, whoever's funding Pratt will have to find another way to get what they're looking for. Since the full Magnus network is self-contained in a local, private system within their building in Toronto, any additional attacks will be directed on-site. So, I need to have a more transparent conversation with our client and rescope this project."

They all piled out of the rented truck and began loading up their chopper.

"Question," interrupted Lance while they worked. "What the hell is a script kiddie?"

Lucas and Raymond exchanged looks of disgust.

"How do you not know this stuff?" demanded Raymond with a shake of his head.

"Because I'm not a geek," the ex-Ranger shot back.

Lucas grinned, and Raymond shrugged since neither was the least bit offended.

"A script kiddie, or a skiddie, is not skilled enough to design their own programs," explained Lucas. "So, they use tools and scripts built by other hackers."

"Got it," Lance replied, looking even less interested in tech-talk than before. "So maybe Pratt's just a lackey here. Maybe we should be looking for the person that developed the program he used."

"Not necessary. I already know who designed the Trojan program," Lucas stated with a dry smile. "It's called AC12 and it's been around for a while."

The others looked at him with various degrees of surprise.

"AC12?" repeated Raymond. "Are you sure? I worked on a few instances at the NSA. It's an ugly fucker, nearly impossible to disarm without wiping your whole system clean."

There was a pregnant pause.

"I'm sure," Lucas finally confirmed. "I built it in my freshman year at MIT."

Two days later, Lucas landed at the Billy Bishop Airport on the Toronto Islands in Lake Ontario. He headed straight into the city to check into his hotel, a short block away from the Magnus Motorsports shop and offices. A couple of hours later, he was unpacked in his room and seated at a table in the hotel's lobby restaurant for dinner. He was scheduled to meet with Marco Passante first thing Monday morning.

Lucas was not a big fan of hotels. During his career as a cybersecurity consultant with the Secret Service, he'd spent many nights in cold, cramped rooms around the world. Even ones as nice and fancy as the five-star Metropolitan didn't come close to the comforts of home. The only advantage they offered, hopefully, was a decent restaurant and a selection of imported beer. Maybe a beautiful stranger to share the bed with for a night or two.

Like the woman who just walked into the room, he thought. Now there was someone who could make this trip more enjoyable. Around five feet eight inches tall, this woman was slender in a tight dress, long, bare legs, and stiletto heels. Since it was April and raining hard outside, Lucas concluded she was a guest at the hotel, possibly alone. Perfect circumstances and exactly his type.

He took another drink from his beer bottle, watching unobtrusively as the hostess directed the attractive woman to a dinner table across the room from his. Her hips swayed gently with each step, and she tossed her long, brown hair with confidence. He relaxed back again, patiently anticipating how the evening would unfold. If she remained alone, Lucas would invite her to join him for dinner.

"Sorry! I'm just going to steal this seat for a second," announced a feminine voice. "These boots were definitely the wrong choice for tonight."

In the chair across from him, all he could see was the flat of the woman's back. She was bent over, doing something under the table, muttering swear words like a trucker. Lucas's lips quirked and he took another sip of his beer.

"Who designs these torture devices?" she added while straightening up.

He followed her hands as she gestured to her legs encased in a pair of very high and very sexy black leather boots. They went past her knees, but the table cut off the rest of his view. Lucas had to resist leaning forward to see where they ended, but his imagination was now fully engaged.

"Definitely a man," he replied smoothly.

She finally turned in the chair to look at him. Lucas paused, caught by the intensity in her large golden brown eyes. He also noticed her creamy caramel skin, pink shiny lips, and a mass of jet-black, curly dreadlocks falling well below her shoulders.

"What?" she asked, clearly confused.

"Those boots were definitely designed by a man," he stated with a wide smile.

She finally blinked, then looked back at her feet.

"You're right. Explains why I can't stand in them for more than an hour at a time," she muttered.

"I don't think they were meant for that kind of action," Lucas added, giving her a wicked grin.

The woman looked at him again, assessing him intensely. Her frank stare was strangely unnerving, but he fought the urge to look away.

"You're pretty," she finally said. It didn't sound like a compliment. "Thanks for letting me get off my feet for a minute."

"Stay as long as you'd like," he offered casually, sipping his bottle again.

Her eyes narrowed, and her gaze lowered to his lips. Lucas felt the start of a low, familiar pulse in the base of his stomach. She licked those plump, pink lips, and the pulse deepened.

"I'm Lucas, by the way," he added, when the silence between them stretched uncomfortably.

She blinked again, then smiled broadly. Lucas stopped breathing, while the pulse deepened to a full throb. Wow, she was gorgeous.

"Thanks, Lucas, but I'm good now."

She stood, allowing him to see her full length. Lucas rose to his feet also, noted her height and soft curves. The boots ended a few inches above her knees where shiny, latex-covered thighs continued, topped with a white crisp men's-style button-down shirt. But only her eyes kept his attention. They widened with surprise as he stepped closer, topping her by at least six inches. Her brows knitted, then she brushed past him without another word. Lucas turned to watch her walk away as the scent of sweet vanilla and brown sugar lingered softly in her wake.

"Lex! Nick's leaving," he heard, as a man from the group at the bar waved in her direction. She was swallowed into the crowd of people.

Lucas looked back at his table, wondering what had just happened. There was no way he had imagined the physical chemistry between them, or her subtle reaction. His body was still humming at a low frequency.

Lex.

In all likeliness, she was here with another guy. Someone from the private party milling around the bar. But the night was young. With any luck, he'd have a chance at round two. Particularly since the other options in the room no longer held any interest for him. Lucas sat back down and ordered another beer as his prime rib dinner arrived.

Over the next forty minutes, he got several glimpses of black locs within the group of noisy men. She talked and laughed with many of them, but none seemed to have a claim on her. He finally drained his second bottle of beer, charging the tab to his room, and headed in her direction.

He was only a few steps from her position against the bar when she said something that must have been very clever, because the three guys around her roared with laughter, one of them almost choking on his drink. Lucas took in her bright smile and the teasing look in her eyes, wishing he could share the joke. He brushed her shoulder lightly as he leaned toward the bartender.

"Stella Artois, please. And whatever she's having," he requested, pointing to Lex's empty cocktail glass.

She glanced at him from the corner of her eyes. He met her gaze steadily.

"Thank you," she said softly when the fresh drink was placed in front of her.

"Club soda?" Lucas quizzed.

She shrugged with one shoulder. "I'm driving."

He nodded. There was a pause. Lucas intended to wait for her to make the first move, ideally to indicate she also felt the attraction and his attention was welcome. It was usually a pretty easy strategy at a bar. But the seconds ticked on and she just watched him with those curious eyes. He cleared his throat and caved.

"How are your feet doing?"

She smiled.

"I'll survive for a little longer, I think."

"Good. But I'm happy to help you out again if needed." His grin was meant to be charming and flirty, but her raised brows made him doubt its effectiveness.

"Really? And how exactly would you do that?"

Suggestive words sprang into his mind, like the offer of a soft bed to rest on and a long foot rub to ease any discomfort. The direction of his thoughts must have been clearly written on his face because she finally looked away. Lucas leaned forward so he could whisper near her ear.

"I'm a gentleman, so I'd do whatever you need me to do."

"I bet you're good at that," she shot back, playing with the frosty condensation at the side of her glass.

"At what?" he probed, now facing her with his elbow resting on the bar. His fresh mug of Belgium draft beer remained untouched.

She rolled her eyes, suggesting he knew exactly what she was referring to. "At doing whatever a woman needs."

"I can only try my best."

Lex looked at him again.

"So, Lex, is it? Are you from Toronto?" he finally asked.

"Born and raised. But I can tell from your accent that you're American. Visiting for work, I take it?"

"That's a pretty accurate guess," he conceded.

"A man like you, alone in a downtown hotel bar on a Sunday night, and looking for company? Not hard to figure out."

"Ouch," Lucas stated with a grimace. "I'm pretty, and a cliché."

"Sorry, I didn't mean it as an insult, just an observation," she added. Her eyes twinkled with amusement, taking the sting out of her words. "Unless of course, you have a wife and kids back in . . . where, New York?"

She took a sip from her drink.

"Alexandria, actually. Born and raised in New Jersey, but I live in Virginia now," explained Lucas, lifting up his left hand as evidence. "No wife, no kids. Not even a girlfriend."

There was a silent pause as they both continued to assess each other.

"Lex. Is that short for something?"

She smiled wide again, her eyes sparkling.

"Alexandria, actually."

Lucas laughed.

"Now, that can't be a coincidence," he replied, leaning a little closer so that her intoxicating scent teased him.

"Hey, Lex, this dude bothering you?"

Lucas didn't take his eyes off her, but from his peripheral vision, saw that the guy asking was a couple back in the crowd, standing over six feet and big, almost as big as his friend Evan. But he looked slow and well into multiple cups of alcohol.

"Are you bothering me?" she asked with a big smile. She was enjoying the conversation. Lucas felt encouraged for the first time.

"I hope so, if you don't mind," he replied with a grin of his own.

"I'm good, Adrian, thanks," she told the other man before facing Lucas again. "I'm leaving now anyway. Thanks again for the drink."

"So early? We were just starting to get to know each other," Lucas protested.

"Sorry, I have to be at work early tomorrow."

Lucas followed her as they made their way through the crush of people pressing close to order drinks.

"All right, I'll walk you to your car."

Lex gave him a funny look.

"Okay, if you insist," she conceded.

"I do. I'm a gentleman, remember?"

They were silent as she handed in a coat-check ticket and got back a long, red raincoat that tied at the waist. He escorted her out of the restaurant.

"My car is in valet parking, so I'm just going to the front entrance. There's really no need to accompany me," she added.

Lucas looked down the long expanse of the hotel lobby, with the main doors at the opposite side. There was plenty of real estate for more conversation.

"No biggie. It's on my way to the elevators anyway," he dismissed with a shrug.

"Giving up on the night already?" she teased with raised eyebrows. "You're walking away from a lot of potential."

"Who says I'm giving up?" Lucas shot back. His gaze said very clearly that she had all his attention.

Lex let out a short bark of laughter, her lips spread wide in a big smile. He was now certain she was enjoying their banter as much as he was.

"Exactly what is it that you think you'll accomplish on this short walk?"

"Nothing. I'm just enjoying your company, that's all," he lied smoothly while he plotted the right words to say that would convince her to stay with him for more of the evening. Maybe even all night.

"Liar. You think you can talk me into sleeping with you tonight," Lex shot back, her voice still soft with humor. "And I bet you're successful with almost all the women you meet. But, unfortunately, I really have to be up early in the morning."

Her blunt assessment caused Lucas to stop his slow stroll. His expression showed a mix of surprise and intrigue. Lex stopped two paces ahead and faced him.

"And as tempting as whatever your offer is, I'm

not what you're looking for. I'm the exact opposite of what you want, Lucas."

He heard two things in her statement: she remembered his name and she was tempted. Lucas smiled, slow and sexy.

"I haven't made you an offer, Lex," he clarified.

"Not yet, but you will."

"Touché," Lucas conceded. He continued their walk, slightly slower than before, and she fell in beside him.

"What do you think I'm looking for, and why is it not you?" he finally asked, genuinely curious.

"The answer to the first question would damage your fragile ego, pretty boy. And the second is way too complicated."

Lucas snorted, not the least bit insulted.

"Try me. I'm tougher than I look, and I've got time."

She looked him up and down, her eyes lingering in some interesting places. Lucas felt like straightening his back and flexing his chest. But he resisted the juvenile urge. Nothing he did would demonstrate just how strong or lethal he really was.

"Okay. But I don't think I can handle it if you start crying," she shot back, her lips twitching with the effort to hold back a grin. "You're looking for someone fun, easygoing, comfortable with a casual hookup. A girl that's not going to have expectations beyond a night or two. A week, tops. And all on your schedule."

She wasn't asking for him to agree, and he wasn't offended. The summary was pretty accurate. Casual sexual encounters required honesty and clarity at the onset or they were bound to go disastrously and uncomfortably wrong. A complication that he never had time for.

"And that's not something you're into," guessed Lucas. "I can respect that."

"No, I prefer casual, actually," she clarified, surprising him with the transparency. "And I'm partial to pretty men without expectations. But I need it on my terms, too. My available time is limited and I don't like to waste it. And that's where it gets complicated."

They had both stopped walking, and now stood side by side in the middle of the marble-tiled hotel corridor. A small number of people walked about around them, but neither noticed.

"I'm pretty sure that's not going to work for you, pretty boy," she continued.

"Let me be the judge of that. I can compromise," he replied softly, completely captivated by her frank statements and overall energy.

She looked back at him speculatively, her bold, golden eyes piercing into his. Lucas found himself holding his breath, willing her to see what she needed in order to make a connection between them worthwhile.

"Was that an offer?" Her expression was deadpan, but her tone was teasing.

Lucas laughed. He liked her. "I believe it was."

"Thanks, but I have to pass," she finally replied. "I don't compromise very well. One of my character flaws, I've been told."

She started walking again, much faster and more determined than before, and Lucas could only fall in step. He felt much more disappointed than he cared to admit. And it was more about the end of their conversation than a spontaneous roll in bed.

"Well, there's no need to decide so quickly," he added when they reached the large revolving door at the hotel entrance. "I might be here all week."

Lex turned to face him, then backed into the open section of the turning door and pushed herself out of the building, her eyes fixed on his. Lucas shoved his hands into the pockets of his jeans, experiencing a rare moment of indecision. She'd already turned down his invitation and was walking away. It was just unmanly to chase after her further. Yet, a minute later, he was following her outside, ignoring the damp, windy night air that easily blew through the fine wool of his sweater.

The valet attendant had already taken her ticket and they stood waiting silently for her car to be brought up. He looked at her profile, then felt her look at his. Their eyes finally locked before the deep, low rumble of a powerful turbo engine vibrated around them. Lucas turned to watch the slow arrival of a late-model Porsche 911 Carrera, tricked out with sexy skirts, matte black sport rims, bright red brake calipers, and a slick storm-gray paint job. It was a beauty.

"This is me," Lex said at his side, and he turned to find her watching the car as it rolled to a stop. Pride of ownership was written all over her face.

"Wow," was all he could say.

She laughed, throwing back her head. Lucas couldn't help laughing also.

"I was serious about my offer," he added seconds later, feeling helpless to stop her from walking away.

Her lips quirked again, and she stepped to his side, close enough to brush against his arm, but still a breath away. Lucas looked down at her face, locked on those incredible eyes, and did what he wanted. He leaned down until his face was close to hers, then paused to gauge her reaction. Lex lowered her lashes and tilted her chin up an inch. His mouth covered hers without a plan of attack, only the irresistible need to touch her, explore the powerful attraction, taste her flesh before she disappeared into the night.

The kiss was open-mouthed and instantly hot, giving her a glimpse of what he had to offer and taking more than he was entitled to. Lucas was rewarded with her quick response. Lex leaned in until her soft curves pressed into his side. Her tongue met his, swirling around with arousing strokes. Lucas Johnson, elite security specialist and practiced bachelor, felt his knees go weak.

His lids were still closed when she pulled back, stepping out of his reach. His breath was caught somewhere between his stomach and throat, dreading what came next.

"Nice to meet you, Lucas," she said softly.

He opened his eyes to watch her walk around her car and slide into the low driver's seat. He was still standing in the cool night air, hands buried in his front pockets, as the sports car disappeared down the street.